GARDEN

OF

EARTHLY

BODIES

GARDEN OF EARTHLY BODIES

a Novel

SALLY OLIVER

THE OVERLOOK PRESS

This edition first published in hardcover in 2022 by
The Overlook Press, an imprint of ABRAMS
195 Broadway, 9th floor
New York, NY 10007
www.overlookpress.com

First published in Great Britain in 2022 by Oneworld Publications

Abrams books are available at special discounts when purchased in quantity
for premiums and promotions as well as fundraising or educational use.
Special editions can also be created to specification. For details,
contact specialsales@abramsbooks.com or the address above.

Library of Congress Control Number: 2022932220

Printed and bound in the United States

1 3 5 7 9 10 8 6 4 2
ISBN: 978-1-4197-5935-2
eISBN: 978-1-64700-568-9

ABRAMS The Art of Books
195 Broadway, New York, NY 10007
abramsbooks.com

PROLOGUE

'DO YOU THINK THIS IS a mistake?'

Charlotte directed the question to her friend Nick.

They were standing by the side of a hole in the ground, roughly two feet deep. It was acquiring more depth by the second as they watched five men shovel great mounds of earth. The men shared a somnolent expression, like their thoughts had reached some sort of impasse and had slowly shrunk in obedience to it. Yet there was a quiet intensity in their movements, a monomaniacal focus.

Charlotte turned to Nick and saw that he was also transfixed by what they were doing. With some effort, he parted his lips.

'I don't know,' he said. 'Maybe you can just say you've changed your mind.'

'But we came all this way.'

'I think you should say you've changed your mind,' he repeated in a whisper. 'They're not going to force you.'

Six members of the research team had accompanied them to the forest, though the leader, Sarah Clarke, was the only person Charlotte had actually corresponded with over the last month. Her own emails had been frantic and slightly scrambled, alternating between acquiescence and apprehension. Sarah was a renowned neurobiologist who had written countless articles on psychiatric disorders and new methods of rehabilitation. Her words had been precise, measured, and they were often abstruse in a way that earned Charlotte's automatic respect. Doctors had always had this effect on her. She knew she was being assessed by a mind much greater than her own, and she was vaguely excited by the idea that her thoughts – those missiles that fired without warning – would finally be defused. She longed for a quiet brain.

The forest was lucid in the early morning light, the trees fixed in positions that appeared very human. Their crooked arms seemed schooled into stillness, with muscles that twitched before the sun arrived. Charlotte had known this strange tension of arrested motion. She had been here a month earlier and she hadn't forgotten those hours.

The momentum with which the men shovelled the soil was beginning to slow. The ground was gaining heat as the sun rose higher, leering at the newly disclosed earth.

Sarah had been tapping on an iPad for a few minutes, and now she stared at Charlotte.

'Are you ready?'

Her voice was calm and instructive. Charlotte stared at the earth.

'I think so.'

Sarah approached her slowly and then lowered her voice.

'Do you remember what we talked about? That you need to—'

'Yes,' Charlotte said in a small voice.

By this point, the men had all turned away and were standing in a uniform line with their backs to Charlotte. Perhaps they hadn't intended to do so with such ceremony, but the effect was vaguely chilling.

One of the men had a large bald head, the surface of which was very uneven, almost lumpy, towards the back of the neck. His skull was shaped in a similar way to— She shuddered, refusing to entertain the thought. She would trade everything to renounce that thought – its source too, if possible.

Nick was still standing beside her and she felt reassured by his presence when she started to unbutton her blouse. She'd often freely changed from one outfit to another in front of him back in her bedroom and there had been no awkwardness. Without looking ahead, she slid her trousers down, then her knickers, the elastic grazing her legs.

As she unhooked her bra, she sensed a new gravity in the atmosphere. She could detect the imminence of something malign, a force that gathered itself for sudden discharge. She couldn't attribute it to any solid presence, at least not any conscious entity.

Nick was staring at her with a questioning look. He appeared to mouth something but she couldn't make out the words.

She placed her clothes on a pile on the ground and felt it again, a reverberation that had seemed remote yet was now fully interred, having passed through her skin. Her spine began to bend and she was forced to curl her neck, as though to lean into the smallness of herself. An intimation of something vast and merciless pressed on her mind, pushing it down then letting it loose. It was like her head had been forced under water to marvel at the void below, then suddenly buoyed upwards at the last moment. In that second she could see all of her thoughts clearly like the overhanging sky.

She took Nick's hand. This was like the last time she'd been here, only now there was an urgency in the way her mind was behaving.

'Now you're going to lie down on the sheet, face down,' Sarah said to her, 'and you're going to have this tube to breathe through.' She picked up the transparent tube from the ground and held it carefully aloft, like a snake. 'I'll hand it to you when you're lying down. Okay?'

Charlotte slowly moved towards the hole and crouched by it, feeling her pubic hairs bristle between her thighs. The men were still facing the opposite way, staring towards the compact darkness of the trees. She thought it looked like she was about to do something indecent, which called for their frozen postures. She crept into the shallow plot and knelt on the tarpaulin sheet at the bottom, which was tough and crackled beneath her calves.

'Take your time, Charlotte,' Sarah said. She was standing close. 'Take deep breaths first.'

'Maybe this is a bad idea.'

That was Nick. His voice was very distant.

'Charlotte?' Sarah said sharply.

She was waiting for her to make a decision.

Charlotte stared at the wall of earth in front of her. An elongated worm was wriggling furiously from the cracks, shocked at the way its world had suddenly shifted. Only minutes before it had spasmed through the darkness, trusting in the mercy of what pressed it and, simultaneously, gave way.

A current of pain surged through Charlotte's back and deposited itself at the base of her spine. She lowered herself on to the sheet and lay face down, shifting her head so that one side of her face was free. The sheet was rough on her stomach and her breasts were squashed in a way that made them hard and heavy. But at this point she could still believe that she was a tenable surface, the limit beyond which the world ticked over, without intruding.

She closed her eyes, took a deep breath and braced herself for the first fall of earth.

Nothing came.

'You need to take the breathing tube, Charlotte.'

Charlotte pulled herself up, shocked that she had almost forgotten. She took the end of the tube from Sarah and lowered it towards the sheet, tugging it bluntly to test that Sarah had a firm grip on her end. She found, at this critical stage, that her trust in authority was compromised by something, that it always would be, right at the moment she needed to relinquish control. For a second, the women stared intently at each other. Charlotte yanked the tube again, which prompted a smile from Sarah, one that seemed to insinuate this lapse of faith was foolish.

When Charlotte was flat against the ground again, she inserted the tube into her mouth, taking care not to bite it. Her whole jaw was trembling. There were several heavy footfalls from on high and she felt a series of shadows blocking the sun, cooling her blood. They were all watching her. She flinched when someone leaned forward and placed a small cotton sheet over her head, tucking it in gently around her skull. She was surprised to feel a small lingering pressure beneath this person's hands before they withdrew them. There was something tender, almost mournful, in the motion that caused her eyes to burn. For a few seconds her eyelids fought to shift the material, beating rapidly against it.

'We're going to distribute the earth evenly, Charlotte, so none of your joints are pressured,' Sarah called to her. 'Your neck will be stiff in this position but, remember,' – her voice grew solemn – 'if you want to get out of there, you have to make a sound through the tube and we'll hear it straight away. We'll not leave you longer than twenty minutes.'

Nobody spoke. After a few seconds a block of earth hit Charlotte's right buttock. It smashed against her skin and took her by surprise. Her heart was pounding against the sheet. She instinctively wanted to roll on to her back, but Sarah had been very clear that she must be facing down.

More people were sending soil down now, the blocks colliding in mid-air and shattering over her skin. The pain returned, a hot prickling that started at the back of her neck and progressed to her tailbone. Though she knew she wouldn't be trapped here forever, the sensation of staring towards an infinite mass was frightening. To stare towards safety would have soothed her instincts, knowing there were only a few metres between her and the open air. But to stare into the depth that threatened her, the world itself and its endless dimension, thrilled her with the knowledge of her frailty. She could feel her body growing taut as it lost its last remaining surface.

As if on cue, her thoughts spiralled into chaos. They evolved at lightning speed and then, at once, began to regress and unwind, to return to their sources. An image of her mother's hands blossomed in the dark, and she strove to clutch them. Her brain was being compressed, forced into a hot centre of awareness.

As her world shrank to nothing, she breathed quickly, sucking the air through the tube, wishing she could expel her thoughts through it. Her ears were ringing with panic.

Silence.

Not silence but the stifling sound, one note, of eternity.

Slowly, her thoughts began to change. Panic no longer stunted them. They seemed to migrate somewhere beyond panic, beyond anything that demanded an emotional response.

There was a tremor across her back. Her mind flooded with darkness, and yet she could see her way. She was sliding, inch by inch, through the earth.

MARIANNE FOUND THE FIRST HAIR one morning after they made love. It was a solid black one attached to the bone of her spine.

Richard only liked to penetrate her in the morning. He required the urgent collision of flesh on flesh, to chafe his body across the surface of another, one that hadn't quite stirred from sleep, and unload himself into the darkness of something that wouldn't follow him out of the door. Then he could throw the duvet back, unfurl himself and stretch towards the bathroom in a clean white arc.

On the morning of his meeting with the director of the company, he buried himself a little deeper into Marianne than was necessary. She had always thought reticence was a fatal error in sex, and so she'd been honest about the parameters in which her pleasure lay. She said it was not necessary to fill her entirely, that she liked a space reserved for her imagination to do the rest. Beyond a certain point, she didn't like him there. Beyond a certain boundary, the tip of him made her sting and she imagined he was pouring something else into her, deliberately crossing the line that divided her joy from his. She felt every sharp turn as he struggled to translate himself, to store this precious, unfiltered data inside of her before it was too late. It was this he eventually hated, that he communicated something to her without knowing what it was, having finally lost the capacity to censor himself.

When it was done, she always wanted to sleep again, whereas he was fortified, recalibrated. She heard him banging the shower door and then the slow thud of his feet as he rotated under the jet of water. They hadn't lived together very long, and yet, in some sense, she felt she could already predict every move of his body. Each small gesture contained an element of violence, as though sheer physical force would end his association with the past. She heard it now as he banged the soap down, clattering the little ceramic dish on the shelf of the shower.

He couldn't tolerate inertia. The queue for the tube, the waiting room of the doctors, any minor form of congestion or delay. She had once forced him to wait in line for an item she didn't want in a shop he couldn't bear, only to change her mind half an hour later once they were five seconds from the till. She'd wanted to see how much anger would amass. Though he said nothing, as was often the case, she had noticed a long yellow vein twitching at his temple. It was a feature she'd never seen before, and which she had evidently lured to the surface, like a worm that had been prodded and was trapped in an endless horrified recoil.

His routine was brutally imposed and rigidly enforced, from the second he woke up to the second he set his alarm. There was rarely any part of him that relaxed, and she could still feel that residual tension on his side of the mattress as she spread her arm across it. His back had made a blunt indentation of itself, an imprint that suggested guardedness and suspense, even when his thoughts were loosely constructed. And yet, there were certain accidents of the body, minor ways it betrayed him.

Sometimes, in his urgency to get ready, she'd hear him cut himself while shaving. The cry she heard from the bathroom was more than just an automatic response to pain. It sounded like the echo of an old grievance, suddenly recalled, leaking through his thoughts like warm blood. Then silence. He'd switch off the razor and she'd hear nothing for several minutes while he, presumably, stared in the mirror.

Perhaps she was too sensitive. Lately she'd been seduced by the idea that every small disruption, every minor delay, was a subtext for something else.

The morning light was beginning to filter through the gap Richard had made in the curtains. Marianne stretched, pushing her fist into the small of her back and arching her belly towards the ceiling. She glided her hand upwards to scratch the space between her shoulder blades. That was when she felt it. A thick hair, about the length of her thumbnail. The pore that held it seemed slightly swollen at the base, and she couldn't stop running her finger over it. It shocked her because of its singularity, and because she was sure she would have discovered it long before it had reached this length.

She got out of bed and moved to the dressing table mirror. She lifted up her T-shirt and stood with her back to the glass, searched for the hair again and twisted to look at it. Often when she felt a lump or a spot on her skin, it never looked as bad as it felt beneath her fingers, and she was often disappointed to exchange one sensory truth for another. But this was every bit as strange as she'd imagined it to be. When she pulled, she felt movement from somewhere far below the surface of her skin. She tugged it again but it was riveted to her back.

When Richard appeared in their bedroom, muttering to himself with a towel around his waist, she lifted her T-shirt up again and revealed her back to him.

'Look. Can you see that?'

'What – oh yeah. Shit.'

For a second, she hoped it would miraculously have disappeared.

'Can you get it out?' she said.

He said nothing.

'Please?'

'Do I need tweezers?'

Marianne rooted through the drawer in her dresser and handed a pair to him without saying anything. This time, she arched her back so that her spine rode through the skin and the hair darted upwards. She sunk her head low and waited.

'I don't want to hurt you,' Richard said.

'Just do it,' Marianne said. 'You won't hurt me.'

He paused, which made her seethe. The delay only served to ply her imagination with the idea of the pain long before it arrived, until it buzzed in her ears and her skin and she couldn't possibly think of anything else.

He pulled the hair sharply in their shared belief that the greater the force he applied to it, the swifter the turnover from pain to recovery. But the hair was trapped and she gasped. He pulled it again and she felt her skin stretching with it. What they saw on the surface must have been a tiny fraction of the whole, which made her worry.

'I'm not doing it again,' Richard said. She heard him place the tweezers on the dresser. 'I'm going to be late. Can't you shave it off?'

'That doesn't get the root out.'

She sat back on the bed and watched him dress. His hair was still wet and she wished it would stay wet. When it came through the stiff circle of his collar, it was dark and complex before the hours wrought their changes. The nape of his neck stayed wet for longer, the sweat holding fast to that groove beneath his skull in between changes on the underground.

'What does it mean?' she said to the crease in his bottom before he pulled his boxers over it.

'What?'

'Why's there a massive black hair on my back? It's weird.'

Richard smiled and buttoned his trousers.

'It's not funny.'

'It's not a life-or-death situation, is it? It's a hair. Just Google "women with hairy backs".' She heard the irony in his voice now. 'I bet other women have had the same issue. You hear of women having hairs in the oddest places. At least you haven't grown a beard.'

She leaned back on her elbows and refused to look at him.

'Go to the doctors if you think it means something. You have to go some time anyway, for your meds,' he said. He had looped a tie around his neck and held it still. 'Why don't you bring it up with Doctor what's-her-face? I'm sure it's nothing. Just your hormones.'

'You're not funny.'

'Sorry. Oh, come on. I'm only messing.'

He waited until his tie was straight before bending low to look at her very closely. She stared back at him with her mouth tightly closed. Then something about his stooped posture, implying contrition, made her pop her lips out so they were full again. He leaned in and butted his mouth there, poking his tongue so she was obliged to part her teeth for it.

'When is your next appointment?' he asked, when he drew away from her.

'Today actually.'

'Well, there you go. You'll have your answer then. Just leave it until she's had a look.'

The first half hour of the silence Richard left in his wake was a relief, until it was not. There was an invisible line somewhere in her solitude beyond which Marianne began to crave respite from herself again. She had adapted well enough to this new climate of self-sufficiency to spot the signs when the solace of being alone turned swiftly into a dangerous solipsism. She had her work, writing features freelance for a magazine, but the amount she was asked to do was slowly decreasing and did little to distract her in the first place. She could sometimes feel her eyes drifting from the screen of her Mac into empty space.

There was a certain place far back in her consciousness where she was liable to fall. And there were so many seconds in the day, too many, to guard herself from. Time has a way of bullying the mind into submission, of breaking down all defences until the thing one cannot bear to think must be born again and again, endlessly reconceived. And she could never bring herself to abort it once it emerged; she felt guilty if she tried, for it only survived through recollection. The thing itself – could she call it a *memory*? – still had the force of a revelation; the event, the *incident* (how formal that word was), that entered her head was tied to a person. There was no longer even a face – Marianne's thoughts orbited a blank spot where the face should have been. She was remembering an impression of someone who no longer impinged on her life with the same sharpness of outline or sound of voice. But her essence, or rather her tone, was still there. Tone survives. What had happened couldn't claim all of her, not all at once. Marianne worked very hard to shift that impression of violence, which she had once considered quite alien and surreal, but the days were long and the seconds longer, so she was beginning to believe in what had happened as though it should have happened all along. Again, she saw the dark track of the underground, the charred walls, the mice that scurried along the rails. Her blood ran cold. The key was to avoid lapsing into reverie. It was a form of abstinence she had taken great pains to practise in the last six months, and which she had still not mastered.

She didn't want to have a shower that morning because then she would have to confront the hair on her back and actually do something about it. *God, it's a hair. Get the razor out and shave it off, for Christ's sake.* There was something faintly reasonable about the idea of showing it to a doctor, to see why it had grown there. She had a wary, ambivalent respect for doctors on the whole. She felt torn between wanting to be studied – for that dispassionate, clinical gaze sometimes excited her very much – and wanting to remain inscrutable, opaque. She had adopted a perverse habit of ignoring anything her GP told her to do. It was all that she had, her autonomy, and she exercised it by revolting against what was expected of her every once in a while, a healthy exercise that revived something of the colour in her cheeks. She felt better when she refused to be well, perhaps because she refused to believe 'wellness' could be boiled down to anything. Wellness – in mind and body – was entirely complex, a mythic state, and she was adamant nobody had the right expertise to bring it to her.

Coming away from the doctor, her ears resounding with instructions on which vitamin supplements to take and the creams she had to apply to a rash that had developed on her hand (the origin of which the doctor wasn't quite qualified enough to determine), she found greater consolation in resisting all of it. It was a passive, peculiar form of power and the reward was more potent. She marvelled at signs of physical impairment, at her command of her own body in simply letting it down. The rash grew flaky and sore and she happily scratched it until it bled. Streaks of blood clung to the cracked knuckles but she didn't want to wash it off straight away. It was evidence. It gave her a licence to pity herself. And she did. She had endless stores of self-pity and she knew she would perhaps one day extricate herself from this dreary, rather childish pattern of behaviour, but for now she wanted to indulge it. She found solace in impairment. It was signs of vigorous health, imperviousness to decay, that frightened her. She held her thoughts in her hands and wanted people to see them.

But once the original shock of something is absorbed into consciousness, it fails to reverberate. As she saw the inflamed skin on a daily basis, she lost the surprise and the novelty of it. Richard was also rather skilled at intervening when she went too far, although the intervention was slightly delayed, as though he had been waiting to see if she snapped out of it without interference. He held her hands in his own and balanced them in the air between them, as though they were no longer alive. *This is mad*, he'd say. *The longer you attack yourself, the longer it will take to heal. You know that. You know the cream will help. I'd feel sorry for you if it was something you couldn't help.*

Her appointment at the doctors' was at 3.00 P.M. She had spent all morning emailing someone she was interviewing for her next article. The piece was commissioned for an issue on 'women without men'. The woman Marianne was interviewing had recently written a book, based on her own experience, about the problem of finding love before she was no longer fertile enough to conceive a child. She did not wish to have a sperm donor. She wanted the man before the sperm, a life-affirming union between herself and another, and couldn't bear to open her legs for anything else. It was a horribly intimate admission of defeat, but Marianne could only respond with the usual stock phrases that professionalism required.

Her phone vibrated on the table. A message from Richard. She ignored it up until it was time to leave for her appointment. Then she swiped the lock screen aside.

Please can you pick up some antihistamines? Run out and nose is streaming. Not a good day for it. x

She was about to put her phone in her bag when it buzzed inside her hand.

Are you going to show the doctor your hairy back? x

She texted back:

Fuck off. Thought you had an important meeting today.

A second later his reply was curt.

Already had it. I didn't get the promotion.

She didn't know what to say but it was nearly time for her to go and she couldn't leave him hanging on her silence.

I'm sorry. Speak soon. x

She panicked when she realised she was running late for her appointment. She had planned to wash her hair very quickly but now there was no time. She couldn't remember if she had washed it yesterday or the day before. She ran her fingers through the roots. She had fine blonde hair, but lots of it, and it never seemed to fall from her scalp like other people's. The hair that collected in the drains of their sink and shower was only Richard's dark, woolly locks and never hers, though there was so much of it. She derived a strange pleasure from the knowledge that it continued to hold fast to her head in spite of what occurred in her life.

She dressed quickly, and when she pulled her T-shirt down, she smoothed the back of her hand across her spine. For a fleeting second, she couldn't find the hair and she was appeased. Perhaps it was smaller than she'd remembered and her brain was simply sensitive, open to panic that early in the morning. Then it brushed her just as she brought her hand back down. It was a thick root, swelling darkly through the skin. And she was certain it had grown in the space of the night.

The waiting room in the Dulwich surgery was emptier than usual. Once she'd signed in, Marianne sat in the corner where there was a wooden box of toys, a desk with drawings to colour in, an abacus and a few cursory pieces of Lego scattered on the floor.

There was a girl, perhaps no older than four, sitting in the hollowed-out dent of a beanbag beside the box of toys. She was lifting the limp figures out one by one, her face impassive. There was a Barbie doll without any clothes to cover her shiny body, and the girl ignored the rest to fixate on this, perhaps repulsed by the slightly mottled and bobbly texture of some of the softer toys. Marianne dreaded to think of the germs those toys had accumulated over time – they must have been heaped in that box for at least twenty years. The girl took the Barbie by the feet and pulled her squeaky thighs apart in a sudden motion that surprised Marianne after the solemn conduct with which the child had taken the toys from their hiding place. She squeezed her head so that the sides of her face deflated under her thumbs and met in the middle. Then she released it and waited to see how long it would take for Barbie's head to pop back.

'Marianne Turner,' a familiar voice said.

Marianne lifted her head to the woman standing in the doorway that led on to the consultation rooms. They met one another's eyes, and Marianne got up and walked across the waiting room towards her.

This was a small interval in which she never knew where to look. If she stared all the while at her doctor while she crossed the room, without breaking eye contact, she'd come across too eager, insinuating an honesty that wasn't there. But looking anywhere else would imply a brattish streak, an instinctual aversion to scrutiny. She was, in fact, half-disciple, half-brat; willing to be studied yet loath to cooperate. She crossed the room, focusing on the space just above her doctor's left shoulder.

'Hi, Marianne, come this way.'

She followed Doctor Hind to her office overlooking the car park. On the desk were three photographs of Hind's children. They all shared her features – a long nose with wide nostrils, heavy-lidded eyes with thick horse-like eyelashes and a large forehead. They bore a resemblance to her but something was always a little off, which was where the individual crept through.

Doctor Hind was, herself, a large-boned and muscular woman in her mid-forties with a thinning hairline. When she sat down, she always sat very far back into her chair so that Marianne had the impression she was ready to immerse herself in someone else. Her large forehead appeared to move, to pulse slightly, every few seconds, as though it contained her heart.

'So, we upped your dosage of paroxetine by ten milligrams last time you were here.' Doctor Hind glanced at the computer screen from a languid distance in her chair. 'How are you doing now?'

Marianne hesitated. The doctor's room was not a place where she could recall the violence of her thoughts with the clarity they deserved. The grey, muted atmosphere of this office, with its sanitiser and paper towels, made her feel like she had imagined it all.

'Well, I found it difficult adjusting in the first few weeks. I'm still not sure whether it's having much of an effect.'

Doctor Hind said nothing.

'I can only say I feel less awful than before – when I'd just started taking the higher dose. But I wouldn't say I feel better than when I was on the lower dose.'

'I would give it another week or so. It does take some time to adjust to the new dosage.'

To Marianne's mind, a lot could happen in a week. A mere minute was long enough for someone to decide to die and then to change their mind at the last. A morbid thought can arrive like a spasm, quick and crucial, and everything that precedes it is disqualified for what seems like an eternity. And vice versa – the trap of consciousness comes undone at the last second and one is released from the most terrible convictions.

Only death makes the last thought irreversible. It does not mean the last thought is a reliable one. *And there is always a better thought, waiting to intervene, if we give it time*, Marianne thought. Her throat constricted as she thought of this, as she always did. She always came back to it. Perhaps Marie had changed her mind before she died. In a split second, she entered that place without really consenting to it.

Marianne waited for Doctor Hind to resume. She was fast becoming resentful of the patience with which she was being treated.

'Have you been feeling calmer at least?' Doctor Hind said.

'Yes. But I can't sleep.'

'Every night?'

'Most.'

'Do you wake up in the middle of the night or just have trouble getting off to sleep?'

'Yes. Both of those things.'

'What time do you go to bed?'

It was like she was a six-year-old again.

'About ten? Eleven?'

'What do you do immediately beforehand?'

Marianne hesitated.

She would have liked to say that she rolled her boyfriend's penis around her mouth – sometimes, in a lazy offhand moment, closing her teeth around it to hurry matters forward – until she rolled over and he spurted a glossy, silver line across her back –

always her back, she preferred it that way for reasons she never disclosed to herself – and then she lay and waited while he went to the bathroom for the toilet roll, which they somehow always forgot to have on hand.

She always felt grievously disappointed as he cooled on her back, though he'd been hot when he landed there. The tight, involving intimacy of a few minutes earlier always concluded with a fatal lassitude. The moment that had held her so quickly in its grasp now scattered her across the night, and she could not see the end of it. She outlived every concentrated unit of time – where all the great things happened, every orgasm – and her pleasure fell into misuse, grew extinct again. There were too many seconds in the day to keep those momentums aloft.

'I watch TV sometimes. Netflix. The news.'

'Try to avoid watching any screens at least an hour before sleep. Phone and tablet included. The glare of the screen slows the process as it tricks the body into thinking it's daytime.' Doctor Hind looked at the screen again. 'How has your appetite been?'

'Same.'

'And are you starting to feel less anxious?'

When she asked this, Doctor Hind looked at Marianne directly, and her head was tilted in an almost reproving manner, as though she considered it a question of will.

'I don't think so. But, like you said, I've not adjusted to the higher dose yet.'

'Yes. But it's important to know whether you've been feeling any violent urges or whether you've felt... irrational.' Doctor Hind lowered her voice. 'Have you considered harming yourself lately?'

'No.'

Doctor Hind glanced at Marianne's hands, which were curled in her lap.

'They're better. The cream works,' Marianne pre-empted.

'And you haven't—'

'No.'

Doctor Hind raised her eyebrows. They had gone grey, though her thinning hair was still a coarse black.

'Do you know what I was about to ask?'

'Yes. I haven't killed myself.'

Doctor Hind's mouth twitched into a half-smile.

'But have you thought about it?'

'Not really. Only as much as the next person.'

This was apparently reason enough to continue.

'I'm just going to check your blood pressure.'

Marianne surrendered her arm and winced when Doctor Hind grazed it with the patch of Velcro. When the arm cuff tightened, she imagined that her arm was growing inside of it.

'Actually, there is something else unrelated I wanted to ask you about,' Marianne said, while the numbers vacillated on the machine. A tiny heart symbol flashed on the screen. 'I was wondering if you could take a look at something on my back.'

'Sure.'

'It's a hair. A really thick, black one. I've never had any hairs on my back before.' Marianne's arm was released and she immediately scratched the part where the cuff had been. 'I wondered also if you would remove it for me.'

'No problem. Let's have a look.'

Marianne took off her denim jacket and bunched it on the floor by her bag, then rolled her T-shirt up over her breasts, facing away from Doctor Hind. She brushed the hair with her hand, having forgotten where it was momentarily. It felt even longer, though Marianne didn't trust her powers of estimation.

The doctor didn't say anything for a few seconds. Then Marianne felt her cold palm pressing against the centre of her spine.

'That's...'

Doctor Hind didn't know how to finish her sentence.

'It's just the one hair, but it's in an odd place so I thought I'd bring it up.' Marianne spoke to one of the plants beneath the window.

'There's another hair. Here.' The doctor placed her finger a few inches higher. She paused and Marianne felt her breath on her back. 'Also, one here.' The finger grazed the back of Marianne's neck, on the rounded tip of the spine. 'They're all exactly the same size, colour and texture, though you don't have thick black hair.'

'Should I be worried?'

'I'd like you to take a blood test if that's alright.'

Marianne let her shirt fall back and sat round to face Doctor Hind.

'What's the cause, do you think?' Marianne said.

'I can't say until we see the results of your blood test.' She turned her face back to the screen of her computer and clicked her mouse a few times. 'Are you free to have one now?'

'Don't I normally have to wait a few days?'

Marianne panicked. She preferred an interval in which she could compose herself for something like this.

'Oh, I'm sure someone will be free to do it. Just wait here.'

Doctor Hind got up abruptly, closing the door with a bang as she left.

Marianne stared at the three faces on the desk. The oldest child wasn't looking directly at the lens of the camera; she resisted her mother, always, in this room. Photographs were fatal, Marianne thought, because they pinned us to the wall of another's consciousness without our consent. And we are never privy to the impressions we're giving of ourselves.

When Doctor Hind returned, she motioned for Marianne to stand.

'There's a nurse free to take your blood now. It won't take long.'

Marianne picked up her bag and jacket from the floor, tucked them under her arm and followed Doctor Hind through the door back into the corridor again.

She was a teenager the last time she'd had a blood test, and her mother had been there. She had started sobbing a few minutes afterwards, which seemed to alarm everyone in the room because the procedure had been quick and the pain was done. She always had delayed reactions to incidents that, after a prolonged state of suspense, she realised had disturbed her in a manner she hadn't anticipated. The prick of the needle had offended her that time because she'd arrogantly assumed it wouldn't.

She'd already argued with her mother that morning and had a test coming up later in the day. She also recalled having an abscess agonisingly close to her anus, which she couldn't bear to admit to anyone, but which she touched every morning to check it was still there, a secret sign of her secret suffering. When she sat before the nurse, she was haughty and aloof, rolling her eyes when the inevitable chit-chat about school began to fill the awkward silence. When she felt the needle plunge deeper into her arm than she thought it would, the heat of her anger died abruptly. It was as though something froze the activity of her brain, a hotbed of thought she'd gathered to herself like a duvet, and she felt a frightening vacancy in its place, a sense of loss, or rather an anticipation of loss – that, without her fury, she had nothing. Beyond hostility, she had no other recourse with which to engage with anything or anybody. And it was only years later that Marianne could make any sense of what she felt.

This nurse barked instructions at Marianne while barely making eye contact. She pressed Marianne's arm at different points and snapped at her to relax.

'It's not that easy!' Marianne said.

She wished she hadn't said anything. The nurse gave her a smile that was not designed to placate her. She also paused, as though she wished to suspend what she was doing, so she could patronise the patient and reveal at the same time that there was no urgency at all. They stared at one another for a few more seconds and Marianne welcomed the return of that ancient adolescent anger. She had never really outgrown it.

Her fist was closed but her veins could not tighten and flex themselves as she wished. She watched the flimsy blue lines across the inside of her elbow as the nurse selected one without letting Marianne know which one. Last time, Marianne had been instructed to turn her head away and look at the wall behind them. This time, she watched because she thought it was essential. The real pain was seeing the shadow of the needle, she knew that now. The prick was bearable, so bearable it ventured dangerously close to pleasure – the rarefied pleasure of having exceeded a limit previously dreaded in the imagination. But the shadow of the needle under the skin – that was different. She hated to see something that didn't belong in her blood, a passing guest, but an intruder nonetheless, and that continued to move without obstruction. When the needle wormed its way back out of the vein, she had an urge to squeeze the spot shut with her fingers.

'You allergic to plasters?' the nurse asked as she placed a sticker on the sample.

'No.'

She was gentler in placing a plaster on Marianne, pressing it down without undue pressure.

'You'll get the results in a week.'

That afternoon, Richard was already cooking when Marianne got home. The radio was playing and he had it turned down low, presumably so it wouldn't dominate his thoughts. He once said he couldn't focus with too much background noise, yet he frequently engaged with news bulletins on the radio, listening out for signs of progress or impending catastrophe in the world – Marianne wasn't sure what his vigilance was really for. He'd colonised the kitchen while she'd been away; there were vegetables out on the work surfaces and on the island in the middle of the room, alongside egg noodles, garlic and a bottle of soy sauce. *Stir-fry then*, she thought gloomily. There wouldn't be any meat.

'Hi,' he said when she closed the door, barely looking round. His face was shiny. 'Got off a bit early today and I'm starving so I decided fuck it – I'm making dinner now.'

Marianne looked at her watch. 'It's five. This is way too early. Why are you home so early?'

He dipped his head towards her when he spoke, and she noticed the parting of his hair was slightly greasy.

'I told Steve I had to leave early. I never ask. He knows I never ask. He also knows he fucked me over today so he couldn't deny me this at least.'

'But why did you need to leave early?'

Richard stared at her blankly.

'Because I wanted to.'

Marianne slapped her bag down on the island and pulled out a chair.

'I don't know.' Richard shrugged. 'Call it nihilism. I deserved that promotion. And to find out that smug bitch, Lisa, got bumped up when she's only been there a year...' He had nothing to say for a few seconds and rattled the vegetables around the frying pan so some of them went overboard.

Marianne didn't have anything to say either. She rested her head on her bag.

'Hopefully she'll get knocked up down the line – that'll even things out a bit.'

Marianne laughed. 'Maybe in ten years.'

With some effort, Richard dropped the scowl that was cramping his face. He turned around and looked at Marianne with that sudden abortive expression, the blankness of purpose, which she knew well enough herself.

'I sound like an absolute arsehole,' he said.

'You're allowed to lose it now and again. Jesus.'

He moved closer to Marianne but something caught his attention on the radio and he cocked his head towards it. A word in particular had been said that distracted him. He turned up the volume.

'*...has been officially declared as a breakthrough in medical science. Doctors are hoping that this is the way forward in treating the most malignant forms of cancer...*'

'They were talking about this before on the BBC,' Richard said. 'Some sort of plant has been discovered that has anti-cancerous properties. They found it in the Lake District.'

'Mum and Dad used to take us to the Lakes in the summer. They were the best holidays we ever had. Marie and I went skinny dipping in the early hours…'

Richard frowned, and she could see he was afraid she'd go into more detail and never stop. She fell silent so he could listen to the broadcast.

'*This is a new breed of angiosperm, a self-seeding one, that's never been seen before. A sample was sent anonymously to the Laboratory of Molecular Biology in Cambridge, for cancer research, where Professor David Sexton was able to test the seed pods of the flower.*'

A different voice filtered through on the radio, more nervous and grasping.

'*It's amazed all of us here. My job is to research the growth of cancerous cells and monitor how they "hijack" healthy cells. What we've learned so far from the seeds of this plant is that they contain a chemical compound that slows down and effectively traps those cells that corrupt the others. It's early days but we're now trying to replicate this compound to manufacture a new drug for future patients, and the possibilities for treating various forms of cancer are endless from this stage onward. This is a huge breakthrough.*'

The former measured tone of the broadcaster returned.

'*We're getting a flood of comments from Twitter. Sarah Rose from Leeds says, "It's time the world had some good news…"*'

Richard was nodding quietly. Marianne snorted at the last part.

'What?' He looked at her sharply.

'Sorry. I just hate Twitter.'

'Still,' he said, turning the radio back down again, 'that is phenomenal. If only it happened years earlier.'

'If only it happened centuries earlier. If only cancer never existed in the first place.'

He stared at her. His shoulders were rigid. She was being crass and there was no reason for it, or at least she couldn't see why she had felt the impulse to be cruel.

Richard's mother was dying of bowel cancer. Radiotherapy hadn't worked, and she'd spent the last few months incontinent. Her death was privately welcomed by Marianne, because she was disturbed that anyone could continue to exist in such a humiliating way. Her spirit had once been sharply erect, like an invisible spear through her spine, propping up her body. When they found her sitting in her own shit one day, when her legs had grown numb, Marianne was unnerved by how little the woman complained. There was no passing stage in which she softened and phlegmatic anger gave way to some last-minute pink-eyed tenderness before the end. She just negated herself. She stopped talking. She stopped looking anybody directly in the eye. She was waiting for the end, the ultimate anaesthetic. To be nothing was her aim, the thing she single-mindedly sat in wait for, driving herself towards that goal as though her will was growing sharp again only for the event that would undo it.

She had been lost in thought while Richard dished up and set out two plates on the counter. His shoulders sloped morosely.

'I'm sorry,' she said. She pushed her bag off the table.

'What?'

'I'm sorry for being nasty.'

'It's fine.'

'It's not. I'm really sorry.'

Marianne reached for his wrist and closed her fingers around it. Richard looked down and placed his hand over hers. They stared at one another.

'I don't mean to be horrible,' Marianne said. She felt a heat rising through her face and clutched his hand firmly. 'I sometimes hear myself saying these words and I don't know where they come from. I hope you know, I really do…'

She had been about to say something that hadn't been said before. They both heard it die in her throat.

She didn't want to say anything that might be false and would eventually compromise her. It was in these moments that she saw the shadow of a truth she had no courage, as yet, to face; that she was strongly disposed towards love, had sensed something like it pressing on her thoughts, but she wasn't certain of its legitimacy. It was more like a flinching passion, born out of sorrow and regret, perhaps even the intimation of loss.

She was effectively mourning the end of their life together while it was still in progress, had barely just begun. And the strength of this feeling was so similar to what she supposed love to be that she was convinced it cancelled the end of itself. She'd feel an intense wave of pity, the kind that made her slightly sick, and her passion would flow back to its source.

She couldn't deny that she felt most strongly towards Richard when he was defenceless. It might be when he told a joke that landed flat in front of his friends, or when his mother spoke over him and pretended he wasn't there. Marianne had a morbid desire to see him collapse under the strain of himself. That was when her 'love' crawled out of its lair to meet him.

She was only truly aroused when his mind darkened, when she saw something that briefly mirrored her own panic and, when they made love, occasionally received it. The force of his body was a shock, not the kind that urged reciprocity but, rather, forbade and crushed it. Her energy gave way and she was gradually nullified, her responses broken down. All along she thought she could expel loss by adopting someone else's pain, diluting hers to lose its terrible potency. When he finally pulsed through, she felt opposed to him and panicked that it was too late to revoke access. Marie was still there. Or rather, she wasn't. That chilling fact was freshly realised in the worst moments, causing her muscles to constrict as it passed through. It was then that she yearned for the purity of her own despair.

This kind of lust was too bleak to constitute real, lasting love. She knew she would have to end it soon. She was presently treading water, waiting for the plunge.

She let go of his wrist and cradled her hands in her lap. He had been watching her closely as she gradually lost composure and sank away from him.

'I didn't even ask – how was your appointment?' Richard said. His voice was even.

'Yeah, it was... I don't know. I said the pills aren't really having much of an effect at the moment. but she said it's normal to take this long. I showed her the hair. *Hairs*. There are three now.'

'In the same place?'

'One is here, on the back of my neck.' Marianne turned her back to Richard and bent her head.

He dropped his fork and stood to have a look. She wasn't expecting him to pull on it, so the pain made her a little sick.

'Hey!'

'Sorry. I just don't like it.'

'I asked *her* to do that but I guess she forgot. Or *I* forgot. I had a blood test after I saw her.'

'Does she know why they're growing there?' Richard asked.

'No. She said she'd probably find something telling from the blood results. I just have to wait a week.'

She nursed a hand on her back, running her palm over her tailbone.

'Did you get my antihistamines?' Richard asked.

'Oh shit.'

'Great.'

'Sorry.'

'It's fine. You had a blood test.'

Marianne frowned at him.

'Well, I can imagine you just wanted to come home.'

'I've had blood tests before. It was the nurse who stressed me out more than the needle. She was an absolute bully.'

'You bring it out in people.' He said it casually.

'Thanks.'

'I'm joking!' he said.

He leaned forward and kissed her. She was always surprised how tender his mouth could be.

That night, Marianne fell asleep watching one side of Richard's face. She thought he was always slightly aware of her in some sense but he was partially submerged, one eye pressed shut against the pillow as he materialised into the unconscious. Or rather, became immaterial, unfettered. She touched his face the most when he wasn't aware of it, or of anything. The eyebrow she could see dived at an angle into the pillow, frowning at nothing.

She wished she was aware of the moment in which she too entered the other side of everything; but, like death, immersion defies recollection. She was awake and then she was not. The gulf in between might have lasted ten seconds, but what she could remember was just a fraction of it. A series of images jerked through the darkness, all of which she'd never retrieve beyond the seconds in which they emerged. Apart from one.

She was in a forest she distinctly remembered from her child-hood, one to which her parents often took her and Marie. It was somewhere in Windermere and she was wet – very wet, not just a little, as though she'd just emerged from the lake itself. And she was alone. She dripped barefoot through the forest, leaving damp footprints. Her hands were dry and dirty from touching the trees for balance. Now and again, a jagged piece of bark fell away in her hand.

Marie's voice came from inside one of those trees. There was a pause when Marianne approached an ash tree.

'They put me here, Mari. They put me here.'

The voice came from a very deep centre in the trunk. Marianne might have believed it if someone told her the hollow extended to the underside of the world. The roots were very high, like Marie was flexing them and she could lift them from the earth.

The voice shuddered and came back low.

'They thought I could rest here – but I asked to be cremated, Mari!'

Marianne saw that the tree was split somewhere from the top and, if she pulled both ends of the bark, there was an opening. But when she reached to peel the corners back, a smell from the inside caused her to fall back.

'Mari!'

She knew, with that fatal certainty in which dreams are construed, that she would see a perverted copy of Marie inside the tree. A glittering mass of bloody limbs and nerve endings that tailed off into the dark. She vaguely recalled the illustrations in her biology textbooks at school, of the human body reduced to its nervous outline. There was a mouth where Marie's voice had filtered through, but it was the helm of something awful that didn't make sense.

She must not have moved her head far from Richard's as, for days afterwards, he claimed he still had a tiny ringing in his left ear. She only came to when he slapped her with a strength she'd never suspected of him.

'Stop it!' he bellowed, sitting up fast. She was burning in her pillow. 'What the fuck!'

She knew then that she'd screamed, because when she stopped, the silence startled her. She sat up too and stared at Richard.

'Why did you hit me?'

'You yelled in my ear!'

He tossed the duvet aside and got up to wander the room. Marianne remembered the image she'd seen seconds earlier.

'Marie.'

Grief came in hot flashes. She ran her fingers through her hair and dug them up and down the scalp quickly. Richard swooped back down to pull her hands away.

'Marie,' she said to him emptily. 'Marie!'

It was coming, and she pre-empted it with her fingernails, now tearing at Richard's T-shirt, bunching it up in her fists. The black spot opened up in her head, and inside of it, the nucleus itself, was Marie and her failure to exist. The revelation grew with every second like a cancerous cell, multiplying so quickly she thought she would grow mad. Marie was outside of the universe. Enormous and infinite as it was, it failed to contain her; it contained no sign of her. The black spot had reached the optic nerves behind Marianne's eyes, and she saw nothing.

Richard was tugging her everywhere he could to stop her free-falling into the space inside her head.

'Marie,' she whispered.

'Ssh. Don't.'

He seemed to know, by gripping her body, how large her grief was inside of it. His arms came up around her neck.

'Don't, Marianne. I've got you.'

She breathed her way into a hoarse silence, gasping every few minutes. Those gasps became less frequent as the night progressed, until she was finally still. He sat next to her with his arm curled around her neck and they watched the bed from the floor.

She didn't feel as though he had her. Everything had lost its grip; the world was slack-handed. Convulsive despair has a quick trajectory and she was released without progressing from it. There was not any less of it to feel from this night onwards, nor was there anything more to be gained from it. So she waited, with Richard beside her, who she knew was also still awake, for the sake of waiting.

MARIE WAS A BLUE CHILD. For the first few months, her head had tiny blue veins that congregated at certain points where Marianne believed the pressure of being conscious was perhaps too much. Her skin was tinged blue. She had blue eyes and continued to have blue eyes. As if she were composed of water, not blood and muscle and bone. Marianne didn't want to hold her so she watched her in the cot and tried to make sense of her. She herself was only five years old, but she felt unusually responsible for this fragile new life.

Their mother, Heather, was more concerned that Marie was generally very quiet. She was too silent for peace of mind. Heather would pick Marie up and cradle her, waiting for her to make a sound that would finally convince everyone she was thriving. She appealed to their father, 'Why is she still sleeping? Why isn't she ready for feeding?' David shook his head and told her to get some sleep herself. But when Heather disappeared, Marianne felt uneasy watching the child with her father. She detected nothing at the heart of his vigilance, no authentic desire for the task at hand. He watched the television set with the volume down and she watched him. His eyes wandered across the striped wallpaper and always settled on the kind of blank space that seemed to relieve him of the continual pressure of thought, one after another, always inserting itself rudely into his head without permission. At least that is what Marianne imagined when his eyes refused to be filled.

She took it upon herself to watch the baby, kneeling at the bars of the cot. It struck her how very wrinkled the child was. The corners of her eyes were slightly puckered and her body had so many lines and folds, as if there were too much skin to start with. As if the body was retreating back to where it came from. Marie did not yet possess the frightening, volcanic energy of a life that must command itself at once; instead, she was passively inclined and sought nothing of the world. She never cried or threw out her little fleshy arms; she was silent and somnolent, existing because she had no choice. This was what pained her mother, though Marianne did not understand at the time.

Heather suffered from the 'baby blues', something Marianne was told did not happen when *she* was born but did when Marie came into the picture. She thought it was an apt description, considering the strange hue of Marie's skin. And forever afterwards, she associated Marie's shadowy body with that unconquerable grief that leaves an imprint in the blood. Heather was given anti-depressants, and for a while she was drawn into a stupor not dissimilar from the one Marie was trapped in. She stopped checking on the child every hour in the night to reassure herself that it had not died. She stopped rearranging everything in the bathroom cupboard behind the mirror. She stopped ringing her mother and then hanging up just in time so as to escape the sound of her voice. The insidious panic about whatever it was she dreaded happening died down.

In its place, she became extraordinarily placid, though nobody confused it with relief. On the contrary, David knew his wife was still living out her private fears under the influence of medication. What nobody would ever know was the way in which she watched her terrors expand and conflate in that cold room of thought without possessing the energy to attend to any of them. Instead, she quivered at night, pressed upon the mattress of these insane realities, all of them hypothetical, feeling them with her body along the seconds, until something in her bloodstream stole her from her crisis. That was the only way she knew the drug was playing its part. It froze her night-marish progress from the moment of conception, seizing the panic that arose from a single thought, right before it peaked. The problem was that she would rather peak than submit to this dull tension, this inability to evacuate anything from her brain in one glorious second.

Marianne wondered whether her own black line of thought began with their mother, whether it was hereditary. She never thought anything of it until the end of Marie's life. In fact, it had been very easy to pay little to no attention to her mother at all while she was a child because Heather disappeared to her bedroom, the only place the children could never enter in the house, when she was sick. 'Sick', Marianne knew now, was a term for something her father wouldn't divulge, and which must necessarily be voided from the girls' memories. Marianne never found it strange that her parents had two separate bedrooms until she began to visit the homes of her friends at school. When she told their parents that her own did not share the one room, she was always surprised by the rueful expressions she got.

She only understood intimacy insofar as Marie was concerned. She did not simply love her sister, she *craved* her. As a toddler,

Marie was golden-haired. She had lost the sleepy blue tinge to her skin. Her eyes widened and the irises were a very pale, icy blue that gave the impression she saw everything with forensic detail. Her eyelashes were long and thick and balanced neatly on her cheeks and eyelids. Her face had the plaintive aspect of one who doesn't know how to process any dark element of life.

When Marie was ten, their father witnessed her running out into the road in front of their house to collect a tennis ball. She seemed to glide weightlessly across the road as if the air carried her like a leaf stolen by gravity. A car swerved to a halt. Marie blinked at the driver when he opened the door, stepped out and cursed at her, his hands shaking. David had watched the incident from the window and ran outside to intervene. Marie's imperturbable demeanour, her refusal to respond to the driver's rage, was evidently taken as an insult. Marianne also suspected that he was disturbed by her in a way he might not have been able to explain.

Afterwards David spoke to Marie about her carelessness. Marianne sat on the stairs and eavesdropped. Their mother was absent – in her room, out of bounds. Marianne plucked the fibres of the carpet, wrenching them free, while she listened.

'I'm sorry,' said Marie.

'But what good is that once you're dead?' he said.

'I would still be sorry. More sorry.'

Marianne frowned at the banister.

'Don't be stupid. Once you're dead, you're dead.'

He always seemed to be spouting these truisms. They had seemed ludicrous at the time but Marianne would remember them sombrely. Sometimes, the truth had more potency when it was trapped in itself.

'I would still be sorry.'

'*Hey*. Stop being smart with me.'

'I'm not. I don't mean to be. I'm sorry!'

There was a pause, and then their father's muffled voice came as though through the wall of Marie's body.

'I want you to be less stupid. You'll give me a heart attack one day.'

'No, I won't. I won't.'

He laughed while he was buried in her chest. He must have been sitting on the futon and Marie had stood to embrace him. Marianne could imagine his balding head from above, where the view of him was the saddest. She was anxious to join them but something about their voices suggested a privacy she couldn't stake any claim on.

Marianne wished she could release herself from the burden of loving Marie. She was accepted as a permanent feature of Marie's world, as consistent as the bed that she slept in and the cereal she had for breakfast. But she was not essential. She was never really sought out or summoned from her bedroom to help Marie pass the time; it was usually the other way around. Marie knew how to be alone, to subsist from some private centre that she alone knew about, abstracting herself without warning. Marianne would wonder where Marie pooled her thoughts, for she never really shared them with anyone unprompted. How was it possible to exist in such secrecy? She was certainly capable of passion but she never verbalised it, never felt the compulsion that Marianne had to divulge her occasionally dark impulses. Perhaps she had none.

As Marie approached adulthood, this quiet insularity seemed deliberate as opposed to unconscious. She was also beginning to recognise the rarity of her condition – that very few people can be truly independent. Marianne suspected a single note rang through her sister's blood and vibrated with silent urgency, humming like a forest with roots that operated predominantly beneath the surface. That earthy silence – where she sought her pleasure without assistance – was her black secret. Marianne envied her that way of existing purely from the inside.

When they went to Williamson Park with their father, Marie would find ways to bury herself. In the autumn months, she would lie on the ground and ask Marianne to heap piles of flaming leaves on her prostrate form. Then she'd slowly extend her arms and legs so that the leaves would fall away again – it was a game and Marianne had to hide Marie's wriggling body. The 'grave game', Marie would call it. There was also a large oak tree that had a hole in the base of the trunk, and she would crawl inside that hollow centre and sit there for hours while Marianne walked through the woods with her father. He used to be a tree surgeon, and he would point out all the species of tree they saw and tell her the Greek myths and legends surrounding each one. They could see Marie's scarlet Converse trainers poking through the tree from afar, signalling to them that she was still there.

And yet she was not really anywhere. She had crammed herself into a space that seemed to have whittled down her thoughts to the bare minimum required to exist. She was quietly satiated by this spot where the walls seemed to pulse. 'It's alive,' she would tell Marianne. She sat inside it like a foetus. The older she got, the harder it was to cram herself inside until she finally gave up and stroked the heavy opening with her hands, bidding goodbye to her darkness.

Once they left the woods, Marie would glide from one activity to another, casting off the last impression – one that barely made an imprint before its erasure – and cleanly inhabiting the present, never quite clutching it or mourning its end in advance. There was no sudden dent in her mood, where the weight of expectation sank in on itself – at least, Marianne couldn't see any evidence of it. Marie didn't seem to accumulate layers of experience like everyone else, like so many woollen garments to be shrugged off at the end of the day, the pockets weighed down with paraphernalia; rather, she swanned through the seconds like they were made of silk, slipping them off as easily as they fell into place, unwrinkled and unblemished.

She would hurl herself on the tyre swing, then lean her head so far back that her hair brushed the leaves on the ground and the blood sank into her face. She'd sit up and stare, mesmerised, if a dog pranced by, always honoured by its reciprocal interest in her. While Marianne and David chatted at the cafe, she would be wholly absorbed in eating, her eyes glazed over, not glancing up until every crumb was gone. Afterwards, they'd visit the butterfly house, where Marie considered every specimen with solemn interest. If an insect landed on her head, she'd remain stock-still so it could find its footing in the strands of her hair. Her concentration, her pleasure too, was absolute. Nothing existed but what was immediately at hand, though she adapted, always, to the loss of it.

She'd sometimes hum to herself, a monotone sound – which was when Marianne could tell she had reached a point of consciousness from which there was no calling her back. There was a chance she didn't realise she was doing it; it was extremely quiet, barely audible in a crowded place. Often Marie would take a breath and the pitch would bounce up slightly, as though her thoughts had moved higher up where the air was strange. Then she'd continue to build on the original sound, recovering neutral ground. Marianne and her parents would joke about it, but it never truly irritated them because it was one of Marie's harmless quirks. That was not to say that it didn't occasionally grow tiresome. Sometimes Marianne would prod her sharply in the back and Marie would then pretend to break her finger off. She was surprisingly strong when she wanted to be.

David's mother lived quite close to them in Lancaster and he would take Marianne and Marie to visit her. She had an enormous garden with a wall of trees at the bottom, and she asked her granddaughters to take care of it for her. She would not think of hiring a gardener to tend to her plants; instead she tasked the girls with watering and fertilising her flowers. They were taught how to prune damaged limbs and how to add mulch to the soil to stop the weeds from growing. She would show them how to do all of this with her trembling hands, lined with veins that criss-crossed the knuckles. Her thumbs were thick and strong like her son's, the nails slightly brittle because she liked to use her hands as much as she could before they finally became too convulsive. Her oak trees were looked after by David and it was something of a religious exercise for her to watch him out there with the girls, preserving that fertile peace. 'I have one Adam and two little Eves,' she said.

Marie spotted the blood first. She called it blood because it certainly looked like it, a dark oozing trail from a split in the bark. The tree was leaking through the skin, secreting its secrets, which dried like honeyed bruises. Marie asked her father whether the tree was poorly.

'It's infected,' he said. 'There must be bacteria in the tree. It might spread to the others.'

He would have to fell the tree to save the others. Something about this course of action frightened Marie.

'It's alright,' her grandmother said, placing her blue-veined hand on Marie's shoulder. 'We'll have a nice fire and burn it.'

They watched David slice into the trunk with a chainsaw, creating two notches from either side so that he could force his way through the centre. Marianne enjoyed the suspense before it eventually gave way. Marie was forlorn, shouting through the noise. As the chainsaw buzzed, she called to Marianne, 'When is it dead?' For a while, Marianne could hardly respond because she couldn't ascertain anything. All she knew was that her father was delivering something from an eventual fatality, a slow-moving demise. That the tree did not complain, did not move or echo its malaise, but stood as silent as ever while the rot ate through its body, made her slightly sick. If the tree had a heart, it was arrested from beating. An intervention was necessary for the others to remain pure.

When the trunk was flat along the ground, its body was a horrible thing. It was not over. Their father stripped the outer bark and sapwood; then he set fire to its long, thwarted limb. The flames licked the body finally to nothing. 'It's for the best,' said their grandmother when Marie began to cry. Marianne was annoyed that she was so sentimental about a tree.

For her eighteenth Christmas, Marie asked their mother if they could have a real fir tree installed in the living room.

'Why?' Heather said.

She was flossing her teeth in the bathroom mirror, gurning at Marie, who stood behind her in the doorway and was visible in the glass. Marianne noticed that Marie's eyes were never drawn to her own reflection. Even when she washed her face. She never caught her own eye.

'Because it will smell of the forest,' she said.

Heather ran her tongue over her gums and watched herself.

'It'll shed all over the carpet. You knock it even slightly, those firs will shed.' She turned and looked at Marie. 'Bit like you with your hair.'

'My hair is tidy,' Marie said.

'It's everywhere. It's in the carpet, the bottom of the bath, the washing machine.'

'What's she supposed to do? Shave it off?' Marianne said.

Heather turned around and spotted Marianne sitting on the stairs, watching them.

'Who asked you?'

'I'm just saying. I wouldn't mind one too. I'll pay for it.'

Heather closed the bathroom door and locked it. Marie looked at Marianne with a smile.

'You're pushy.'

'Someone's got to be,' Marianne said.

A week later, Marianne found a small fir tree at the garden centre and brought it home once she'd finished work at the stationery shop in town. She'd taken a black velvet ribbon from the shop – for some reason, she wasn't inclined to go for the usual festive colours – and tied it round the trunk before Marie came home from school. She put it in Marie's bedroom.

When Marie arrived, she ran up the stairs lightly as though her feet barely touched the floor. Her face was patchy from the cold; one cheek was much pinker than the other and, Marianne thought, there was something blue beneath the skin when the colour died down. In the past year, she'd begun to turn blue again, and it was only then that Marianne recalled the strange hue of her skin in the early years. It was not like a bruise, more like the ghost of a violent sensation, felt internally, where the blood had left an imprint when it gathered behind the face, peering through the skin as one might press oneself against a window. Marianne didn't know whether she'd imagined it, twisting her memory of things to persuade herself that life has a way of revealing the truth to you before it occurs.

When Marie saw the tree, fat and full, in the corner of her bedroom, she sank to her knees, then brushed the back of her hand along the branches in a gentle manner, like she was stroking a cat. There was a sudden earthy smell, which she had activated, like the tree was emitting pheromones. For the first time, Marianne found Marie's joy vaguely irritating. It was just too much. It defied any mature and reasonable distance from the thing. Instead, she plunged herself towards the absolute physical limit of it, touching every branch and brushing them against her face.

'Calm down. It's a *tree*,' Marianne said with her arms folded.

That same month, Marianne noticed that Marie's calves were covered in large bruises, some of them already turning yellow. And she was noticeably paler. Her eyelids were traced with tiny blue veins that seemed to bleed into her line of vision.

'What the hell have you been doing?' Marianne asked her.

'I don't know. I guess I bruise easily.'

The way her skin changed its colour so readily disturbed Marianne. She also spotted a small purple mark behind Marie's ear, shaped like a comma. She fancied her sister's body was communicating something to her without Marie's consent.

She was not the only one troubled by what was appearing. Marie's form tutor, Miss Grady, rang the house one afternoon when Marianne happened to be at home, having finished early at the shop.

'Could I speak to Mrs Turner?'

'She's not in. Sorry.'

'Ah, are you Marie's sister? Is it – Marianne?'

'Yes.'

'I'm her form tutor, Jo Grady. I was just calling to discuss – to talk about a delicate matter but one that is quite serious.'

Marianne said nothing, so Mrs Grady continued.

'I'm worried about Marie. You must have noticed she has a rather large number of bruises, and she is looking – unwell. Very thin. She doesn't appear to me to be in a fit state for study and other teachers have noticed that she seems very tired in her lessons.'

'I—' Marianne was struggling to find anything useful to say. 'I have noticed the bruises but she says she doesn't know what's caused them.'

'Has she seen a doctor?'

'No. She rarely does.'

'I wonder – how are her eating habits?'

'Fine. She eats,' Marianne said sharply.

'She doesn't limit her food intake in any way?'

'She's not anorexic.'

'I'm sorry. I don't want to seem like I'm prying but – as I said – I *am* concerned for her. She's clearly not well.'

Marianne looked out of the kitchen window. Their small garden was prickly and cruel without flowers and, unlike the other gardens on their lane, which bore fairy lights and flashing LED reindeers, this one held a compact darkness. The gloom immediately below their window made her push the phone deeper into her skin.

'We can take her to a doctor if you think someone should—'

'Oh yes, I do. She should be examined. I also think she should spend the rest of the week at home. I know this is the last week before term ends but I look at her and – I think she's struggling. She needs to get her strength back over the Christmas break.'

'Okay. Is she in a lesson right now?'

'No. She's actually just sitting in reception. I left her there to call you. Do you want to speak to her?'

'Yes, please.'

Marianne waited. She refused to look out of the window.

'Hello,' Marie's voice materialised.

'Hey, is this true then? You're falling asleep in class?'

'No.'

'But you're knackered. And the bruises – people are starting to notice.'

'Yes.'

'Are you coming home now?'

'I think so. Can you pick me up?'

'Of course.'

There was a pause.

'Are you – how come you haven't said anything?' Marianne said.

'I don't know. I don't want to go to the doctor.'

'You have to. I'm going to take you there today.'

'No – there won't be any appointments available.'

'I'll book an emergency one.'

Marie groaned.

'I'll be there in half an hour.'

The surgery was full but Marie was admitted to see someone straight away – a dark-haired woman with very small eyes who watched Marie carefully as she escorted her from the waiting room. It occurred to Marianne that perhaps she should have gone with Marie. *But she's old enough to go on her own.* Then she descended into bitter thoughts. The fact of the matter was that she was losing patience with Marie and her complacency. Perhaps an illness of some sort was necessary to force her out of it. She watched the double doors and hoped that Marie would emerge at a loss for words.

Was it complacency? Marianne wasn't always sure. She recalled a dream Marie had once told her about, only because she'd been asked to write about one for a homework assignment. It was about a year ago now, though Marianne had often thought of it since.

Marie had described how she wandered into a doctor's surgery, seemingly by accident – though surely everything in a dream is some sort of casualty of logic. She had instinctively known that she needed to be operated on, without knowing why. The surgeon welcomed her with an elongated smile, almost too large for his face. The reason for her operation then dawned on her. There was a hole in her brain. It needed stitching back up immediately, otherwise she'd lose her mind. The surgeon told her that there would be no anaesthetic as it was dangerous to put her to sleep at this point, that she had to hold on to her thoughts while they operated. 'I could see what he was doing as he was doing it. My eyes had gone – inward.' She felt the shadow of his scalpel before it plunged through the membrane. The hole was immediately conscious of an intruder and began to glide away from the point of incision, resisting all attempts to pin it down. The surgeon then took a saltshaker and began to sprinkle great crystal shards on the wound where he'd sliced Marie's head open.

It was a bizarre dream and they'd both laughed about it. Marianne was once convinced Marie had invented it, just so she would be able to produce something macabre, the sinister Freudian tale her teacher obviously wanted from such an exercise. But she also felt, in hindsight, that it was too weird to be the product of design. She didn't think it was fabricated – or rather, it was a fabrication of unconscious origin. And she didn't know which one was worse.

When she came through the waiting room doors, Marie was clutching her arm. Marianne knew at once that the nurse had taken blood.

'It's likely a deficiency of something – iron maybe,' she said on the way home.

'When do you get the results?'

'Don't know. I can't remember what she said.'

'Fuck's sake, Marie.'

Marie flinched as she always did when Marianne swore.

They didn't say anything to their parents. But when they were eating at the kitchen table, Marianne had the compulsion to say something even if it wasn't kind. She noticed how different Marie looked under the overhead light, while the muscles in her face were in motion as she ate. And she also realised that she wasn't alone in noticing the difference. Heather also stared, deep in concentration, at the blue hollows of Marie's face, turning the meat over in her mouth in a rigid manner, her jaw shooting quickly from one side to the other.

David spoke about his mother, telling everyone that she was beginning to forget what day it was, that she presumed Christmas was already over. Lately, whenever her social worker came to visit, she found the old woman packing the tinsel and baubles away. Every time, the social worker put everything back again and laughed it off, but after the fifth time, she gave in to the woman's furious conviction – that the new year had begun and she was tired of God and Jesus taking up space in her house. Marie gazed at him for long periods at a time, her knife and fork perfectly crossed in the centre of her plate.

'You're not hungry?' Marianne said to her.

'No. I'm not feeling well.'

She had never said anything like this in her life.

Later, when they were sitting in Marie's bedroom, she confided to Marianne of a tight swelling in her chest.

'Can I have a look?' Marianne asked.

Marie lifted her jumper, which was large and lumpy. Her ribcage heaved through the skin like the shadows of splayed fingers. And there it was – the thing that had been oppressing her all this time. A lump beneath her left rib cage, hard as a stone.

'Shit.' Marianne pressed it lightly with her fingertip.

Marie squirmed under her touch.

'Did you show that to the doctor?'

She had the decency to look ashamed. 'No.'

'You're an idiot! Why *wouldn't* you?'

'I don't know.'

Marie lay back on her pillow and watched Marianne with a quietness that chilled them both.

'I wish you'd take things more seriously,' Marianne said finally.

She returned to her room and tried not to think about Marie, but it was impossible not to. There were countless thoughts she wished she could erase but they only seemed to grow in significance and threatened to repeat themselves. The panic that had once informed them was suspended for a time but now she knew it was hovering below the surface, waiting to insert itself again.

She recalled the years when she used to cross the landing to Marie's bedroom, enter without knocking and sit on her bed.

Marie always woke very quickly. Marianne asked her questions that were frank and fearful, as though she was convinced her younger sister was closer to the truth than she was because she seemed to exist instinctively and without effort. 'I wish I knew when I was going to die,' Marianne once said to that dazed expression against the headboard, 'then I could be ready for it. Not knowing is worse. I hate not knowing when I'll be over. Do you think we'll end up somewhere else?' Marie barely ever gave a coherent answer, but she held on to Marianne's knee. It took Marianne years to realise there was nothing conciliatory in the gesture. While Marie had a vaguely theoretical interest in what Marianne said in her moments of darkness, she didn't respond as one who had ever shared it. The concept of the afterlife was lost on her because she didn't *really* believe in death. The hand on Marianne's knee was an attempt to mute her, to keep her thoughts still. Marie didn't want to be embroiled in them.

Throughout Marianne's teenage years, she lost herself to that peculiar panic. She could never absolutely guarantee that she would be alive in the next second. She could only positively assure herself that she had happened, not that she would continue to happen. The idea of becoming lost forever would create an immediate tension in her head, as though she was bound to prepare for it now while she could, her consciousness pooling at the limit, gathering speed for a route it would never enter. She wondered whether the fact that she thought about it so often held her in good stead. She was also convinced that there were secret methods to prolong herself, that certain practices, like moving symmetrically through the world, with both sets of limbs matching one another, would lengthen her existence, while others, like losing sleep, would bring death a second closer at a time. She was locked in herself without really wanting to be released, knowing that light-heartedness was something she would simply never grasp, for grasping types never fare well and remain trapped in their fixations.

Marianne did not attract the kind of disciples that her sister did, those who gravitated towards calm energy, a prevailing lightness of temper. Marianne drove everyone away with her rigid silences. Her sister was silent most of the time too, but she negated herself without tension. Marianne dropped out of company like a stone. In fact, she often felt the vertigo of one who slips and loses their balance yet never gets used to it. *I live in panic*, she thought. *I live in dread of every day.*

But Marianne had lived through adolescence without pricking herself to death. Once she left home for university, her raggedness disappeared, her edges softened. The library was a genuine haven for critically minded people with a quiet resolve to learn and her thoughts no longer spiralled discursively into darkness, rather they moved at a steady pace. Her essays were methodical and concise. She made plausible friendships for the first time. Spoke with an authority that arrived from nowhere.

She began to write freely, unprompted by any assignment, recording her thoughts so they would be stored for posterity. Posterity, to Marianne's mind, meant the offspring of her ever-evolving consciousness, this mysterious code that adapted to different contexts and produced myriad editions of herself, all of them flickering into being at different stages of her life. She tried to pin down something of her essence even while it was still so tenuous, so that she would commune with that version of Marianne at a later date.

At university, she filled herself from the bottom up, growing into what she once thought was a dead end – though she kept this growth to herself, preferring to exist three quarters below the surface. Writing was a mechanism for relief, a stable method of attending to the dark part of herself, keeping it in check by assembling the right words. And sometimes it was enough – the relief of translating something of herself in as precise a fashion as she could manage was enough to satisfy it, without even finding an answer. She was her sole audience. Whereas before, she had craved company, now she resisted it, skipping nights out for time spent alone. It was worth the quiet growth of her inner life, and she knew it wasn't the only condition available to her but, significantly, one she had chosen. She had only been frightened of being alone when she'd had no other option.

Growing up with Marie had taught her not to share that secret store of feeling and expect much in return. Sometimes at university, lying awake in her bedroom, she granted herself a private audience and strained to make sense of the raw part of her psyche. It was fruitless but far less agonising than what had occurred previously. At least she was no longer in danger of misappropriating someone, fastening her fears on to another's consciousness and trying to reel it in towards her. She hadn't been able to do it with Marie, and the effort had cost her.

ONCE RICHARD LEFT FOR WORK on Monday, Marianne was due a Skype call with the editor of *Empowered*, Anna Mason. She carried her laptop downstairs and placed it on the kitchen counter, though she wasn't sure why it seemed the right place. Perhaps it was that the kitchen offered an impression of industry with its glossy surfaces and appliances – most of which Richard had bought, including the coffee machine from Harrods – and any other room bore little resemblance to a professional environment. Marianne angled the screen towards different parts of the room before settling on the coffee machine as a backdrop. She'd decided to wear a black and white polka dot shirt and, for the first time in weeks, she was wearing mascara and had applied a generous amount of concealer to the areas of her face that had become slightly grey, especially under her eyes, where the skin was turning blue then yellow like a bruise. She heard the chirpy dial tone and waited for Anna's face to emerge.

Anna wasn't looking at the screen when she appeared on it. Typically, Marianne thought, she was keeping her at a carefully considered distance, even in the short time she'd allotted her for a one-to-one. She had a vertiginous head, inverted towards the chin, with a large, shadowy temple.

'Marianne, hi. Just bear with me for a sec.' She turned again to talk to somebody just out of view of the webcam. 'Please don't presume you have the authority to make that kind of decision. You pass it by me. The interview is too long and I asked you to remove the part about her mindfulness campaign on Instagram because it's all cliché. Besides, we covered all that last issue. You know which bit to focus on.'

A woman's voice mumbled something in reply but Marianne could only catch the words 'off the record'.

'There's no such thing. Please do as I ask. I'm relieving you of your conscience, alright?' Anna laughed towards Marianne as though she was colluding with her. 'I'm in a call, Michelle. Send me the piece once you've made the edits.'

The door closed and Anna faced Marianne directly.

'Right. I read the interview,' Anna said. 'We're not running it for this issue.'

'Really? I thought you said—'

'The tone is all wrong. This issue is supposed to be about new beginnings.'

Marianne said nothing. Anna waited before carrying on.

'The woman in your interview doesn't seem invested in anything other than finding the right man to raise a child with. Has she seriously considered other options? Adoption? Sperm donors? And she hasn't stopped to consider the benefits of childlessness. Embarking on new adventures, travelling the world, sleeping in with a hangover at the weekend. She has a wide network of friends and a big family but she acts like none of this means anything until she's found her soul mate. Everything begins once the child begins. Why would our readers want to hear this? What good does it do to know about a woman who refuses to live for herself? There is no angle here that feeds into the hopeful spirit of the issue.'

'But it's honest. She admits she's not hopeful about her prospects but won't disguise it with any bullshit.'

'Nobody wants to read that.'

'I do.'

Anna paused and Marianne wished they were speaking on the phone. Her shirt was tight under her armpits, causing them to sweat.

'How are you doing at the moment?' Anna said. It was hardly a question, delivered in a flat tone.

'I'm better.'

'Are you in therapy?'

'No. I don't think it's something I'm interested in.'

'Fair enough.'

Anna probably genuinely meant it. Marianne couldn't imagine her advising anyone to see a therapist.

'We're considering doing an issue on trauma and PTSD down the line,' Anna continued. Marianne knew where she was going. 'And it might be fruitful, or in some way *cathartic*, for you to write a piece. We'd use it as one of our main features. Include a by-line on the cover.'

She paused and waited for Marianne to insert a reply. There was none. So she continued.

'If you were to write about your experience—'

'And say what? What do I say?' Marianne interjected. She was feeling sick.

'It's been six months. Perhaps this is the time now for some sense of closure – by writing about your sister—'

'No,' Marianne said.

She had never been abrupt with Anna, but she was no longer interested in the consequences. Anna couldn't cross the line where Marie was concerned.

'I don't want to write about her. I don't owe it to anyone.'

Anna was about to speak and Marianne broke in, 'I don't owe it to *myself* either.'

'Right.'

Anna had her hand on her mouse now and Marianne suspected she was being demoted to one of several tabs on Anna's screen. At least she wasn't on view. She raked a hand quickly through her hair and scratched her scalp.

'Marianne, I'm going to be frank with you because it's the least I can do,' Anna said, not quite looking at Marianne but presumably at her inbox. 'We're considering limiting your input to the magazine.'

'It's already limited.'

'Yes.'

'So when you say limiting, you mean reducing to zero input.'

Anna paused. 'It's been six months. You haven't been to the office in all that time. Showing your face now and again is important and you've missed a lot of key meetings which outline the direction of the magazine. You've had a lot of sick days and you don't really give us any advance notice for having the day off. One day tends to become *a week*. In that time, you just go completely offline, never answer your phone, so none of us can reach you. And as for deadlines…' There was a hollow pause as though to create suspense, but nothing in Anna's face or voice had changed. She clearly couldn't be bothered to create the desired effect. 'They're not being met. I've given you several extensions for the piece you're working on at the moment. And you still haven't mastered the *right tone*.'

'I know.'

'I really thought you might have seen a therapist by now. Or someone who can at least prescribe something that will help you.'

'I'm on medication.'

'I mean, what do they call it – hypnotherapy?' The way Anna's pupils moved informed Marianne she was looking at her again on the screen. 'Don't you want to try it at least? So you can travel into London again. Seeing your colleagues might be motivating.'

Marianne said nothing. She couldn't think of anything to say that would profit her in a larger sense, and she wasn't interested in the smaller sense.

'I *am* sorry, Marianne,' Anna said in a softer tone that was alien to her. 'I don't know what to say.'

'Neither do I.'

Anna let go of the mouse and appeared contrite for a moment.

'Look, if you want to meet for coffee soon… It's the least I can do. You've been a solid writer for us. I want to help you. I can talk to people – check around for the best clinic in London, pull some strings, see which psychotherapist has a new opening on their waiting list.'

'No, really. I'm not interested.'

The silence made them both uncomfortable. The door opened in Anna's office and Marianne saw a woman about to enter. Anna turned abruptly.

'OUT!'

The door closed and the woman was gone. Marianne felt mildly honoured.

Anna turned back to her and her face began to assume its usual tightness.

'Think about what I've said, about writing for our issue on trauma.'

'Anna, I'm not traumatised.'

'Well, I can't dispute you on it. It's not my place. But there's a reason you can't take the tube. Right?'

Marianne said nothing.

'You won't move past that episode if you don't at least admit to yourself that you're deeply affected by it in a way that is preventing you from returning to work and doing your job.'

'I thought working remotely was fine.'

'To some extent. But we both know the ones who succeed here are those who network and hustle, and show up to all the fashion conferences, health and beauty festivals, feminism work-shops and award ceremonies. Nobody has seen your face in half a year.'

Marianne couldn't meet her eyes. 'I realise that.'

Anna looked into the right-hand corner of the screen.

'I'm going to have to leave it there. We'll keep in touch, alright? I might have to move around a few meetings but I'll make sure we have time for a catch-up. Dinner perhaps. Somewhere in your neck of the woods.'

'Sure.'

'Look after yourself.'

After speaking to Anna, Marianne took a shower. She stripped and threw her shirt in the laundry, then changed her mind and stuffed it in the little bin under the bathroom sink. Then she stared at herself in the mirror. She was paler than she realised. The concealer hadn't really concealed anything. In fact it had settled on her skin without reducing the puffiness, creating the impression her eyes were sinking. She had never been a stranger colour. She turned around so that her back was facing the mirror and peered over her shoulder.

Along the ridges of her spine, not one, not three, but a steady line of hairs that grew all the way up from the tailbone, just above the crack of her bottom, towards the middle of her neck. There were too many to count. Perhaps as many as fifty. She felt duty-bound to count otherwise she'd be admitting defeat. If they defied a limit, they had become as essential to her form as the hairs on her head.

She pulled a handful from the middle of her back and watched the skin rise without releasing them, growing redder the harder she pulled. She turned and rooted through the cabinet behind the mirror for a pair of tweezers. Precision didn't make it any easier; the pain was simply more concentrated. She took a pair of nail scissors next and tore through the hairs so quickly she clipped her skin several times. It wasn't until the blood reached the line of her bottom and curved into the darkness there that she dropped the scissors into the sink.

The shower was still running, so she washed her hands and waited for the hairs to disappear down the drain. When she stepped under the shower head she took her razor from the floor where Richard had knocked it over and straightened so she could steady it on her tailbone. In a quick, savage motion, she raked it along her spine. It split the skin instantly, but it was necessary; the skin had to be broken for the roots to give way. She sliced herself continuously in this manner, reaching over her shoulder to razor the top of her back, then parting her buttocks to shave as close to her anus as she dared, frightened that they would begin to grow there too. Thankfully, this part was clear. But it took her several attempts to wrench them from her back. They were so thick she couldn't believe the pores on her skin were wide enough to contain them.

The sting was almost unbearable at first but she soldiered past it, raking the blade over her back without allowing herself a second to recover, censoring the part of herself that was witness to what she was doing, barely registering the damage. It was a task that could only be completed with mindless industry. The ridges of her spine enforced a rhythmic rise and fall. Sometimes a cluster of hairs presented a bigger problem and halted her progress; she had to use her fingers to eke them out from the torn skin. Then she grew careless. She could no longer keep the razor straight. *What does it matter?* she thought. She swerved off course, catching a mole she'd forgotten she had, somewhere on the right side. There was a burning sensation. She carried on.

This lasted for much longer than she later wished to remember, and it was much easier than she'd thought it would be. Far too easy. It was the cloudy blood on the floor of the shower that shook her from the spell. She gasped and dropped the razor. With a trembling hand, she managed to switch the water off.

'Oh no,' she said quietly. She sounded stupid to herself.

She ran, dripping, down the hallway to retrieve a pile of towels, all of them regrettably white, and carried them back to the bathroom, trailing a steady line of blood along the carpet. Her legs began to quake. Her hands went next. And she couldn't find her face in the misted mirror, confused and aggrieved by its opacity.

Then she suffered. The pain had finally arrived. Marianne saw strange shapes on the back of her eyelids, bathed in red shadow.

The sting was spreading towards her chest, as though the hairs had roots extending towards the end of her life, creeping inward and curling round the vertebrae like ivy to an arbour. A taut network of invisible lines existed and she'd barely scratched the surface of it.

She lay on her stomach with the towel pressed to her back until the fibres dried in the blood, knitting themselves to her skin. It would be hell having to pull it off again. She rested her left cheek on the tiled floor, and then switched the pressure to her right. Then she grew cold.

The phone rang and she wondered whether it was worth answering. But it might be Richard. Her joints were stiff when she lifted herself up and the sting returned like a whip. She moved slowly along the hallway with the towel hanging from her back like a cape. Every time she moved her arms and legs, the sting broke through so she tried not to move her upper body, keeping her spine erect. Her hair was still wet and she realised, with horror, that it was trapped beneath the towel. She scooped it all up in one hand and tugged the ends off her back.

The phone stopped ringing.

She picked it up, gasping as the sting rippled along the ball of her shoulder. It was an old phone that came with the flat, though she wasn't sure why neither of them had thought to upgrade it. There was something antiquated now in the absence of a name or customised image that accompanied the call, something hostile about the caller's veiled identity. Her fingers were slightly numb, so it took a while for her to dial the number that would trace the call. It wasn't Richard, though she recognised the number as a local one.

Then it occurred to her it was most likely going to be Doctor Hind.

She'd placed the phone in its cradle again so when it rang out a second time, she shuddered. Perhaps the more blood she'd lost, the quicker she gave rise to panic. Everything that seemed anodyne, even slightly offensive in its mundanity – the unmade bed and the wardrobe door hanging off its hinges, the phone itself with its knotted white coil – now presented a very real threat to her continuing existence in the room. The red eye of the machine flashed out of time with the ringing, and she was convinced it was trying to translate something, a malice beyond comprehension, between each interval of sound. She snatched the phone to her ear.

'Hello?'

'Hi – what's up with you?'

It was Richard. Marianne placed her hand on her chest.

'Nothing. Sorry.'

'You sound angry.'

'No.'

'I just called to check up on you. How was the thing with Anna?'

'She's letting me go,' Marianne said quietly.

There was a silence at the other end. Marianne thought she heard him swear to himself.

'What the hell is wrong with her?' he said. 'Is she so heartless that she can't give you more time?'

'I've had time, Richard.'

'Yeah, but she hasn't a clue how much you've suffered.'

'I'm not writing what they want.'

He was breathing heavily, which she hated. 'Why are you – what's got into you?'

'What?'

'You don't sound like you care. I bet you didn't even fight for yourself! Why not?'

'I *don't* care.' She said this quickly but there was a lump in her throat. 'I was relieved actually...'

At that point, she felt breathless, like she couldn't muster the energy to speak. And she'd lost her train of thought; it seemed to be branching off in different directions, little offshoots ending nowhere. The pain was terrible.

'I want to lie down.'

'Are you alright? You sound faint.'

'I feel sick.'

The pain was starting to develop a rhythm. It was one note, a throbbing bass. She could hear its passage, a wave of sound in her blood that caused the cells to spiral upwards. Something pulsed forwards, rippling across the gap from spine to skin in one fluid movement. Inside these undulations, Marianne found relief in being materially vague. She was so taken in by it, she had an urge to answer Richard with something other than her mouth, to speak through the palm of her hand. For a second, she couldn't recall what it was that released the thought into words, and the divorce between the two paralysed her.

'Hey!' The old petulance returned to his voice.

'Sorry,' she said automatically.

'Are you drunk?'

'No.'

'Your words are slurred!'

'I feel sick.'

'Okay, sorry.'

Richard lowered his voice suddenly. Marianne knew someone in his office must have wandered close to whatever secluded part of the building he'd gone to to phone her.

'Just lie down for a bit. I'll try and come home for seven but might have to stay longer. Are you going to be alright? I'm sorry I snapped.'

Marianne frowned at the bed and said nothing.

'Ah shit,' he said. 'Can I call you back? I'm supposed to be in a meeting in five minutes.'

'Don't. There's no need,' she said.

The pain had subsided, briefly, but it was a second in which her anger took charge. It was always there, endless reserves of it.

'What?' he said.

'I've nothing else to add!'

'Right. Look, don't be upset. Don't do anything drastic.'

'Like what?'

'Mari, please don't be angry at me. I'm on your side. I just – have to go.'

She couldn't bear it when he announced he had to go and then still had plenty to say, almost as though he was prepared to be chivalrous in spite of pressing demands. Sometimes she was convinced he made these things up, that he had a meeting any minute or the phone was ringing, so that she might think him so compassionate to continue the call for as long as he could to ensure she was alright. And why *wouldn't* he be on her side? What other side was there? What did he mean by that?

'Bye, Richard.'

She didn't wait for him to say goodbye. It gave her a tiny thrill to cut the call without ceremony.

Then she saw herself in the mirror on the wall.

The blood had dried along her forearms and she'd managed to smear it over one side of her face. Her hair was also dark with it.

But when she turned around to view her back, her nausea returned – not because there were streaks of blood but because there were none. There was a series of lacerations, all of them conveying a manic energy, applied without precision, some as far out as her shoulder blade and hip bones. But they were so faint she might have scratched the skin weeks ago. There was no blood. The scars criss-crossed her spine like the scratches of a biro over a false sentence.

WHEN MARIE'S BLOOD TEST RESULTS were ready, she was summoned to the hospital to see a haematologist.

The underlying gravity of this phone call, its complicated balance of power – in that Marie knew nothing, but somebody now knew something and had deliberately withheld that information on the phone – was enough to make anyone fret, though there was no malice in the process. No deliberate cruelty in adhering to protocol. Marianne knew how doctors managed to terrorise their patients simply by maintaining that formal distance, reducing one to the status of a client waiting in line for a petty transaction, as opposed to someone hanging by a thread, unable to proceed without the facts or function without their pills.

Marie finally explained what was going on to their parents. And she did it on the morning of the appointment, while everyone was still *in medias res*, mid-conversation, half-ready for work and still sluggish from sleep. David took another gulp of his coffee but he looked like he regretted it; he winced as it went down and then his cheeks grew blotchy. Heather exhaled slowly and rested the pads of her fingers in the corners of her eyes. They might have been bracing themselves for an unannounced visitor, something that threw their plans into disarray, as though the sheer unpredictability of life was what had immediately saddened and appalled them. Marianne could tell they were brimming with questions, but Marie's answers were stilted and vague, like her thoughts weren't connecting that morning.

Preparing for the appointment resulted in a panic over trifling matters – being held up in traffic during rush hour, whether they would find a spot to park – perhaps to delay a greater anguish that wasn't readily voiced. Heather deliberated whether they should all accompany Marie – was it tempting fate if they came to the hospital en masse? Would they trigger some sort of catastrophe that wouldn't otherwise have existed by assembling in a frightened, expectant manner for it? How superstitious they were in thinking they could circumvent the inevitable. Heather finally decided that they would all go together to confront whatever it was that was lying in wait. And they tacitly agreed not to talk on the way there.

When Marie was called in the waiting room, she followed the doctor to her office with Marianne and their parents in tow. There was nothing in that corridor with its neatly carpeted floor and fading photographs of previous doctors on the walls to suggest anything other than a bland continuity, a safety in datedness.

'Take a seat,' the doctor said.

She must have been used to people eyeing her for clues as to their future, for she had a habit of ducking her chin down and turning slightly away from everyone when she spoke.

'Marie, the blood test shows that your red blood cell count is low. Your bone marrow stem cells are creating too many white blood cells that are DNA mutations and don't work in fighting off infection. These are leukaemia cells. It's a very rare type and it's referred to as hairy cell leukaemia. Young people like yourself don't usually have it but your symptoms – the weight loss, the bruising, the exhaustion – did point to something wrong with your blood cell count.'

David grasped Heather's hand. Marianne was struck by the disparity of their expressions. Her father's mouth sank so low that she saw new lines emerging where she'd never noticed around the corners. Her mother frowned deeply. The frown guided everything else, her eyebrows bending towards the tiny crevice above her nose.

'Hairy cell?' she said.

'It's called that because the faulty white blood cells have very fine hairs when seen under a microscope,' the doctor said. The colour rose in her face. 'I want you to understand that this is not a severe form of cancer – it's very slow to develop and chemotherapy treatment nearly always gets rid of the leukaemia cells.'

'Will she need chemotherapy?' David asked.

'Yes. Having seen Marie's full blood count, she will need to go through treatment straight away. She can be treated as an outpatient and we recommend a drug called pentostatin which is injected every two weeks.'

The word *chemotherapy* had silenced everyone. Marie began to frown but her face wasn't used to the expression. The bone of her temple grew dark under the overhead electric light.

'But – it's not serious?' David said.

'It's not severe no. HCL isn't like other forms of cancer. It's gradual. Easy to control. The cancerous white blood cells halt the progress of healthy white blood cells that fight off infection in the blood, so it puts you at risk of infection and anaemia.

Basically, the body isn't very good at defending itself. But chemo-therapy will redress the imbalance. There are side effects, of course, but remission shouldn't take long and you won't have to stay in hospital for the duration.'

David's face was slightly contorted. He kept looking at Marie, but she was looking at nobody.

'So…so, it's not serious? What stage is it at?'

'We don't give this type of leukaemia a *stage* as it's not aggres-sive in the same way other types of blood cancers are and we can treat it depending on the health and the physical state the patient is in. I would like to do a physical examination just to check if there are any signs of swelling in the abdomen.' The doctor turned her head to Marie. 'Sometimes, if the spleen' – she positioned her hand over the left side of her ribcage – 'is swollen, this could mean that abnormal cells are building up there too. The spleen is a major part of your immune system and removes old red blood cells, so if it's not functioning because of HCL, you're more susceptible to infections.' She looked from David to Heather and back again. 'I'd like to carry out that examination on Marie now – so if you could all wait outside?'

Marianne got up first as nobody else seemed eager to comply. She was beginning to grow tired of the collective apathy in that room; her own impulses were dangerously sharp. She held open the door for her parents and looked at Marie before leaving the room. Her sister was frowning at her lap.

In the corridor, they sat and watched the door.

'I can't believe she didn't say anything about this sooner,' David said.

Then, without warning, he began to cry, rubbing the back of his hand roughly over his mouth. Marianne exchanged a horrified glance with her mother.

'Dad, you heard what the doctor said. It's not a serious form of cancer.'

'It's still *cancer*. Just look at her – the bruises – I knew something was wrong!'

'You knew but you never said anything,' Heather said calmly.

'I didn't want to upset her or pry. She's sensitive.'

'She's nothing of the sort and you know it.' Heather's voice had a bite to it. 'She's careless and thinks nothing of herself, or anyone. Her brain is switched off half the time.'

'Mum,' Marianne warned.

'I'm amazed she went to the doctor in the first place—'

'I took her. Her form teacher rang the house a week ago because she was concerned. She said Marie was always tired and she was struggling to get through the day. People notice things.'

David held his mouth with his hand as though he was censoring himself.

'You *are* hard on her,' Marianne said suddenly to her mother.

'She makes me angry.'

Marianne understood why she was hard with an instinct sharpened by years of accidental intimacy.

When she next looked at her mother's face there were tears running down it so quickly that Marianne felt a sudden pain in her chest. She reached for her hand without thinking, and it seemed to dislodge something. A dry croak left Heather's mouth. She didn't move the rest of her face; it was trapped in its previous semblance of anger.

'I don't mean that,' she said quietly.

David seized her free hand and held it tightly. She couldn't bring herself to look at him.

'It's fine, Mum,' Marianne said gently.

'No, it's not.'

'Heather...' David began. Then he had nothing else to say. Something was weighing down his words.

They continued to sit in silence for a few minutes more. Marianne could feel her mother's hand growing cold. When the door opened again, David stood to attention straight away. The doctor motioned them back in.

'Marie's abdomen is swollen and she tells me it's been painful for a few weeks now,' she said.

'What does that mean?' David asked.

'It means the spleen may have a build-up of the leukaemic cells. If this is the case, we can test what treatment she will need by doing an MRI scan. It may be that she will need keyhole surgery to remove the spleen, but we'll wait for the MRI before making any further decisions.'

'Didn't you realise something was wrong?' Heather said to Marie.

'Yes,' Marie said. 'I thought it would go away.'

'It's common for patients to resist being examined,' the doctor said. She looked directly at Marie. 'You shouldn't feel bad about it. It's good that we're getting it sorted now. This is not an aggressive or typically life-threatening form of cancer. Treatment is very easy.'

'When does she have the MRI scan?' David asked.

'The radiographer will get in touch and send the details of your appointment in the post along with some routine instructions and information.' The doctor turned to her computer screen and began to type. Everyone was silent for a few minutes. 'Marie, are you aware of what the MRI scanner is? Are you comfortable with small spaces?'

'Yes.'

'Because there is an option to take a sedative if you don't want to be awake during the process. It takes up to an hour but it's painless – you just have to lie still. You can even listen to music.'

She smiled and everyone propped themselves up on that smile. It had a redemptive quality because she was a medic and surely she was opposed to giving out false signals? She had nothing to gain from lying and everything to lose. But perhaps these things are accidents, nervous tics.

Marie had listened to her diagnosis without conveying what she thought about it. She was slightly more solemn than usual, but that vacancy Marianne hated was still there. It was there in the car on the way home, a silence that bore no sign of unease. David and Heather spoke about her fate like it was another passenger in the car, gesticulating wildly. Heather took the wheel because David was talking very fast and she sensed there was something slightly dangerous about the manic energy with which he spoke. He was dispensing with words in a hurry while he was brave enough to do so. He had somehow managed to steer the conversation on to Marie's funeral, feeling his way along every dark possibility, baiting himself with new objects of fear until his panic reached a peak none of them had known to look out for. Marianne had never seen him hurt himself like this. Heather shouted at him to stop several times, but she gave up because he was taking them with him, with or without their consent. She had the wheel, but he was steering them, and his panic directed the way.

'She always was in danger. I *knew* something would happen to her,' he said, and his veins stood out in his forearms like the little winding roads in one of his Ordnance Survey maps. They seemed to move across the skin as he rerouted his thoughts.

'Perhaps she was born with it. Perhaps there was nothing we could do.'

'Of course there's nothing we could have done,' Heather snapped. 'Cancer cells don't appear because of inadequate parenting! Will you be *quiet*.'

'She's too young to go through it,' David said after a moment's pause.

'Oh, for god's sake.'

'Dad, stop,' Marianne said from behind. 'You heard the doctor. It's not a serious form of cancer. Most people who have it go into remission. It's *not* fatal.'

She turned to Marie, who stared at her father in the mirror overhead.

Their father's meltdown on the journey home from the hospital had driven Marie even further into her silence. Only now there was something lonely in it. She was signed off from college for the last week of term, so she had the house to herself when everyone else was at work. Heather was around the most – she was a part-time cleaner – but Marianne knew they avoided one another around the house. It wasn't a large house so there was only so much distance they could maintain without secluding themselves in one room for the entirety of the day. Marianne would never know how they passed these hours.

Marie received her appointment for an MRI scan a few days after seeing the doctor. The morning of the scan she looked paler than she'd ever been. Her eyebrows and eyelashes, normally so light and feathery, were growing dark, and there was a density in the bone of her brow that Marianne was slightly in awe of.

Though she had lost weight, her head seemed to have grown and acquired an austerity where the bones peaked through the skin. She looked several years older, and it had only taken about a month for the change to take effect. Marianne was beginning to find it impossible to look directly at her.

'I had a strange dream in the night,' Marie told her while she ate her cereal. 'You were in it.'

'What did I do?'

'I don't think we were ourselves. I was trapped somewhere underground –' she clenched her teeth around her spoon which always made Marianne wince '– but I wasn't really separate from the ground. I was *grounded*, like scattered. And I couldn't speak. Then I felt the soil parting and, even though I couldn't see you, I knew it was you parting it.' She rested her spoon calmly inside the bowl. 'You were burying yourself to find where I was.'

Heather scraped her keys loudly across the kitchen counter and sighed.

'We'll be late if you don't hurry up,' she said. 'You've taken fifteen minutes to eat a couple of mouthfuls. Come on.'

Marie shared a glance with Marianne. Years later, Marianne still struggled to interpret it. She wondered so often whether Marie was afraid right there and then – whether panic was at the root of her refusal to eat. Or perhaps panic arrived much later, after a long period of arrested development. Marianne had since witnessed how a young brain becomes old, worn down by fear, in a matter of seconds. But she recalled no signs of disturbance, no reason to be disturbed by Marie, in those few days before the scan.

When she got home after work, she found her mother first. Heather was watching the garden through the kitchen window.

The day was growing dark already and there was a frostiness outside that pressed on the lungs and made it difficult to breathe. Marianne's face was riddled with goosebumps, and she could feel her lips begin to crack. She had expected the house to be warm already, but when she walked through the kitchen, the room was chilly.

'Why's the heating not on?' she asked her mother.

Heather was still standing with her back to Marianne.

'I forgot to put it on,' she said.

'How aren't you freezing? Where's Marie?'

'I'm just not. My blood is hotter than yours. She's upstairs.'

'How did it go?'

Heather pressed on something in her hands. It was a tube of hand moisturiser. When she rubbed the cream into her palms, Marianne smelt something she didn't like. Heather had a penchant for foul-smelling ointments.

'She couldn't keep still. Said the noises the scanner made were upsetting her. She was given a sedative, so she probably doesn't remember most of it.'

Marianne nodded and was about to head upstairs when she heard a strain in her mother's throat.

'Please leave her alone.'

Marianne stared at her mother's oily hands, which she rubbed with increasing force.

'Why?'

'It's not good to always be fussing. She has it from her father. She doesn't need it from you too.'

'Are you serious? She has—'

'Oh, don't keep saying it. I know what it is. I also know that she's –' Heather looked appalled for a second '– she abuses herself.'

'What?'

'Some of those bruises I've seen now, some of them are not...
random. She has been hurting herself.'

Marianne stared at her in horror.

'No, she hasn't. Why would you think that?'

'Marianne.'

She was turning to leave but her mother came quickly forward
to intercept her, and, for a second, Marianne believed she was
going to be shaken – those hands were gleaming and the creases
in the palms looked deeper once she'd oiled them. Instead,
Heather placed her hand on Marianne's arm and stared at her.

'You need to look out for yourself. Nobody else will. You' –
the hand gripped her – 'need to live for *you*. Marie doesn't think
about anyone, not even herself. You can't make her the centre
all the time.'

'*You, you, you*. That sounds completely selfish to me.'

'It should be. I wish *I* had been more selfish.'

Heather often said things like this and Marianne never got
over the shock of hearing it. She took refuge in the idea that
her mother had little control over what she said because of her
illness. But her thoughts took a darker turn when she was
obliged to consider the origin of it.

David had once told Marianne that Marie's arrival into the
world changed everything. Heather was horrified how difficult
she found rearing a child in its raw state, having to root out that
phantom maternal instinct, the self-sacrificing urge, which she
did not possess. 'I'm not designed for it,' she had told Marianne
once. She had held her hand tightly as she said it and Marianne
forgave her everything, as she always did. 'I'm too selfish.'

Perhaps Marie was a blue child because she was not supposed
to emerge.

It was with a guilty conscience that Marianne slipped into Marie's bedroom that night. But Marie had, for the first time, come to Marianne, asking for company. Her silhouette filled the slit in Marianne's door, darkness pressing on darkness.

'Please can you stay in my room tonight?' Marie whispered.

'Why?'

'I don't want to be alone.'

Marianne obeyed, marvelling at what Marie had just said. She quietly padded after her and when she slipped into the room, she saw the tiny lights on the Christmas tree were still on. The battery must have been dying as they were on a low light, and every now and again they lost themselves completely in one synchronised blink. It lasted less than a second. They had also lost their colour-changing function and were fixed on a final red glow.

'You want a new battery for those?' Marianne said.

Marie lifted the duvet, inviting Marianne to lie beside her on the bed. The mattress was cold, though Marie had only left it for a minute. She curved into the foetal position, her middle travelling away from Marianne while her knees came surging back with their shadowy bones. 'The lights sometimes blink three times in a row. Then nothing for hours. Then they go off altogether and, just when I think it's over, they're back again.'

'That sounds boring.'

'It is. I can't sleep so I've become obsessed with counting the blinks.'

'Morse code.'

'Exactly.'

They were silent, their heads parallel to one another. It was nice to listen to each other's train of thoughts in motion without hearing exactly what they were.

'You ever hear about those people who become so paralysed in their bodies that they can only move their eyeball and blink?' Marie said. 'That's the only way to speak.'

'Yeah – it's horrible. What's worse is that they feel obliged to exist anyway, like they lack that final bit of courage.' Marianne turned and couldn't see where Marie's eyes were as the tree lights had disappeared, this time for a longer interval. 'If that ever happens to me, you have my permission to put me down. Don't even check to see if I change my mind at the last minute. Just do it. That is the *ultimate* version of myself speaking for any future version that lacks courage. I'll write it down.'

Marie laughed. 'You can't decide anything for your future self. When the time comes, your future self is the ultimate version, isn't it? What you are is *when* you are.'

'No.'

'Really?'

'I wouldn't say that about Grandma. She's never been less herself.'

'I don't know.'

'She is maybe a quarter of herself now. Not even that. She would hate to see herself now.'

'I miss her.' Marie's voice sounded mournful. 'I miss her gentleness. When she came out of hospital she was all hard and brittle.'

'I know what you mean.'

'They messed with her.'

Marianne was surprised how agitated Marie seemed. They'd never discussed their grandmother at length before as neither of them had wanted to affirm anything had seriously changed.

'Grandma confides in me sometimes when we go to see her,' Marie continued. 'She said that when she was in hospital, a nurse once advised her to just *relax* and let go of her thoughts. That meant she was being told to die.'

'She lies about so much now. And her illness makes her confused.'

'Well, *I'm* on her side.'

Marie said this in what Marianne thought was a forlorn voice. There was no anger in it.

'I believe her,' she added. 'Nothing good comes of going to see a doctor.'

'Well, that's just rubbish,' Marianne said sharply.

They were silent for a few minutes.

Marianne's attention was eventually drawn to what Marie was doing under the covers. She lifted the duvet slightly and saw Marie's hands pressing down firmly on the side of her chest. It was distended at a point close to her ribs.

She had told Marianne that the swelling was like a pulse where the build-up of blood, the rising pressure, never fell into reverse. It was like a prolonged inhalation of breath. She was so uncomfortable that she had daydreamed about puncturing it herself with a sharp object.

It haunted her, that much was true, and Marianne had never realised it so much as when she spent that latter part of the night lying beside her. Several times that night, Marianne was about to drift off when she was alarmed by the outline of the duvet, because Marie had twisted herself in such a way as to diffuse the tension in her side. Sometimes she arched her back on the mattress so that the duvet rose very high next to Marianne, a surreal white slope in the gloom.

Marie had never struggled to sleep before in her life. That knot in her chest claimed all her attention, her movements, her breathing, and she was trapped in each second. She had never been so anxious for something to be over. It seemed as though her body had absorbed time itself, pushing each second out until it might burst, then racing ahead so that she thought she had plummeted out of life altogether. That was when she gasped quietly. It took only a second to realise her body gripped her as it always had. How strange to think she could have lost it.

Marianne grasped Marie's wrist.

'You have to be well,' she said. 'Stop letting this happen to you.'

'What am I supposed to do?'

'Stop lying about how ill you are. There's no point in being secretive.'

They were annoyed and confused with one another, so they both slept facing opposite sides of the room. Marianne continued to search for sleep without finding it. Marie continued to toss and turn until, finally, she wept. Marianne hadn't heard her cry before and, for a moment, she was relieved. Then her relief turned quickly into remorse. She pretended to be asleep after that, but she was secretly alert, highly sensitive to any noise that came from the other side of the bed.

The result of the MRI scan confirmed that Marie had an enlarged spleen as a result of the hairy cell leukaemia. The doctor explained to David and Heather that she needed open surgery; the spleen was too large for a partial operation. The surgeon would need to disconnect it from the pancreas and the body's blood supply before removing it altogether.

When she was told this, Marie began to fidget. The doctor, with her small and inscrutable eyes, sensed there was an element of panic that Marie wasn't used to dealing with – panic that had never existed before and wasn't used to being contained – so she directed every other comment to their parents and, frequently, Marianne, whose neutral expression invited honesty.

'Many people live without a spleen. But Marie will have to be extra careful to avoid infections. Antibiotics might be given for at least two years after the spleen is out – often they are required until a patient is twenty-one-years old but that might not be necessary. It's life-altering but –' she looked directly at Marie '– this is something that you can adjust to if you make sure you continue to get the right medication and you're vigilant, you make sure any symptoms of infection are reported to your GP straight away.'

'When does she have the operation?' David asked.

'As it's a critical case, she can be seen the day after tomorrow. The operation takes between two and four hours.' She took some documents from her desk and was about to hand them to Marie when, on second thought, she gave them to Heather. 'Please read these – they cover the risks and benefits of the operation in more detail. There are also instructions there for what she needs to do tomorrow morning.'

The doctor had finally redistributed all her attention to Heather instead of relying on Marie's concentration. David was rubbing his thighs up and down, ruching his trouser legs until the sight distressed everybody and he sensed a pause in the conversation that was directed at himself. He wanted to touch somebody – Marianne knew that by the useless strength of his hands, patting himself in an effort not to become still, for if he became still he would be stranded in thought again.

He did not like hospitals because he had spent so much time listening to his mother denounce them, threatening mutiny if she was ever taken there again. 'Let me die in my own bed,' she'd often snapped at him. 'I don't want anyone messing with my organs. Rather be dead in a heartbeat!' People often conducted bitter tirades against what they thought was a fate worse than death, a confinement they hadn't consented to, yet when death came just close enough to prise those thoughts from a precarious brain, the monologue was suddenly very different. *We think we know how to die or withstand pain with dignity, but we don't*, Marianne thought. *Nobody is ready and nobody knows how to be brave.*

Sleeplessness made her susceptible to everything. The smallest things were loaded with terrible meaning when she was tired. She could not remember the last night she had slept easily. But that night, in Marie's bed again, she sensed another threshold in sleep, one that was located somewhere in the gap between hyper-sensitive thought and somnolence.

There was a moment of panic that Marianne would remember the next morning – a moment in which she knew she was falling asleep but a sharp prick of consciousness brought her back into the room and into her life. All of this – the Christmas tree winking feebly by the window and the cardigan hanging off the chair with long wispy hairs attached to its fibres and the sleeping form on her left-hand side – was deceptively timeless, an illusion that might end at any time and that she couldn't afford to lose. She was afraid, monumentally touched by her ordinary exist-ence. Her sleep had acquired an unusual density that stifled her and made her forget she was alive, as though life was so distant a memory it could have been falsely implanted. There was a depth inside herself that yawned for more every night, swallowing her memories and depleting her thoughts, whoring her out to a void she knew would last forever. When she woke, she dilated like a pupil, rising out of a black centre.

ONCE MARIANNE LOST HER JOB at *Empowered*, she felt almost that she understood the meaning of the magazine's title for the first time. She had always baulked at the idea that the content they curated bore any relation to what that word implied. But when she was released from the obligation to uphold these values – of solidarity towards all fellow women, regardless of character; of an atavistic pleasure in the messy parts of the female body; of natural scepticism for male authority – once Marianne was ejected from their party, she felt a visceral hatred of it. An ancient hate she'd taken pains to bury while she was there. She felt *empowered* now that these overlords of female autonomy had deemed her powerless. She threw all the corporate clothes she had never liked in the bin and shredded her office files. She soaked her ideas for new features – complete with brainstorming diagrams – in the bath. She considered burning things but thought it seemed too hysterical and designed for an audience, of which there was none. She revelled in her privacy, her regressive instinct – released at last. She no longer had to pretend she was anything other than what she was.

Sleeplessness returned. It came with renewed force now that she had nothing during the day to appease the empty part. She knew now that insomnia wasn't sluggish by nature – it was sharp and piquant; her sense of herself burning in her own body as though she'd only just realised it was a terminal residing place. She wandered downstairs in circles, moving from one room to another, so that she could escape that encroaching climax – of what, she didn't know. When she was lying horizontal, it moved more quickly through her brain. She felt her spine grow taut as though it would progress that way, down her vertebrae. The hairs had also returned. Sometimes, when she caught herself in the act of sleeping – like she had betrayed her last thought by letting go of it – and came, with a shock, back into the room, she could feel the hairs without touching them, could feel the pores opening as they surged through. The more she fretted, the faster they seemed to grow. Sometimes, she looked over at Richard and realised, with horror, that he would never see any of this. He could not be called upon to exorcise whatever it was that gripped her.

And yet he was patient with her while she was out of work. He bought her flowers from Marks and Spencer and booked a taxi for Bodean's in Soho, a place he'd ordinarily refuse to consider but one Marianne liked for its pulled pork and barbecue ribs. She hadn't been into central London for months and was once again dismayed by its horrible vitality: the voracious energy with which young people darted the streets; the raging taxi drivers; the bulging crowds filtering out from the underground station at Oxford Circus; the homeless man pissing against a wall as he leered at everyone who walked past, rolling himself idly between purple, scabbed fingers.

'I want to go home,' she said when she'd finished her steak.

'We've been here forty minutes.'

Richard was still halfway through his swordfish and capers. She couldn't stand the pace at which he ate and had an urge to take the fish with her bare hands and finish it for him.

'I hate where we are.'

'We're only here because of you,' he said pointedly.

She watched a large table of girls in their twenties behind them. They were laughing with the kind of complacency she knew she would never have.

'You know, Dylan has been asking after you,' Richard said.

'Right.'

He frowned, and she registered something punitive in his expression.

'And Rosalie,' he said. 'You should get in touch. They're worried about you.'

'I don't want to see them just yet.'

He put his knife and fork down, which made her groan inwardly. They would never leave.

'You can't be like this forever,' Richard said. 'You can't shut everyone out. One day, they won't bother.'

'I don't mind.'

'You will. You have to try and get *out* of yourself.'

'I don't think I'm really *in* myself.'

She was sounding childish and she blushed. Richard simply stared at her in disbelief. She caught something cold in his eyes, which she still wasn't used to seeing.

She was suddenly stifled, hot and clammy. The room was noisy, the people striving for one another – laughing, lurching, grabbing hands and slapping backs.

'Let's just go.'

'What about dessert?'

'I don't want any.'

'What about if I want some?'

Marianne stared at her lap mutely.

'Alright. Fine.'

When the waitress came with the receipt, Marianne cringed at how quickly Richard gave her the fifteen per cent service charge in spite of her getting their order wrong to begin with, the sulky manner in which she spoke to them and the half hour it took for her to glance over and recognise he was signalling for the bill. She knew that the easiest course was the silent one. And yet, she railed silently against it, this mechanical politeness and the desire to impress strangers, maintaining the deception, always, of good will. It was embedded deep in Richard's psyche, so foreign to her own.

She knew he was irritated by the same things as she was. She only had to see that vein pulsing on his head to sense the strain of saving face. Why could he never openly admit he hated people's guts? That he couldn't bear to be dismissed, overruled, ignored, patronised, ridiculed – no matter how subtle the insult, how difficult to prove if challenged? And not just to Marianne but to the source of his outrage. She couldn't feign civility in the same way that Richard could, because it required a tact she no longer possessed. She'd lost the ability to project the best version of herself and to protect the worst, to stop it from leaking into her life and contaminating previously clean spaces. Those small daily injustices would give rise to tensions that grew like an ache in the small of her back. It was a gradual increase of ill will towards everything and nothing. A hostility so vaguely directed that she was always finally dismayed by it rather than emboldened. The trajectory was long and difficult but her hate always curved off before she could do anything with it.

A week after she visited Doctor Hind, Marianne received a letter in the post. She was instructed to ring the practice immediately to discuss the results of her blood test. Strangely, she had given Marianne what seemed to be a mobile number instead of the standard line for reception.

She had only just got up and hadn't eaten anything before she opened the letter, so she felt light-headed as she dialled Hind's number. She wandered into the kitchen with the dial tone clamped against her ear and opened the bread bin for a tea cake. Marie used to eat them and Marianne had fallen into the same morning routine, applying a liberal amount of butter then some grated cheddar cheese. She plucked a currant from the bun and popped it in her mouth when Doctor Hind answered.

'Doctor Hind speaking.'

The fleshy fruit was trapped between Marianne's teeth. She picked it out with her nails, which caused a second's delay.

'Mm, hi – sorry. It's Marianne Turner.'

'Marianne, thanks for calling. I'm glad you got in touch so quickly. I'd like you to come to the practice as soon as possible to discuss your blood test.'

'Oh, okay. Is it bad news?'

'It's nothing of any grave concern but it would benefit you to know the score sooner rather than later.'

'Okay. When—'

'Are you free to come by this morning?'

The raisin had left a tart flavour in her mouth. She swallowed again.

'It sounds really serious if I don't even need to make an appointment,' she said.

'Please don't be worried. I happen to have a cancellation this morning at eleven, that's all. Are you free to come by?'

'Yes.'

'Excellent. I'll see you in a few hours.'

When Marianne put the phone down, she continued to make her breakfast. She cut two teacakes in half and squashed them flat before pushing them in the toaster. She stood on her tiptoes to watch the red glare inside the metal slots.

Then she panicked. What Doctor Hind had said wasn't reassuring in the least. *It would benefit you to know the score sooner rather than later.* It was also highly unlikely there was an available slot for her this morning because someone had cancelled. The Dulwich surgery was very limited on the number of appointments it could offer, as there weren't many doctors, and they were largely unforgiving about attendance. She switched the toaster off at the plug and ran upstairs to get dressed. In twenty minutes, she was out of the door.

Once Marianne checked in at the surgery, Doctor Hind called her in almost immediately. When she appeared at the double doors, her expression was entirely different from her usual cold, formal manner. The muscles of her cheeks had slackened and her eyes were sharper. Marianne followed her down the corridor. She realised that Doctor Hind was sweating though it wasn't particularly warm today. The back of her neck was damp, causing the ends of her hair to curl.

'Right, Marianne,' she said as they sat down, 'I'll cut to the chase. Your blood test revealed a deficiency in iron to start with.'

'Right.'

'But that's common enough and you can take supplements for it, which I've recommended in the past.'

'Yep.'

Doctor Hind turned her back on Marianne to stare at her computer monitor.

'The real problem here is that there is an extremely low count of white blood cells. This means you are more likely to get infections because your immune system isn't doing its job. It's the blood of someone who is very undernourished and –' she dipped her head in Marianne's direction '– generally very run-down.'

'My diet's not bad,' Marianne said. 'And, yes – I'm *run-down* if that's what you want to call it. But I have been for months. Ever since…' She felt her throat constricting and paused. 'What does it have to do with the hairs on my back? Why are they there?'

'Your body is reacting like that because it's under stress and it feels it needs to build itself up again, create an outer layer. People suffering from anorexia often have more hair on their forearms and faces because the body has little body fat to keep itself warm. This is similar in nature, only in your case, your trauma has caused your body to react like this. It's a defence mechanism for loss of another kind, something more than body fat. There have been other cases, but not many.'

Marianne was at first relieved that Doctor Hind wasn't interested in maintaining eye contact. But now she perceived Hind's behaviour, this staring at her screen as though Marianne weren't present in the room, as perverse. She was still staring at the same document, though there was only a very small paragraph on it in such small font that Marianne couldn't decipher anything from where she was sitting. And there was a line at the end that might have been waiting for a signature.

'I don't have PTSD. You've never diagnosed it,' Marianne said. 'Perhaps – is there a chance this is some weird side effect of the paroxetine or something? These other cases – have those patients been on the same medication? Why wouldn't I have heard about it? I've read all the forums and blogs online. Nobody ever mentioned it.'

'Everybody's case is entirely different. And this is really nothing to do with the medication you've been taking.'

Marianne was surprised at herself. She was ordinarily coldly opposed to any suggestions that she shared the same fate as the average clinically depressed person. She had always clung to the safety of her essential difference, that her total immunity to any cure, holistic or medicinal, was somehow proof she had evolved towards a higher state of consciousness. She had taken a perverse refuge in knowing herself to be helpless.

But Doctor Hind's diagnosis chilled her enough to abandon this line of thought. She clung to the safety of being a statistic, wishing she had read something online about this happening to someone else.

Doctor Hind finally turned around to face her. She took a brochure from her desk.

'What I suggest, what I *highly recommend*, is that you spend some time at this place.'

She passed on the brochure and Marianne found herself staring at a photograph of a luminous garden. There was a statue of a naked woman crouching in the middle of the photograph. Several large, white cherry trees were planted around her. Printed in gold lettering above the statue: NEDE.

'What is it?'

'It's a kind of health retreat, if you will – a rehabilitation centre. It's in the Wye Valley, in Wales. Have you ever been to Wales?'

'No.'

'You'll love it. The grounds are beautiful. The House of Nede is where guests stay. It's completely solar powered. It has different rooms for relaxation, meditation, massage. It's a new venture. There is a very long waiting list.' Doctor Hind looked at Marianne intently. 'But for special cases, patients can be admitted more quickly.'

Marianne flicked through the pages, though there weren't many. The first half of the brochure consisted of photographs of the garden, or what was referred to as 'Upper Nede'. Trees spiralled towards the sky, providing a heavy canopy of leaves so the photographs revealed spaces that were dark and cool but also vaguely amorous. There were statues of men and women with eyes of a dark red stone. Turning the pages, she saw quotations, which she found quite tedious.

'"Healing comes only from what leads the patient beyond himself and beyond his entanglement in the ego." Very Freudian.'

'It's Carl Jung, actually.'

Marianne landed on a photograph of a large building that was entirely transparent on account of having glass walls. It looked like a giant greenhouse. There was a room with a pool and sauna, and a cafeteria with a bird of paradise tree angled towards the ceiling. Almost every room was filled with unusual, violently coloured plants. She was surprised by the contrast between the intricate garden and this minimalist, modern space that the building offered. The plants inside its rooms were so wild and dramatic that she could imagine being exhilarated in their presence. She recalled a trip she'd made a few years ago to Kew Gardens and how much pleasure she'd taken in those exotic glasshouses, the damp warmth, condensation running down the glass. In those rooms, she was atomised by the heat, flooded through with something foreign to her body.

She was appeased by these photographs. They implied peace without the obtrusive presence of a doctor. However, Marianne realised something was bothering her.

'Why are there no guests – patients – in the pictures?'

Doctor Hind followed her gaze.

'These were taken very early on, before the place was open to the public. It's still very much in its infancy – Nede has only been open for a year.'

'Who runs it?'

'It's an independent venture, managed by a small group of psychotherapists. They were given funding by a medical charity to research the therapeutic impact of a natural resort without artificial stimuli – no electronic devices, no internet, no contact with the outside world. Most of the guests have left a stressful environment in the city for something more than peace. They come looking for self-transcendence, an antidote to the hyper-active consciousness. It's almost like a Buddhist retreat – this is the kind of language the therapists speak.'

Marianne closed the brochure and turned again to the image of the crouching woman on the front.

'How much is it?'

Doctor Hind smiled. 'There is no charge. This is a project funded by the Medical Research Council. An experiment. As I said, it's still in its infancy and guests being treated are in effect volunteers in this experiment, taking part in specialised and unique treatments. It involves some work on your part. It involves entering into a dialogue with these people.'

'Are you trying to put me off?'

'Not at all. I actually thought you'd be brave and sensible enough to agree to it.'

Marianne hesitated.

'Can I think about it?'

'Of course.'

Marianne was sceptical about wellness retreats and didn't believe one glossy brochure could radically change her mind. Yet once she returned to the flat, she couldn't stop thinking about Nede. She would be there for a month, according to the brochure. It involved no great sacrifice as far as she could see. What Nede would offer her was a radically different environment – which was what she craved. She could use this time to procrastinate, to delay the business of getting on with her life. And perhaps she would find some solace in knowing herself to be entirely unreachable.

Yet, when she googled the place, nothing came up. There was no Nede in cyberspace. She decided to ring Doctor Hind, as she had been told she could do so if she had any further questions.

She pressed the phone into her cheek until she heard the woman's voice on the other end.

'Hello?'

'Doctor Hind, it's Marianne. Turner.' She hesitated. 'I just have a few more questions about Nede.'

'Of course. I expected you might. Go ahead.'

The doctor's voice was nowhere near its usual crisp tone. Marianne wondered, briefly, if she had the wrong person on the line.

'Right. Well, for one thing I don't understand why there's no website.'

'Nede is an exclusive resort. As I said, patients are referred privately and it's not advertised beyond that. It's really in an early stage but there are plans to broaden its reach, invite more patients over time once the resources are there. It's nothing to be concerned about though. Just means you'll be given extra care and attention!'

'But how do I really know I'll be looked after?'

'The doctors are some of the best in the world,' Doctor Hind said passionately. 'It's headed by Sarah Clarke, who is a prominent neurobiologist from King's College. The doctors on site are very professional, considerate, well trained. There's also a team of staff who run the kitchen and all other facilities, yet the whole experience is designed so that you feel almost self-sufficient. If you don't want to do any of the activities, that's up to you. You can take your experience of Nede at your own pace.'

'Right.'

'Some of the guests actually end up offering to participate in various research projects at Nede by becoming "Friends of Nede". They like it so much there, they never want to leave!'

'Right.'

'You'll enjoy the comforts on offer there but you *are* obliged to take part in a series of interviews with a psychiatrist, that's all. And they're conducted once or twice a week.'

'But how will this seriously help me?'

Marianne had spoken out of a desire to remain cynical. She still could not believe what was on offer. Yet she could feel herself being drawn to it by degrees. She only needed one final push.

'Marianne,' Doctor Hind said gravely, 'you don't have to go. This is entirely up to you. I'm offering to sign you up because it's proven to be very effective for other patients who have similar conditions.'

'What's my condition? I still don't get it.'

'You've been through a terrible time. You need to be reacquainted with your life again, given a purpose. But you need to deal with your loss first, to process it and see what's on the other side. Nede is very good at getting you to decompress. It's the right environment, has a sort of purging effect, if you will. You'll feel calmer, healthier. And – if it doesn't work, what have you lost?'

Marianne said nothing.

'You don't lose anything by trying this out. But you could gain *a lot* from the experience.'

'I guess.'

She suddenly didn't know how to end the call. She wanted to sit in silence for a moment.

'Thank you,' she said shyly.

'No problem. Just get in touch once you've made a decision. We can talk it over on the phone or send me an email. It's up to you.'

Marianne was now essentially afraid of her own volition. It would have been easier if her hand was forced, either for or against, then she could not be liable for her own mistakes.

When Richard came home, she showed him the brochure immediately. He read it through and then he looked at her with an expression that made her desolate.

'You really want to go there?' he said quietly.

'I don't know. It's an idea.'

He sat down in the living room. The sofa creased with his weight, which suddenly seemed enormous because of the tiredness inside of him. He flicked through the brochure again.

'It's just – not you,' he said.

'What do you mean?'

'This is not something I'd have thought you wanted to do. *Ever.*'

Marianne came and stood behind him, glancing down at the garden in his lap.

'I don't have to pay. And it's a month away from—'

He stared up at her sharply.

'From what? Please don't say life.'

She was silent.

'You don't have a job anymore. You need to find something. Being here alone has fucked up your head,' he said.

Marianne's eyes began to burn and she gripped her mouth with her teeth. She did not have anything fruitful to say.

'Look, just...' He scratched the back of his neck savagely. 'Ah, I don't know. Take some time off to go home and see your mum and dad.'

'You're bored of me being here.'

'I didn't say that. I just think you're stuck in a rut.'

She faced him and wondered seriously who he was.

Occasionally, somewhere in the early hours of the morning, there was a shade of consciousness she sought, one she sensed dawning inside of him. She felt the surrender of his body, the way it curled meekly into her back. He was clearly awake because there was something tentative about him, an intelligence behind the care in which he curled himself around her. It was in this tiny portion of the morning, the part before sleep is fully drained off, that she believed in him. She couldn't recall the last time she'd felt that conviction, that Richard would guard her from the nakedness of her thoughts.

That night, she slept in the guest room. She hadn't touched the bed since Marie had last slept there, and she sank her face into the duvet to see if she could smell anything. There was nothing. She could only trust in the invisible imprint, the outline of a body that she was careful not to disturb. After an hour of waiting for sleep, she gave in to restlessness and slipped back downstairs. She picked up her mobile and dialled her parents' number.

The dial tone sounded and she wondered who would answer.

'Hello?'

Her father spoke and she felt that constriction in her throat again, that tightness. He sounded weary, confused – it was one in the morning – but there was also an element of carefully controlled fear. The kind of fear he'd known once before and which he kept below the surface. If it ruled his thoughts, he would never get anything done.

'Dad.'

'Mari.' The panic rose then. 'Are you alright?'

'Yes.'

Then she cried. She sobbed until she couldn't breathe, barely making a sound down the phone. He must have heard a strange silence inflected with tiny gasping noises.

'Mari. Hey, Mari – don't cry, love.' He spoke in a small voice. 'Ah, Mari, I do miss you.'

'I miss you too,' she said. Her tears were wet on the surface of the phone against her cheek. 'I miss you all the time.'

'Why don't you come home?'

'I want to. I will.'

'Good, we were hoping you would. Your mum is in a bad way.'

Her breath came out in a shudder. 'Are *you* alright?'

'It comes and goes,' he said. She knew what he was referring to.

'I'm coming home, Dad. But first, I'm going to this place – it's for people who are going through a bad time and need a break. It's a health resort in Wales. My doctor recommended it.'

He paused and she grew frightened.

'It's just for a month. And then I'll come and see you. I want to stay a while this time if that's alright.'

'Of course it's alright. You can stay here for the rest of your life, Mari.'

She couldn't bear it any longer. She said a shaky thank you and then she told him she had to go.

DAVID AND MARIANNE WENT TO find Marie in the hospital the afternoon after her operation. They were told she had left the operating theatre and was in recovery, that her mother was speaking to her. Marianne smelt her mother's perfume in the corridor before they found the right room, a floral, masculine scent that she had always found to be an assault on the senses. She noticed her first in the room, sitting straight-backed in a chair beside the bed with her hands crossed in her lap. Marie was lying without moving, facing the window on the left side of her mother. There was an IV line feeding into a vein in her arm.

'Surprise!' David said in the doorway.

Heather got up and found another two chairs, which she dragged into place on the other side of the bed. She was wearing a ribbed black jumper and skintight jeans, and moved with a sinuous elegance that seemed out of place.

'How are you feeling?' Marianne asked Marie.

'Alright. Just tired. Glad the swelling is gone.'

'Doctors said she'll be here at least a few days before she can come home,' said Heather.

David got up on impulse and leaned over to kiss Marie on the forehead. She gave him a babyish smile and seemed, for a second, to come back to herself.

'I'll be out for Christmas,' she said.

'Good. We'll put up that bloody tree to celebrate.' He was suddenly galvanised. 'And whatever you want this year, just say. I'll get you anything. What do you want?'

She looked at him and then her eyes slid towards her mother with covert fascination.

'I want a haircut,' she said.

'Eh?'

'I want a new hairstyle. Short.'

He hesitated and glanced at Heather. 'Sure! You can have a Vidal Sassoon makeover. Why not. It's just hair, right?'

'Exactly.'

'But you love your long hair,' said Marianne.

'I want a change.'

She was bright and effusive for the first half hour of their visit but then, gradually, she dipped into a non-committal silence. Everyone noticed, but David wanted her attention for as long as possible. His voice rose every time he saw her eyelids lowering.

'Come on, she needs to rest,' Heather said to him.

'We'll be back tomorrow,' he said.

He leaned over to kiss her again, but he accidentally placed his hand on her chest. She twitched beneath it.

'David, careful,' Heather snapped.

'Oh god, sorry.' Then the sadness returned to his voice. 'I'm glad you're alright, Marie. You look after yourself, okay?'

'What else is she supposed to do here?' Heather said quietly to Marianne.

He leaned over to kiss Marie again but Heather tugged his arm.

'She's tired, for god's sake. She wants to sleep.'

He gave her a look that Marianne had never seen before. His whole head seemed to shake.

'I get it,' he said. 'There's no need to snap at me here, Heather.'

Marie's eyes flickered briefly. Then she appeared to dive into a very dense form of unconsciousness. It was not quite like sleep, but something else that preceded a final state. Instinct forbade them to leave her, but visiting hours were nearly over and a nurse reassured them that she was in recovery mode and some sleep would do her good.

Marie was released from hospital after four days. When she arrived back at the house, she seemed to forget where she was straight away, as though she'd been taken to another place of captivity. Heather opened the door to the living room for the big reveal – a large fir tree in the corner of the room with glass decorations hanging from the branches. David had added silver tinsel as a gaudy final touch.

Yet the tree was frowned at by Marie. She stared at it for a long time without moving into the room.

'Don't you like it?' Marianne said.

'Yes. Christmas has already been and gone though,' she said.

'No. It's the day after tomorrow.'

She was sore and carried herself differently. She seemed agitated by something they didn't see in their house. She roved around the rooms as though hoping to find what it was she thought of as an intrusion, a displaced object or entity. They followed her, maintaining their distance. When she arrived at the foot of the stairs, she was suddenly tired of everything. She was hostile, wary of being stalked and apprehended. She looked at Marianne as though to say, *Are you still here, watching me?*

'You look tired. You should rest now,' David said.

'Okay.'

She then slept for the rest of the day and well into the night. On Christmas Eve, she still wouldn't be disturbed. Nobody wanted to wake her and hoped her strange mood would dissipate overnight. Sleep seemed to be the only solution for her sluggishness, yet Marianne was not convinced it made her any better – it only exacerbated her tiredness. Her eyes were growing dull and she had that peculiar endogenous expression of one who is trapped inside themselves. She came downstairs as though she were sleep-walking and wandered into the kitchen to drink a glass of milk. Then she ate a quarter of a slice of bread. Later on, Marianne heard her retching in the bathroom.

On Christmas day, Marianne slipped into Marie's room to wake her. She immediately smelt something strange.

'Marie?' she whispered. Then she raised her voice slightly. 'Marie.'

Marie's head turned slowly towards her, and Marianne felt a rush of panic. The hair fell away to reveal a face so white she thought there was no blood beneath the skin at all.

She sat on the edge of the bed and pressed her hand on Marie's forehead.

'Marie,' she said again.

Marie's eyes opened in an instant, which took her by surprise.

'Are you alright?'

Marie prised her lips open.

'Yeah. Just tired.'

'Have you been taking all the antibiotics?'

She nodded and dipped her chin down into her neck as though to bury herself into her body for more sleep, but Marianne tapped her on the arm.

'Hey, don't go to sleep. It's Christmas!'

Marie managed a smile.

'Are you going to get up? Mum's making breakfast. She's got waffles on the go. Syrup and everything.'

'Okay.'

Marie pulled herself upright and looked around the room. Then she shivered.

'Are you cold?' Marianne said.

'Yeah.'

Then her eyes went out – at least that was the only way Marianne could describe it to herself. She sunk back on the pillow, crushing Marianne's arm.

'Mum!' Marianne called.

Marianne whipped the duvet back. The sheet on the mattress was damp and she also noticed that Marie had vomited in the night. There was a brown soupy puddle on the carpet on the other side of the bed.

Marianne ran downstairs and found her mother standing at the kitchen sink. David had placed his arm around her waist and they were leaning warmly into one another as she held a saucer suspended in mid-air. Their posture would have consoled Marianne in any other situation. It was something she would later cherish, extracting it from the day's events like a hand in the dark.

'Something's wrong with Marie. I think she's dying,' she said.

She had not meant to say this but it forced its way out. They turned and their faces changed very quickly.

They followed her up the stairs, feet thumping on the carpet. On entering the room, David began to sob. Marianne watched her parents tugging at the limp form on the bed like they were attempting to break parts of her for safekeeping, fighting over the contents. David took her arm and Heather curled her hands around the edges of her face. Marie opened her eyes then closed them again and continued to do this repeatedly, blinking herself back into the room.

Marianne rang the emergency services and stated the problem, stopping between words to catch her breath. The woman on the end of the line waited patiently for her to finish speaking, then said that she would send an ambulance to their house so Marie could be taken to A&E.

'What do I do?' Marianne said. Her voice was high and she couldn't breathe.

'Keep her conscious for as long as possible. And try moving her arms and legs to prevent blood clotting. It sounds like sepsis.'

'Oh, okay,' Marianne said. Tears were falling from her eyes and they slid into the space between the phone and her cheek. 'Thank you.'

What happened in the next hour was to be painfully scrutinised for the rest of Marianne's life. The hour held Marie's consciousness in its grip and proceeded to brutalise it. Her pupils grew so large that they forced the blue irises back until she was seeing things as through a void. They had tried to move her from the bed but she fell to the floor, her limbs slack. Her lips turned blue.

She had not been that blue child for a long time and Marianne's heart stopped when she saw the change. Her father ran downstairs to see if the ambulance had arrived, paced the bottom of the house, ran back upstairs to check on Marie, and repeated this sequence until they thought he had gone mad. Heather crouched over her daughter and held her wrist, stroking it with the other hand. When she heard David shouting as he spotted the paramedics closing in on the house, she jumped to her feet and ran to join him.

Marianne stared at Marie. Her eyes held a monumental truth.

'It's okay,' Marianne said. She gripped Marie's arms. 'You're not going there.'

Finally, the words came.

'I don't want to die.'

Her voice was young in its admission. In her face was a final recognition of what it meant to be lost forever, to fall out of existence like a stone. And she was helpless to erase the consciousness of it before consciousness itself was erased. Marianne experienced a sudden vertigo, something she had felt when she spoke on the phone earlier. That suffocating height to which thought had climbed before a sudden plunge. Marie had always trusted in the hospitality of the universe. How could it dispense with her? The idea of herself, that terribly precise formula which she alone knew, being misplaced forever like a secret script, gave license to an almost erotic intimacy, a burden of love for herself in her last moments. She knew who she was and she saw the imprint of herself for the first time, tunnelling into it as far as she could go while she still had the effort of mind to do so. She clenched her fist and forced herself to stare at the face in her line of vision. She saw Marianne as one would see God.

Two paramedics came and carried her downstairs where a stretcher was waiting for her. She seemed to lose consciousness again as they hauled her into the back of the ambulance, but it was impossible to tell from a distance. Heather asked if she could sit beside her. David and Marianne could follow in the car. One look at her father informed Marianne that he was entirely incapable of driving. His hands were shaking so badly that he pressed them to his face and seemed tempted to bite himself as a means of distraction.

'Dad, I'll drive. Come on,' she said.

She pulled out of the driveway after the ambulance and saw the neighbours watching them warily over the wall. They had never really spoken to this family or adopted any kind of rapport with them, so their sympathy seemed ill-placed, though David nodded as they drove past. Their children, whose names they didn't know, were about to step out of the house, but the couple abruptly turned and marshalled them back in.

The way forward was bleak. The roads were empty, which lent the ambulance a ghostly tension in its passage. Marianne took heart from the fact that she could drive with such command of herself. She felt her grief mounting beneath the dividing line of thought but trusted in the division, her ability to partition all thought that prompted panic. *Just think of practical things. The speed limit, the colour of the sky. Will it rain? Does it matter? The road, concentrate on the road.* If she panicked, she would not be able to stop. She was quietly conducting herself on the inside, sending every terrorising notion to another part of her mind to deal with later, letting all the banalities flow through for now. Her father was consoled by her ability to console herself.

The ambulance pulled up to the entrance of the A&E department and Marianne watched her mother stooping from the double doors. Her face had turned grey. The paramedics pulled Marie out and turned her towards the building.

'David,' Heather called.

She darted towards him and took his arm in hers. He noticed it in a very abstract sense but couldn't bring himself to react. He stared at Marianne.

Once in the A&E unit, a series of nurses descended upon Marie, and Marianne lost sight of her. She wasn't conscious anymore. They pinned an oxygen mask to her face and proceeded to insert an IV line in her left arm. The last image she had of Marie before being ushered out was one in which she sensed nothing of her sister, no sign of any struggle beneath such complicated efforts to restrain her.

The three of them waited in a room just off the corridor. A doctor came to speak to them after ten minutes and announced that she had extremely low blood pressure. He asked whether she had been taking her antibiotics since her operation. Heather replied that Marie had always told them she was doing it, yet it was also true that nobody had actually witnessed her taking any. The doctor said they were giving her antibiotics and fluids through a vein as well as vasopressor medications to increase her blood pressure. He said the words 'septic shock' several times. When he told them to stay calm and left them again, Marianne looked to her parents and saw that they were staring with the exact same vacancy at the poster for inflammatory bowel disease on the wall.

After half an hour of silence, Heather announced her intention to get a coffee and asked if David would go with her. He didn't seem to hear her until she repeated herself sharply.

'Mari, will you be alright for five? Do you want anything?' he said.

'No. Thanks.'

Left on her own, she didn't know how to organise her thoughts. It was strange that whenever she thought of Marie in that room, something censored it at the last minute and her mind recoiled. It wasn't because she was afraid to assess Marie, it was more that she was losing the energy to do so.

She was glad to be alone in this sterile, impersonal space. And she knew she would have the rest of her life for despair to resume itself. Inside of this interval, Marianne was still free of it. She refused to entertain it for as long as she could manage, suffused with a passion for sleep, for apathy and inconsequence. Her thoughts were drawn frequently towards the image, already relegated to the back of her mind, where Marie lay open for eternity on the carpet of her bedroom. That was when she sensed a split occurring between what she felt now – a paralysing numbness – and what she would eventually feel once this subsided, what she would not bear but somehow tolerate by virtue of continuing. She covered her eyes with her fingers and pressed the lids so that her eyes began to ache.

Heather and David returned with their drinks and sat either side of Marianne. She listened to them sipping their coffee tentatively and wished she had asked for one. David burned his mouth with too great a gulp and winced, then proceeded to do the same thing again. She cringed for him, for his propensity for self-sabotage. For her own too. She felt a pang of hunger in her chest and she needed the toilet. But she did nothing. She leaned into the pain of both, craving the emptiness of her stomach to somehow cancel out the strain on her bladder. She wanted to be compromised by something else. She thought that if she could withstand these minor privations, relieving herself only when she chose, she was safe from any sudden misfortune.

This logic buoyed her. She could circumvent Marie's fate by taking on her own share of suffering. She pressed her legs into the edge of the plastic chair where the surface was rough and scratchy. She pulled the roots of her hair from her scalp and felt the corners of her eyes lift.

'What are you doing?' Heather said. She had been watching Marianne from the corner of her eye.

'Nothing. I need the loo.'

She couldn't hold it any longer and was suddenly acutely aware of the likelihood she was about to wet herself.

'Toilet's down the corridor on the right,' her mother said.

She moved slowly so as not to disturb the weight of her bladder with any sudden movement. By the time she reached the toilet, she just missed pissing on the seat and slapped her bottom down violently. Once the pressure was gone, she felt a startling relief. Then she sobbed.

When she returned to the waiting room of the emergency unit, her parents weren't there. She panicked and then saw her father leaning out of the door of the room where Marie was.

'Mari, come quick.'

There were a lot of lines feeding drugs to Marie's bloodstream. Her face was squashed beneath a respirator so that her mouth was slightly parted. Her eyes were shut but her head was tilted so that she seemed mesmerised by the ceiling, apprehending its surface inside the static gloom of her eyelids.

'Her blood pressure is still very low,' the doctor said. He had a large, fleshy face and eyes that seemed to sweat rather than glisten. 'There is a lot of blood clotting, which has reduced blood flow to her internal organs, so she's not getting enough oxygen. We've got her on a breathing machine and we're feeding her vasopressors to increase the pressure in her blood. She's stable for now but she'll have to be monitored in intensive care for at least a few days.'

A nurse was looking at the screen of the ventilator. The small green lines mounted in random places, and Marianne wondered whether there was some part of Marie's brain that was privy to her peaks and troughs. The numbers on the right-hand side of the screen meant absolutely nothing to her. She felt it was a matter of urgency to pinpoint where Marie was in that room, in her body. Was she exerting any conscious energy not to die, willing herself whole? There was no longer any violence in her. But where was she? What was she conscious of?

'Will she be alright?' David asked the doctor.

'I can't say for certain. We're hoping she'll be stable from now on.' He stared at the nurse as she adjusted the fluids over Marianne's head. 'It's good that she was brought here straight away. A few more hours without treatment – she would have certainly died.'

David stared at Heather and she took his hand in hers.

The doctor explained that Marie was under such heavy sedation that she was not likely to regain consciousness for hours. *But at least it didn't slip away*, Marianne thought. *It's trapped somewhere.* She had a peculiar desire to talk to Marie while she was still comatose, to discuss everything with that part of her that was secluded from the state she was in. She wanted to sit next to Marie and share her vantage point, but simultaneously watch her lying in front of them, as a separate entity. For she was convinced that Marie was not there at all, that she was spying on them from a calmly resigned distance.

Her condition worsened that night. After Marianne and her parents had left the hospital, at around half past twelve, Marie abruptly slipped into an abyss. The nurse on the night shift heard the single note of her heart monitor and quickly realised there was no activity on the electrocardiogram. Her brain also went silent. She was given CPR and connected to a life support machine, as well as a ventilator, to help her blood circulate. The doctor was kind enough to explain to the family only once she came back round that Marie had died for two minutes. Once her heart was beating normally again, they were in a belated stage of grief for a death that was already over. They had missed their cue.

It took Marie two days to regain consciousness. She happened to re-enter her life when they were there surrounding her. Marianne had touched her sister's wrist and, as though prompted, Marie opened her eyes and stared at her. She seemed to have no concept of who they were. Her eyes were heavy, but they managed to centre themselves on Marianne's face. Then the muscles in her cheeks tightened.

It was perhaps the only time that Marianne and her parents cried in unison, within seconds of one another. They lapsed into the same darkness of feeling.

When Marie was discharged, the doctor explained to them about post-sepsis syndrome. She needed to take antibiotics every day to fight off infection and would likely have a range of symptoms, one of them being poor cognitive function. Rest was the priority and also rehabilitation, to some extent.

Marie was weary of herself and silent. She moved slowly, ponderously, without paying very much attention to where she was putting her feet, so they had to assist her with the smallest things to begin with. The first few days consisted of a rotating schedule of sleep and medication. All that was required of her at this stage was simply to exist without relapsing.

She always spoke more when she had just awoken. One morning Marianne heard her gasp behind her bedroom door in the early hours. When she entered, she braced herself for a repetition of that morning when she smelt something awful: her memory of that smell had changed, convincing her that it was not just vomit but something else. Instead, she saw the dim outline of Marie sitting upright in the darkness, staring blankly at the wall opposite.

'What is it?' Marianne asked from the doorway.

Marie turned and was surprised to see her sister. She reeled back slightly in her skin, her eyes struggling to refocus as though everything was suddenly too close for her to take in properly.

'I was in a garden and I was being followed,' she said quickly. 'Then it was a forest.'

Marianne moved irresistibly towards the bed and sank down.

'It was full of red light. Light coming from the trees, like it was coming from their insides. I was being chased.'

Her eyes held the tears for a long time before finally shedding them, so that she saw Marianne like she was a fluid, dissolving slowly before suddenly becoming sharp. She was very still and was evidently tied to her stillness; when Marianne touched her shoulder and pushed it slightly, she wouldn't relinquish the tension inside her body that made her sit that way.

There was a quiet obduracy at play that Marianne didn't like. Perhaps because there had been very little time between the two states, from heavy sedation to full-blooded consciousness. For Marie was filled with thought, the kind of thought that had leaked out of her brain and now ran through her blood. She existed in the thought and vibrated with it, frightened of retention and frightened of release. She looked at Marianne.

'I was running really fast but I wanted whoever it was to find me. I was really scared they'd stop looking,' she said.

'It's over now,' Marianne said.

'It's not.'

'Marie, you're safe,' Marianne told her.

It required a great deal of convincing, but Marie finally believed her.

To some extent, Marianne struggled to believe it herself. Marie might have died for a small time but she had surpassed death itself, seemingly without having made any conscious effort to do so. If consciousness was down, how then did she navigate? For two minutes, she was nothing. How could all of her thoughts and memories not have been deleted in that interval? They were miraculously intact.

After reading more about it on the internet, Marianne found an article that explained how the neurons went silent for a limited period, storing their internal charges in wait for the return of blood flow. It was referred to as a 'wave of darkness'. Instead of being a consolation, it was a source of great disturbance to Marianne – that consciousness could resume itself so readily. She thought it was a betrayal of her sister in some way to think this. But she also wanted to believe, in the abstract sense, that death was absolute and that it couldn't be retracted. She did not like to think that one could be pronounced dead and then pronounced not dead after all. There was a ghoulish aspect to the second phase of living.

Marie's appetite changed when she left the hospital. Though she was weak, she was hungry. She had a sudden and aggressive craving for meat, mostly red meat. There was still so much uneaten food in the fridge, which had been bought for the festive period, and Marianne caught her raiding it several times a day, leaning on the door and pulling slices of cold meat from under the cellophane, dangling them into her mouth and snatching them from her fingers in an angry compulsion. She'd developed, in the space of a week, an avaricious streak, a way of holding herself that was meagre and suspicious. She watched the television screen with an irate expression, frowning around the room from time to time to reassess its contents every few minutes. She complained she was hungry and tired, which was true, but she told everybody as though it was somehow their fault. And then she'd grow silent again, sometimes midway through her complaint, her eyes paling until there was no expression. She was nullified within seconds. Something outside of her consciousness repeatedly entered it without her permission and proceeded to attack what had always been there. When she came back round, she was kinder to everyone and had forgotten what it was that had agitated her. Marianne wanted to hunt for the second before she forgot, the last thought she had before she was submerged in that wave of darkness. Something was happening to her.

'The doctor mentioned she might have some memory loss,' Heather told Marianne. 'I wouldn't worry about it. She's still in shock.'

Their parents had been invited to a party for New Year's Eve. They had been friends with Jon and Mary Taylor for many years and David knew Jon originally through his former job at Bowland Tree Services. Marianne had always liked Mary because she was very attentive to everybody and always brought out a side of her mother that nobody else knew to look for. They had a large house, which Marianne and Marie used to visit when they were younger.

Marianne remembered the enormous oak tree in the garden that she'd climb with Mary and Jon's son, Dylan. They used to hear the low murmur of adults talking through the open window as they curled their legs around the branches. This house excelled where Marianne's failed because it felt as though it was lived in without tension or subterfuge. It was a calm space, but not so carefully organised that it couldn't contain distress. Heather had often felt at liberty to cry in that house when she couldn't find the nerve, or perhaps the momentum of feeling, to do so in her own.

'We won't go. They'll understand,' Heather said. She was staring into her wardrobe and biting her lip. Most of her dresses were green or grey or charcoal – never quite black – and she suddenly seemed very tired of the image of herself she'd always crafted. 'We shouldn't leave Marie.'

'I'll look after her. I know what to look out for. I know what pills she needs to take,' said Marianne.

Heather said nothing and tugged at the sleeve of a white blouse with a high Victorian collar.

'Mum, please. You should go. You and Dad haven't done anything for ages.'

Her mother eyed her coldly.

'I don't know if I want to.'

'Please. I promise Marie will be alright with me.'

At about eight that evening Heather finally relented, though they were already an hour late. She wore a very dull outfit in the end, a coffee-brown dress that was creased at the back and a pair of suede boots that were scuffed at the toes. She wore no make-up, though her face was shadowed and her skin still grey. Marianne didn't know whether this was something to admire – that she was not a slave to artifice and wished others to see her naked face as it was – or something to be concerned about, for surely she knew she looked very unwell. Perhaps she wanted to flaunt her sadness to legitimise it. Mary would see her and know at once that she was suffering. It was a shorthand way to reveal her sadness without having to assemble the words, because that took time and consumed a great deal of energy, which needed to be conserved for other things. For choosing what to wear, for example. Marianne wished her energy had not been so misplaced in that instance.

'Have a great time,' Marianne said to them as they were on their way out. 'Happy new year.'

David was putting his coat on when he looked in on them both, Marianne eating a bag of popcorn on a beanbag by the tree and Marie lying under a blanket on the sofa.

'What are you guys up to tonight then?' he said. 'Are you going to watch all the *Lord of the Rings* films back to back?'

'No. Those days are over, Dad,' Marianne said.

'Shame.' He smiled. He looked at Marie. 'You'll be alright, love?'

She looked at him blankly.

'Yes,' Marianne answered.

He looked downcast when he left them. All it took was a second of silence from Marie. Heather was similarly strained when she stooped to hug them both. She asked Marie if she was still in any pain and Marie shook her head.

'Ring me if anything happens,' she said to Marianne quietly before leaving.

When they were gone, Marie admitted she was, in fact, in pain.

'Where? Your wound?'

'Everywhere. Just lots of dull throbbing.'

She wouldn't turn her head to look at Marianne, perhaps
because the effort was too much, so Marianne came and knelt
by the sofa. She could see a line of sweat across Marie's forehead
and her upper lip.

'You're too hot? Shall I turn the heating down?'

'No. I'm hot then cold again.'

For the next couple of hours, Marianne sat beneath Marie
on the floor and flicked through the channels on the TV. She
settled on a documentary on Britain's coastlines and thought
vaguely about how much she wanted to be at sea. It was a
bland, romantic impulse that lacked conviction. Her imagination seemed to have lost its forcefulness. Now and again she
glanced at Marie, who was drifting in and out of sleep. Her
face was growing slack again, like when she was sedated in the
hospital.

There was, Marianne knew now, a very marked distinction
between a face that is animated by the content of a dream and
a face that empties entirely so that you instinctively feel there
is nothing happening within. As though all movements grind
to a halt, stunted by something a little deeper that dispossesses
the brain of its timeline. Marianne recalled those times she
herself woke from a heavy sleep. It was a kind of paralysis she
strove very hard to recover from. For a time, she thought it was
brought on by the sameness of her days, the monotony of her
routine, the details of which were scattered through her dreams,
maddening repetitions that filtered through and found her again:
an odd phrase she'd heard recently, the fading pattern of her
grandmother's carpet, a lurid headline from the news. But
Marie's rest was different. It might have been entirely blank,

uninfluenced by any memory. Her features hadn't softened; instead, they were frozen in a position of cold neutrality. Marianne watched her and tried to imagine whether conscious-ness was flowing through a dark channel, or whether it was a stagnant pool of tension, the current circling the same spot. Marie would often wake up and still seem stultified, never recharged. Whatever the brain did to flush itself out during this time, it might not have happened for Marie. The shadows beneath her eyes became more pronounced with every passing day.

It was eleven o'clock when Marianne got up from the floor, feeling stiff. She needed to be diverted by something and she craved nostalgia. Sitting in the same position and poking her sister every ten minutes to see if she would respond had depressed her. She realised she had been keeping great reserves of pity on hold that she'd been waiting to use on herself when the time came for it. She recognised her tendency to squander feelings on someone else, but tonight she would rescue what last good thoughts she had of herself before they passed on and were finally irretrievable. It brought on a maudlin impulse for her childhood.

She left the room momentarily and headed up to the attic, where all the family albums were kept. She studied the photo-graphs in their shiny sleeves, alone, sitting on the upstairs landing with the leather book in her lap.

One photograph gave her pause. It was taken about ten years ago according to the pencilled date on the back. 'Aberystwyth, North Beach', her father had written in neat letters beneath. It wasn't a scene she remembered. Her mother was sitting on a jetty with her feet hanging very close to the water, the arches extended so her toes were pointing straight down. She looked as though she was poised to disappear. Though she was in the slightly blurred recesses of the photo, her head was clearly turned towards the two children frolicking on the beach in the foreground.

Marie was posing in a manner that Marianne had completely forgotten about. Her hands were behind her back, legs parted as far as they could go, chest thrown out, head cocked downwards and to the side. Her eyes were demented and forced open very wide, her mouth in a rictus grin. The pose was vaguely suggestive of irony or at least self-awareness, a brash imitation of an excitable child. It was just clever enough without being mocking, so closely aligned with her ecstatic, preposterous mood as to be real. She was both within and without, posing and projecting what was already there. She'd dialled it up a notch because she knew it would please her father, whose finger occupied the corner of the frame as a hot pink blur. The slightly dazed, inebriated expression in their mother's face confirmed the silliness of everything, as well as the ease with which they'd behaved with one another on that trip.

It was only ever on holiday that Heather had been susceptible to those emotions, namely those in which she found her family an essential component of herself. There was a rarefied quality about these excursions to the sea, a way in which common grievances dissolved. As though the salty air ground everyone down to their native instincts, which were fundamentally peaceful. Marianne was not one to sentimentalise the past – there was a meanness in the way she sometimes viewed it, guarding herself against harmful fabrications – but she still sensed those people in her blood, the silly child on the left and the wistful girl on the right. Her own face, a little more defined with the onset of puberty, was not as wildly contorted as Marie's, but there was a relaxed quality about it. Her eyes were closed, and she was laughing easily like she knew the day would be safe. There would be no unexpected twists, no abrupt changes of atmosphere. The climate of that photograph was perfectly hospitable, conducive to hours, perhaps days, of happiness while its warmth remained. That this was a foreign feeling for their mother was difficult to read in that picture. Heather's face seemed *right* in softer focus, like this was her basic setting, her natural state. Yet how swift was her reversion to harmful habits of thought. How quickly that false temperament, the one that automatically resumed itself once they returned, how quickly *that* then seemed the natural order of things. The holiday had tricked them, and they would continue to fall for the trick every time.

Marianne slipped the photo back into its sleeve. She was being cruel in her thoughts. Perhaps it was not the quantity of those moments that counted but their exhilarating quality. Still, the suddenness, the strangeness of happiness could also be its downfall. The rare intensity of a moment could cause everyone to fumble, to launch themselves at it with too much vehemence, too much anxiety, until pleasure itself was lost in the effort of maintaining it.

A selfish impulse prevented Marianne from wanting to share these photos with Marie. But she felt it was a burden to look on the past alone. Reflecting on shared experiences in isolation only compounded the fact that it was over and couldn't be revived. When she came upon a photo of Marie as a smiling, white-haired two-year-old with pink cheeks, she carried the album downstairs to the living room.

'Marie, look at this,' she said loudly.

Marie was awake this time and she was frowning at the door before Marianne had appeared there. Marianne thrust the open book in her face.

'Look. Baby you.'

Marie smiled but she didn't sit up, so Marianne perched on the edge of the sofa and proceeded to turn the pages.

'Oh my god, we're in the bath. With our pecks out.'

Side by side, Marianne's skin was so much more solid in that photograph. Marie's small body possessed that old blue transparency, a reluctance to materialise. She was three according to their father's handwriting, and Marianne was eight. It annoyed her slightly that she'd been photographed in the bath at this age. Sometimes their father might have gone too far in his quest to document everything they did together.

She fast-forwarded to the years Marie was in primary school. Marie's face had settled into its heart-shaped mould and her eyes were so light in the morning sunshine, standing with her head slightly bowed on the front doorstep, that the camera had failed to trap the pigment. The resulting image felt undernourished, not quite as vital as it should have been. Her hair, however, looked like it was blissful to touch, soft and feathery and full around her shoulders.

'God, your hair was so light then,' said Marianne.

'And it's always long,' Marie said. She sat up a little. 'Same boring long hair.'

Marianne stared at her, dumbfounded. She had never heard Marie complain about her hair and had always assumed she was as in love with it as everybody else.

'I want to cut it.' Marie looked at Marianne urgently. 'I'm sick of it. It makes my head itch.'

'You haven't washed it for a few days, that's why.'

'No, I want to cut it.'

'Dad said he'd book an appointment—'

'Don't need to wait for that. Let's do it now.'

There was that same angry compulsiveness in her voice that Marianne had witnessed in her eating habits recently. Her hair was certainly lank and stringy because she hadn't washed very often, finding it painful to do so without help. And it was darker too, almost mousy now with age and recent oiliness. But it was so much a part of Marie's image that Marianne was afraid to give her consent.

'I think you'll regret it,' she said.

'I'll do it myself – or you can do it. Bear in mind you will do a better job from the back.'

'But how short?'

'Let's see.'

Marie picked up the remote control and flicked through the channels. She paused when she came to the BBC footage of the New Year's Eve celebrations in London. A female presenter was shouting at the camera and kept pushing strands of her hair out of her face with the wind.

'Her hair's awful,' Marianne said.

'Not her. The woman on the right.'

The woman she was referring to was standing at the front of a crowd of people in Trafalgar Square. Her hair was closely cropped and her ears were quite large.

'Jesus – no.'

'Why not? It really is just hair.'

'Then why cut it at all?'

Marie twisted the dry ends of her hair in her fingers and stared at it dispassionately.

'Because I don't want it. I can't sleep and it's there around my neck and face.'

She was bored of talking about it and heaved herself off the sofa. She hadn't changed her clothes for the last few days either, and Marianne didn't like to say that she was starting to smell of dried sweat. She silently followed Marie out of the room and upstairs to the bathroom. Marie opened the cupboard beside the sink and found a pair of scissors. She handed them to Marianne and then turned resolutely to the mirror to watch herself.

'Marie, I can't. Why can't we just wait for the hairdresser to do a better job?'

'Because I'm bored of waiting for everything.'

'At least wash it first.'

Marie sighed and turned the tap on. Marianne stared as she put her head under the cold water without waiting for it to warm up and scrunched her hair in her fist until it was all wet. She looked up and Marianne passed her the shampoo bottle. Then she spurted it into her hand and scratched it into her scalp. It was quick, frenzied, careless. She didn't bother cleaning the ends. By the time she had washed it out, she was fully engaged in the task at hand. Her face had flushed slightly. She towelled her hair dry and threw it aside.

Marianne began slowly. She trimmed about five inches of hair from the bottom, which had grown to Marie's waist. She flattened the ends between her fingers to see if the line was straight.

'Come on. Just hack it off.'

'Yeah, right.'

'Right, then.'

Marie snatched the scissors and flicked her hair over both shoulders so she could see it in the mirror. To Marianne's horror, she really did hack it off. She bunched one part and snipped it at the level of her chin. Then she did the same on the other side, only snipping it higher. The hair fell in dark wet waves over the sink.

Marianne could see that Marie hadn't the will to stop herself. She was convinced Marie's dismay at what she was doing was linked with a morbid impulse to carry on with it. She kept pulling strands in her fingers and cutting at random points. Her scalp rose beneath the roots.

'Marie! *Stop it.*'

Marianne made a swipe for the scissors, but Marie held on to them. She was almost smiling again but Marianne didn't understand the humour in it. She fastened her hand on to Marie's wrist in a pincer grip and they both watched the scissors fall into the sink. The hair cushioned the fall so it made no sound.

Marianne had a very real dread of Marie and what she would do next. Her face, with that wildly uneven body of hair around it, had stopped moving, but the tension inside of her was building. She was ranging in and out of some dark centre, launching herself at the physical world with haste and then reeling her energy back in again to prosper from the inside. Marianne sensed in her an unwillingness to be consoled ever again, a desire also to bring things violently to a head.

Marianne was glad the scissors were down. She silently picked them out of the sink.

'Well, you've just made yourself look awful,' she said. 'Mum and Dad will kill me when they come back.'

Marie shook her head jauntily and continued to stare at her head from different angles.

'I like it,' she said. 'My head feels lighter now.'

She turned to Marianne and smiled. Something of her babyish nature came back in the smile.

'I'll tell them I did it when you were in the other room. They can only blame me.'

'It's not even straight. *Anywhere*.' Marianne pulled at some of the ends, which were beginning to dry around Marie's chin. 'The right side is totally shorter.'

'Give me the scissors then.'

Marianne reluctantly consented. She remained close to Marie's elbow so that she could pull her hand away at any moment. They both watched as Marie gradually overcompensated on the left side so that it was uneven again. They were both fascinated by the speed at which her whole head seemed to change, how the bones of her face reached a sharper climax. She ended up with a rough version of a pageboy haircut, though the bulk was unevenly distributed.

Marianne finally stepped back and looked at it from every angle.

'It's a bit better.'

They gathered the rest of the hair and put it in a plastic bag for the bin. Now that her hair had dried, Marie was pleased with it and kept swinging it to and fro. She was no longer submerged in it and her face was in closer range to everything. Her eyes appeared larger, older. Marianne could not stop looking at her.

Marianne had known to look out for signs of confusion, disorientation and forgetfulness and she took consolation in the fact that this was what the doctor had warned them about. There was certainly something feverish about Marie. There was also a powerful compulsion towards something that was making her ill and that gave out before she was finally compromised by it.

When midnight was close, Marie grew solemn and retentive. Marianne couldn't say anything to lift her spirits.

'Do you want to go to bed?' Marianne asked her after a while.

'Yes.'

Marianne took herself to bed too. She couldn't sleep because she was aware Marie wasn't asleep either. Eventually, she heard their parents enter the house at around four. She was surprised to hear her mother stumbling up the stairs, sniggering uncontrollably. Even her father began to laugh, although his voice was quieter and slightly more dignified. It took a very long time for them to reach the upstairs landing, and when they did there was a moment of complete silence while they must have stood there for a few minutes.

Marianne couldn't imagine anything that they could be doing on the other side of her door. She discounted the likelihood of anything amorous happening in the darkness of the hallway, because the timing was completely wrong. Her sleep-starved brain was filled with bitter thoughts towards them, towards Marie too for cutting her stupid hair. And herself for watching her do it.

In the morning, Marie came downstairs at eleven to take her antibiotics and painkillers. Heather was still in bed and Marianne and David were sitting in the kitchen drinking tea and eating pancakes. When Marie entered, her hair looked even more lopsided after sleeping on it.

David turned and yelped, spilling his tea on his trousers.

'Shit! Marie! *Shit!*'

It would have been funny had he not looked entirely devastated. He continued to stare at her without making any effort to close his mouth.

'I did it myself,' Marie said blithely.

David turned to Marianne, but she had been expecting his anger.

'Dad, she wanted it done. It looks nice enough, doesn't it?'

He scowled at her. Then he turned again to Marie and seemed to lose sight of whatever it was he needed to say to her.

'Fine. Yes. Take your meds.'

Marie didn't linger and took her pills dutifully by the kitchen sink while they watched her. When she was gone, David rounded on Marianne.

'You let her do that?'

'There was no stopping her,' Marianne admitted. 'Honestly, I've never seen her want something that passionately before in my life.'

'So what – would you let her burn herself with hot water? Cut herself with a knife?'

'Dad! Cutting your hair isn't a form of self-abuse!'

Although she was defending Marie's behaviour, she was secretly relieved he saw it for what it was.

'How was your night, anyway?' Marianne asked. 'I heard you come in,' she added provocatively. 'You sounded pissed.'

He smiled and scratched his head, pretending to be embarrassed.

'It was nice. Your mum enjoyed herself.'

'Good.'

'You know' – his voice lifted – 'Dylan was there for the first hour or so.'

'I haven't seen him for over a year.'

'He's based in London now. Peckham, I think. He's been working for a tech start-up company and he's doing really well. *Really* well by the sounds of it. Promotions come thick and fast when you're in that line of work. Coding, I think he said.'

'I can imagine.'

'Anyway, he's got a girlfriend now. Rosalie. She works for a new women's magazine. *Endeavour*? I can't recall the name of it now. Something beginning with "E". A strong title for strong women. That kind of thing. Its office is based in Soho, right in the middle of London. It's relatively new so I don't think they have any sort of track record in sales yet, but it sounds exciting. Dylan said they're still hiring and they're looking for interns too. Probably involves a bit of grunt work to start with – admin, filing, mailing, et cetera. But I thought – hey, Mari could do that!'

She thought she was moderating her face quite well but she must have given something of her cynicism away; his own bright expression fell when he surveyed her response.

'Obviously it's a starting position. It's practice for the real thing. If you don't want to write for a women's magazine, that's okay. But you want to write, to express who you are – right? Why not start here and at least get a leg in the door somewhere?'

'But where would I live? How could I pay rent anywhere? I'd be earning nothing as an intern. Who knows if they'd hire me permanently?'

David smiled. 'Well, Dylan might let you stay with him! I bet he would.'

'*What?* No. He already lives with his girlfriend.'

'She'd probably be happy to put you up. She's your age and surely she'd understand how hard it is to find work up here.'

Marianne bit her lip and said nothing. Her father's relentlessly good opinion of everybody was entirely at odds with her own misgivings.

'Look, think about it,' he said, leaning forward to catch her eye again. 'Dylan won't be looking for anything in return.'

Marianne had known Dylan for most of her life. From the age of five, she had played with him in that luxurious back garden while the adults drank coffee in the conservatory and forgot to watch what they were doing.

Though their friendship had long since evolved from rooting for worms in the soil and goading one another to eat 'just the tip', or tying one another up to the oak tree until someone nearly wet themselves, Marianne always found him a little too regressive, a little late in growing up and leaving that childish spirit behind. He liked to tell them stories about himself that were evidently embellished. He once told Marianne he'd lost his virginity to his maths teacher. He said it while they were playing ping pong in the garage at the Taylors' house. The sound of the little ball bouncing delicately across the table sounded silly after his apish grunt in swinging the bat. Especially since Marianne was terrible at it and knew that he only liked to play this with her *because* she was terrible. A very dishonest campaign for victory. But then he was fifteen. And he liked her, maybe more than he knew how to say.

He would never really know the depth of her reliance upon him: that he granted her a temporary release from the emptiness she felt in being vastly less visible to the world than her sister.

'Should I call him?' she asked her father.

'Yes! He'd love to hear from you. You've got his mobile number, haven't you?'

'If it hasn't changed, yes.'

She got up and kissed him gently on the top of his head.

There was no urgency to call Dylan right away. But she also knew that if she didn't marshal the courage to do it now, she would prolong it for as long as she could. She restlessly stalked the house from one room to another, frantic to begin her life and frantic not to. She was afraid of seeming desperate on the phone. She would act casually if her life depended on it. But then it didn't – it required force, exigence, passion. Her desire to make something of herself had gradually disappeared over the last few years and she'd become susceptible to derelict patterns of thought. She remembered her mother's angry tone of voice when she'd told Marianne to think more of herself and less of others, but it was a very difficult task to accomplish, primarily because she was useless at surmising who she was.

That afternoon, she left the house and traipsed up to Williamson Park, to walk among the sycamores and cypress trees. They were starkly elegant without their usual volume of leaves. The sky was grey but sharp and lucid. Marianne felt the outlines of the trees receding as her vision slowly narrowed to the tip of her shoes. Then she began to examine the space inside her head.

She had that timeless sensation of falling without ever wanting to reach the bottom. She was frightened of the immensity of what was there, how many square inches of darkness she consisted of. All those seconds in which she'd been alive, all of them stored in this great backwater, some glittering close at hand, others plunged in obscurity. Then she sensed a frightening pressure, something pulverising her share of existence and sweeping her into a greater abyss. She felt a numbing disbelief, where *Marianne* was nothing but a flimsy device, a ghostly echo receding as the blood surged in her ears. She didn't like the sensation of leaving everything and everyone behind as she tumbled into this vast space with the same tightness of breath as when she passed the door of her mother's bedroom. It was like drowning in something denser than thought. Something vaguely resembling euphoria once she stopped struggling against it.

When she came back round from her stupor – she hesitated to call it *meditation*; it seemed more punishing and perilous – it was to other identities that she merged, huddling close to them for protection. Marie filled her from the core. Almost every thought over the last few weeks had been directed towards her, and to her mother and father too. Her family were bound to the tenuous outline of herself like flies in a web, their every movement causing the fibres to tremble.

'HERE'S YOUR DETOX JUICE. WE'LL arrive at Nede in about five hours.'

Marianne turned to the man who held out the drink. She had just settled down on the coach after stowing her bag in the luggage compartment.

'Sorry, what is it?'

'Coriander, lemon and ginger. Coriander draws heavy metals from the body, so it's good for cleansing the system.'

The man was fairly young, blond, freckled. His voice was light and ebullient though the tone wasn't reflected in the expression on his face. He had walked down the aisle of the coach with glacial ease, not really making eye contact with any of the passengers.

She took the drink, which was a bright green, and swirled it in its bottle. Most people around her received their drinks enthusiastically, marvelling at the colour. One woman smiled to herself, brightening at the promise of a good purging. Marianne noticed that everybody on the coach had come alone, unaccompanied. They looked at one another shyly, not quite ready to make any small talk, too immersed in themselves to venture out.

She took a swig of her juice after realising the blond man was watching her expectantly. When he turned away, she put the top of the bottle back on, frowning.

'Do you like it?' A woman with dark hair and glasses had spoken to her from across the aisle.

'Not really. Do you want the rest?'

The woman smiled. 'Are you sure? That's really kind of you.'

Marianne handed her the drink. The woman thanked her again and then she drank it with great, noisy gulps. She turned back and smiled sluggishly. The smile lingered for a while after the thought that prompted it disappeared. It dawned on Marianne that the exchange might evolve into a conversation and she turned away to look out of the window before it could happen.

She took Marie's black velvet ribbon out of her pocket and wound it round her finger. She would never tie her hair with it; instead, she kept it close for no apparent reason other than to bind it temporarily to herself. She had been told not to bring any personal possessions to Nede but she relaxed in the knowledge that she alone knew what the ribbon was. It also redeemed her memory of Marie because it was an object from her earlier years. For when Marianne remembered her now, she recalled two people. She had learned to create a shortcut in her mind to leap cleanly from one version to another. She associated Marie's healthy, full head of hair with her mental aptitude, her happiness. When she thought of the final edition, the estranged part of Marie, she saw the bare bones of her head. The ribbon was located in a safer part of history.

She fell asleep not long after she got on the coach. Her dream was meagre, malnourished. It kept disappearing so that there was no narrative, only a series of images that had no connection to one another and that she could see only as shadowy outlines. Everything was infused with green light as though she were staring through the epidermis of a giant leaf. Then the sun came forth and burned through the membrane. Inside that heat, she saw thousands of cells swimming in front of her eyes, vying for her favour.

The coach hit a bump in the road and she woke sharply. The dream lingered with a strength she hadn't anticipated, but perhaps it was because she literally couldn't move and exercise it off somehow. She cursed herself for trying the juice, as she imagined its taste had somehow trespassed into her unconscious, dulling her sleep with its nasty flavour.

The coach was rumbling along a country road and she wondered where they were. The hills were strewn with sheep and little rivulets of water bubbled down the earth. The woman on her left was asleep but it wasn't a light doze. She had craned her neck to the side so her jaw was upturned and a line of saliva glittered down her neck. She was also mumbling something but it was nonsense. Marianne wondered whether sleep reordered language or created a new lexicon that never stored itself in memory. She turned around and realised that everybody else was asleep. Some of the passengers who were sitting together and who had initially behaved with a great deal of reserve were now leaning against one another, their heads reclining cheek to temple. Her neighbour was definitely the most disturbed sleeper. She exuded a sweat that smelt like it was coming from her thoughts – wherever they were now. It was trapped in her pores so her face had a sallow shine. Marianne briefly considered waking her.

The coach turned off into a forest and began to shuttle idly along a narrow path. The darkness was heavy on the eyes and

Marianne thought she could smell the juices of the pine trees. The air was sodden, subterranean. She kept waiting for someone to wake up and see how different the landscape was, how quickly their route had changed. She began to feel lonely in her tension, wishing she could share it with someone. And then she began to enjoy it. She grew glad of the intimacy with which the forest pressed itself upon her eyes alone.

She lapsed into it like it was a further stage of unconsciousness, one in which she trusted. A sea of pines, their needles blocking the sky and scattering the ground. It was a heavy place, vast and vital. She could understand why there was such a practice as 'forest bathing.' It really felt as though the shadow between the trees, briefly broken up by flashes of light through the canopy, could be reasonably absorbed in the bloodstream. She shivered in her seat.

The coach had wandered on to a gravel path and there was a very high security fence with barbed wire lining the edge, where it came to a halt. Marianne looked around her to see if anybody else was awake this time. Again, she was disappointed. She saw the driver consult with a security guard dressed in black who stood by the large iron gate. The guard looked at the passengers briefly and nodded. Then he spoke into an electronic device. There was a five-minute wait. Once the gate slid aside, the way was clear and the coach continued.

The path opened out and the trees formed an avenue inside the security walls. At this point in the journey everyone began to stir from sleep and stare through the windows. Everything was sharply imposed, the greenery, the light, the crunch of gravel, the oncoming glisten of something pure through the leaves, and it had a distinctly sobering effect. There was a communal silence, solemn yet feverish from the way people shifted in their seats to see the view. Eventually they reached an enormous clearing and Marianne finally saw the frontier of Nede, sectioned off from the forest.

It was the size of a small castle. She had already seen from the brochure that its two floors were transparent with giant glass walls, but she hadn't anticipated just how bold this decision was. She could see guests emerging from the swimming pool on the ground floor, their white bodies glistening from afar, others sliding into it with sinuous ease. She had to try not to gasp when she realised the swimmers were naked. And they were not shy about being so. One woman was reclining on a chair with her arms folded under her breasts as though she had forgotten that nudity ever had a sexual dimension. She sat with her legs slightly apart, her crotch airing itself. Tropical plants dominated the entire ground floor of what appeared to be a self-contained ecosystem. The heads of flowers were enormous and some of them almost reached the ceiling, their petals thick and rubbery, the ovaries fit to burst. Scarlet kaka beak, angel's trumpet and red-hot poker, waxy anthurium flowers, their yellow tails erect in the centre. There were leaves like heart-shaped tongues, lapping the sunlight through the windows. There was something lascivious about them, an engorged quality where their outlines never stopped expanding.

There was a garden behind the house, which Marianne had seen in the brochure, but the coach pulled up at the front entrance. Everyone stepped out and the blond man directed them through the double doors. Some people inquired about their bags, which were still in the luggage hold of the vehicle. The man said they would be taken up to their rooms, 'if you used the tag with your name and identity number, like I asked'.

Marianne looked around at the group – there were about fifteen of them in total.

The woman behind the reception desk wore a pair of glasses with thick blue frames. Her eyes were small inside the lenses but the pupils moved deftly. When they entered, she scanned each person quickly, the pupils snapping from one person to the next without settling on anybody.

'Welcome to Nede,' she said. 'If you will just wait here, I will go and get your guide and you'll be given an induction.'

She left her desk and disappeared through a door, her heels clacking on the floor. The ground they stood on was a dark stone that wasn't entirely even, rising and falling between the cracks. They waited in mutual anxiety for her to return, not wanting to look at one another.

When she came back, she was followed by a woman wearing a blue gown with rolled-up sleeves. Her skin was brown and liver-spotted, and there was a layer of downy hair across her forearms. The hair on her head was light and woolly, tied in a thick plait which had sprouted and frayed as it drifted across her back. She had brown eyes with liquid black centres.

'Hello, everyone. I am Doctor Gail Cedon. I'll be your guide as well as your point of contact if you ever need anything during your stay. If you step this way, I'll lead you to the lounge.'

She was neat and compact with a narrow frame. When they followed her through the door along a corridor, Marianne had the impression that her shoulder blades were arching closer together to save even more space and her plait was trapped between the muscles.

She opened a door at the end of the corridor and they entered a large, luminous room with a small pool and fountain in the centre. There were clusters of plants with red veins running through the leaves. Marianne remembered her father telling her about them. She had forgotten the Latin term but knew they were referred to as 'nerve plants'. The tributaries had a pinkish glow along the underside and burned brightly on the surface.

The fountain was a sculpture of a small-breasted woman whose arms were outstretched in a gesture of profound relief or despair. It was graphic but strangely consoling. The water streamed through small slices in her wrists and her throat. Because she was delicately constructed, the water dribbled from her body rather than cascaded, and the sound was gentle and sedate. The surface of the pool was barely disturbed.

There were angular wooden chairs around the edges of the room and everyone sat down, leaving an obligatory space between one another. Doctor Cedon took her own seat on the edge of the pool. She did not seem to mind that the sleeve of her dress dangled in the water. It floated towards the centre, where the sculpture stood feeding the water through her veins on a loop.

'It's great to see all of you and I'm thrilled you've decided to come to Nede,' she said. She made sure she levelled her gaze with every guest, moving her eyes towards a different face every few seconds. 'Everybody who comes here has made a brave decision in doing so, but also – we like to think – the right one.' She smiled. 'There are a variety of different ways to relax here, to acclimatise yourself – the pace at Nede is very different from the life you've lived so far. And there are exercises that will help you adjust to your new environment. Ideally, we want everyone to participate. After all –' she smiled at a young man who was just then loosening his shirt collar '– you have very kindly agreed to loan yourselves to this project. We want to learn from you.

This is a dialogue, between patient and doctor, guest and host, where an element of absolute trust is required.'

She sat up a little and rubbed her hands together.

'Okay – some brief rules. Not too many, don't worry. All electronic devices must be handed over to reception. That means phones, iPads, laptops, et cetera. Cameras and any other recording devices must also be handed over. I know it will be difficult for some of you – you've probably become accustomed to checking work emails routinely and scouring the internet to pass the time. Loading evidence of your day on to Instagram and monitoring how many likes it accumulates.' A few guests smiled wryly at each other. 'But you'll spend your time differently here. You are here in the pursuit of balance. And it can only be achieved without the distractions of modern life. Nede is a refuge from artificial stimuli, and – most importantly – from the ego. The largest distraction of all.'

Here she paused and her face divested itself of its former expression until it was blank. Marianne thought she looked as though she'd finally let go of the instinct to please her audience. Their attention was locked in place and the woman knew, with sudden ripe satisfaction, that their thoughts were no longer in danger of wandering away from her.

'Dismantling the ego is the most difficult thing of all,' she continued. 'But you can only be renewed this way – by letting go of your identity. The earth, it wants to hold you. Your consciousness is a strangled root and we have found a way' – her voice slowed down and Marianne felt the hairs on her back begin to twitch – 'to stretch it out. Further than ever before.

'You are about to re-enter the world you once knew as violently as a newborn child. Where consciousness is brand new and timeless. You will learn to empty your grief, your memories, your fears. Every terrible memory that informs who you are. We are going to help you lapse out of your pain – and out of yourself. The two are inextricably linked. I expect most, if not all of you, have come to rely on your misfortune as a symbol of your identity – perhaps you understand the allure of marking yourself as different or incompatible from the rest of society as possible. Anti-depressants and therapy haven't dissolved the source. What possibly can? A horrific event has detained your consciousness, then re-formed it so that your thoughts grow steadily around a single black spot in time. That black spot has sent your thoughts over the edge, winding into the darkness, crawling through your dreams.

'It's not cowardly to think of death at this point, to wonder whether it would be a better fate. But I understand you're all still tied very much to life and simply wish to find a way to continue as cleanly as possible. Nede offers you a blank slate. A chance to begin again without any recollection of your life. It requires a certain kind of courage – to forget who you are. To pour your memories out of your brain as though you never actually occurred. But it's the only way you'll become fully conscious again. And bind your new consciousness to the universe.'

Her words had shuddered then softened towards the end of her sentences. Everybody was watching her without really grasping what she said, listening with that vaguely hostile uncertainty – the belief that it couldn't possibly apply to them. The language was abstract enough to lock them out of its meaning. But Marianne was also mindful of what was growing on her back. The hairs that had grown steadily along the ridge of her spine, curling slightly in the night at the point where her dream entered its final phase.

It was clear Doctor Cedon was not going to say anything else, but her silence was voluble. She held it for a long time, and then finally gestured for everyone to stand by turning her palms upwards and lifting them at either side of her body.

She gave them a tour of the ground floor. The building was thick with that earthy, tropical smell and the heat of the sun was fairly extreme through the glass walls. Marianne was drawn to the idea that they were roaming a large botanic conservatory. There were vine plants that clustered the door frames, dangling their tendrils overhead. They came across a tree, which Marianne overheard someone referring to as a handkerchief tree, the white petals hanging softly. One room was a library, the bookcases lining the middle of the floor in symmetrical rows, with small breaks in between. Inside each gap, a trachyandra plant was placed. Its name was engraved in the stone pot that held the roots. The leafless tendrils looped and wriggled from the earth like a series of frightened worms. Their inertia seemed impossible.

The so-called 'meditation chamber' was the darkest part of the building, located in the centre of the ground floor. It was a long room with oak-panelled walls that gave off a sweaty shimmer without the light. When Doctor Cedon threw the switch, they saw rows of succulents positioned on tiered shelves against the walls. '*Haworthia cooperi*,' Cedon muttered when someone inquired what they were. Marianne found them faintly disturbing: she thought they looked as though they might explode. The leaves were like bubbles of molten glass. This room was different from the rest of the building in that the atmosphere was close and stifling. It was nothing to do with the heat; rather, the walls were heavy and gothic, reminiscent of ornate church pews.

It was past lunchtime, so there was only a handful of guests eating in the cafeteria. The room was clean, modern, sleek. There was no food displayed for guests to choose from. Instead, there was a bell on the counter to summon the server from a private room beyond a pair of double doors.

Somebody caught Marianne's eye in the cafeteria, without her catching his. She was thankful he wasn't looking up for it took her a minute to compose herself. She recognised Eric first in total disbelief – it was a strange coincidence, after all, that one of Marie's old college friends should be here at the same time as her – and then with the kind of relief she had been aching for without being aware. The blond hair was shorter and his face was slightly different, a little fuller, which made him look older and less anxious. He was dressed in the same grey clothes Marianne had noticed all the guests wearing, other than her own party of new arrivals – a plain v-necked T-shirt and linen trousers. He was eating a bowl of soup, his right elbow propped on the table and his left hand barely gripping the spoon, holding it with a slack wrist. He stared at the same spot on the surface of the table, his eyes never wandering from it.

They took a lift to the second floor, where they were directed to their bedrooms. Marianne's room was littered with cacti, some standing sentinel around her bed. *Myrtillocactus chichipe,* the plant pots read. At the end of the bed someone had laid out the grey clothes she presumed were her own uniform. She noticed her bag had been left, as promised, in the room. Finally, she was alone.

She sat on her bed and stared at the cacti.

'Jesus Christ,' she said under her breath.

She wondered whether to go back to the cafeteria to see if Eric was still there, but the prospect agitated her. There was every chance he was, given how slowly he had been eating. But she had been informed that she was allowed half an hour's rest before she would be summoned for a consultation with Doctor Roberts. She wondered whether there was some sort of time-table outlined for her entire stay.

The foot of the bed faced the glass wall which overlooked the back of the house. Now she saw how the garden, with its long shelves of privet and birch trees, its fountains and mytho-logical sculptures, met the edge of the forest through which they had come. A decorative wrought-iron gate divided the two plots of land, divorcing the garden from an untamed wilderness. The pine trees towered above the gate and blocked her from seeing anything else, giving her the impression that nothing existed beyond that insular darkness. The road along which they had travelled, and which ran the length of the garden and disappeared into the trees, was on the other side of the security fence with its razor barbed wire mounted on welded wire-mesh panels. This fence ran along both lengths of the garden, its brutal structure contrasting with the starkly elegant gate at the end, leading on to the woods.

The hairs along her back were itching now and she reached under her shirt to scratch her spine, digging her nails into the skin. She stood up from the bed to find that her legs were shaking. She was hungry and thirsty, aching from spending most of the day in a sedentary position, drifting between states of consciousness.

She saw another juice had been left in her room on a bedside table. She reached and took it. The bottle was still cold and must have been left there just before she came up. She would have preferred anything else but her throat was dry and the liquid inside the bottle seemed to glitter. She removed the cap and, with the fatal compulsion of an addict, gulped the whole lot down in one go.

It didn't look or taste like the last drink. In fact, it barely had any flavour at all. It might have been water. However, she immediately felt sharper, more expansive. She crouched to unzip her rucksack and rifled through it. She had wanted to check that something was there a few minutes earlier, but now she couldn't remember what it was that she'd needed to be sure of.

Someone knocked on her door. She walked over and opened it to find a young man in a white shirt and trousers staring at her. He was much shorter than her, and his hair was oily, raked across his scalp from a high hairline.

'Hello, Marianne – Doctor Roberts is ready to see you now.'

'Right. Do I need anything?'

'No. Nothing.'

They stared at one another for a few seconds and Marianne suddenly remembered what it was that she now knew had been taken from her bag. Her pills were nowhere to be found.

'If you'll come this way, we'll take the lift to the basement floor,' the man said. His eyes were full and shining.

Marianne followed him to the lift. On their way down the corridor, they passed a young woman who was sitting on the floor outside room 306. The man stopped abruptly and looked down at her.

'Are you 306?'

The woman had been muttering softly to herself and she met his eyes without really turning her head. She shook it and carried on speaking. She believed it was a dialogue, that an interchange was happening, and they had evidently intruded the space in which it was conducted. The veins were prominent around her forehead.

'Are you waiting for someone?' the man asked her. The woman nodded softly.

He drew a key from a small white leather bag that was belted around his trousers and which Marianne had only just noticed.

'She's not there now,' the woman said in a thin voice, shaking her head. 'She's not been there for weeks.'

The man opened the door and Marianne could see a vacant room beyond it, the same as her own. The cacti were deformities in that half-light, trapped in a strange orgiastic climax. He closed it but the woman had grown disturbed by what she hadn't seen.

'She's been gone too long,' she said quietly, as though to herself. 'Someone needs to look for her.'

'That patient has gone back home,' the man said slowly. 'You can't stay here forever.'

He said the last statement with a hint of irony and well-intentioned humour, but it spiked the woman's anger. She looked at him from beneath a pair of heavy brows.

'She's not gone home. She's been taken.'

The man looked at Marianne and smiled apologetically.

'I'm really sorry. Some of our patients are quite unwell and often confused.'

He patted the woman's shoulder and his tone was suddenly quite different.

'Shall I find Gail? Which number are you?' he asked her kindly.

She shook her head and sighed, staring ahead furiously. Marianne thought she had never seen someone so deeply incarcerated in their own delusions.

'Will she be alright?' she asked the man.

The woman lifted her eyes slowly to Marianne, mining her face for information. Her eyes were sharpening, sizing her up.

'Have you just arrived?' she asked.

'Yes.'

The woman sat up a little straighter then, and Marianne felt a cold prickling feeling at the back of her head.

'Don't give your thoughts away to them,' the woman said in a strident voice. She began to massage the small of her back. 'Don't let them have your thoughts. You won't get them back, I'm sure of it.'

She gestured with disgust towards the man who was standing over her and his face fell slightly. It was an expression of gentle commiseration, perhaps even of disappointment on her behalf, which Marianne wasn't sure she liked.

'You need some sleep,' he said gently and made to touch the woman's arm. She shifted away from him, her face set in its fury. 'Shall I send for Doctor Cedon? She'll take you for a walk around the garden if you like.'

'I'm not a geriatric,' the woman spat.

Marianne thought that she was perhaps in her forties. She had thick, curly black hair, a square-shaped jaw and large, questioning eyes, one of the pupils slightly off centre.

'I'll come back as soon as I can,' the man said. His eyes were earnest as he stooped to face her, but as soon as he straightened up and walked away, beckoning Marianne to follow, he closed them and raised his eyebrows in a dramatic show of tension.

'Sorry about that,' he said to Marianne after a few seconds. He smiled conspiratorially. 'She's upset because she made a friend here and now that friend has gone back home. She's very upbeat normally. In fact –' he looked at his watch '– in about half an hour she'll be off for a swim or reading a book in the library like nothing happened. She has a lot of dips in her mood, none of which are permanent.'

He took Marianne to the lift at the end of the corridor. Once inside, he used a small key fob to select the basement floor. He continued to explain to Marianne that the woman would be looked after and that she shouldn't worry about her. Patients came to Nede with a variety of mental illnesses and bipolar was a common one.

'Is she taking her medication?' Marianne asked him.

He stared at her and smiled. 'Of course.'

The lift dropped and the doors opened. This floor was dark and the stone walls were uneven. The smell of earth was unbearable and Marianne had the impression the ceiling would fall and cramp them into the darkness.

'It's a bit grotty down here,' the man said. His keys were glinting through his fingers. 'But this won't take long, don't worry. Then you can return to the light!'

He laughed, and Marianne felt a sudden sharp pain inside her ribcage. The man's voice was receding. The darkness had the effect of dismantling both their outlines so she couldn't be entirely sure of his presence, only the occasional glitter of the keys and his quick, shallow breaths.

She felt dimly that she was falling into the pit of herself. Her eyes were in her chest and her heart was pulsing through the membrane of her past. The heat of the underground was rising through her blood. A wall of suited bodies, their hands clutching the silver bar overhead, the hard edge of a suitcase against her back. She felt that old myopic fear worming its way through her lower body as she fought her way to the doors. *Please, move aside!* The white-hot certainty of death. Her bowel shuddered. *Stop! Someone stop it!*

'Are you alright?'

The man was clutching Marianne's arm and she realised she had been in the process of slowly crumpling to the floor.

'Oh sorry. Yes.'

'You must be tired after the journey. This won't take too long, don't worry.'

She allowed herself to be hoisted up. She strained her eyes to see what was in front of them, but it was difficult as they were facing a black door and she was only vaguely certain of its existence. A woman opened it at the first knock and the sudden light made Marianne feel like she had materialised again.

'Marianne, come in.'

The woman stared at the man who'd escorted Marianne. She had a broad face, the features large and evenly spaced. Right then, her expression was entirely neutral, and yet something about its stillness, its suspension, must have frightened the man. He nodded and was gone quickly.

Doctor Roberts's office was stuffy and disorganised. There were no plants in here and Marianne found herself relieved by their absence. Instead, she saw books and files on overloaded shelves. The woman indicated a chair on the other side of her desk for Marianne. She then seated herself and looked at the screen of her computer.

'I'm just going to ask you a few routine questions about your health and medical history. Nothing too serious. And then I'll ask you a bit about yourself. Okay?'

She stared at Marianne and in the stillness of her face was a growing warmth. It lifted the tone of her voice.

'Let me explain. You see, Nede is a health resort, but it's also a clinic that makes assessments of its guests. Guests are also patients who need something more than relaxation. If you needed some time off work or a change of scene, you'd just book a flight to Santorini, right? Nede is entirely unique. It offers a kind of training to recalibrate your mind forever. I know Gail will have mentioned this already. It's also important that I know about your mental health so that we can ensure you get the best out of this place. Referrals are only given to patients with serious psychological damage. But it's the kind of damage that can be reversed.

'You don't have to answer all of these questions. But it will help you in the long run if you do give clear answers to the best of your knowledge. Down here, in the *underground*, I like to do a bit of light probing into what makes you *you* – excuse me for sounding crass. Up there, you'll be able to relax and let go of all these neuroses that have such a tight hold over your consciousness. But here, I study the source. As I said, this is not an interrogation and I'm not going to force you to speak if you don't want to.'

Marianne began to sweat. The hairs on her back were unpleasantly damp.

'Right. First question,' Doctor Roberts began. 'What made you decide to come to Nede?'

'My doctor offered me an invitation.'

Doctor Roberts smiled and her face instantly lost its light neutrality. The smile was sardonic and gave away the knowledge that she was being subtly derided.

'And why did you accept the invitation?'

Marianne paused. 'I wanted to escape things for a while.'

'What things?'

'My job. My boyfriend. My flat. Myself.'

On the last word, Roberts's smile grew rigid.

'Can you identify the source of that feeling? Any significant event that prompted the desire to escape?'

Marianne knew Doctor Hind must have passed on her history and wondered why she had to be asked directly.

'Yes. My sister died. About seven months ago.'

'How did she die?'

The question wasn't tempered at all. It was naked and Marianne was glad of it.

'She killed herself. She jumped off the platform on the underground at Victoria station,' she said quickly.

The words did not sound like they belonged to her. It was a foreign statement, made strange again after so many months of avoiding having to state it. The words had fallen into disuse, but they came back with chilling ease, with the same surreal and biting clarity. Her heart was beating fast.

'I understand that this is difficult to answer and you might not wish to. Why do you think that she felt the compulsion to do that?' Roberts asked.

Marianne swallowed. Her throat was tightening.

'She'd been very ill and – she couldn't get her state of mind back.'

'Could you tell me about her illness?'

'She had cancer. Hairy cell leukaemia. She had a splenectomy and she got sepsis afterwards – she went into septic shock. She died for two minutes in the hospital and when she came round, she was…different.'

'It's a hugely traumatic experience and very few people manage to recover from it emotionally.' The doctor's voice was in a minor key now, carefully pitched. *Too careful*, Marianne thought. 'Was she younger than you?'

'Yes. Eighteen. She'd be nineteen now.'

Again, Marianne felt a tightness in her throat that forced the words back. She was afraid of being seen like this and, on impulse, she pressed her hands lightly against her face. She breathed through her skin, taking herself in so as not to let anything out, resting her little fingers in the corners of her eyes. Doctor Roberts was kind enough to wait for her to compose herself. She had begun to write notes, her silver ballpoint pen flashing across her desk, and seized the opportunity to get all these last details down while Marianne was silent. Marianne saw what she was doing through the gaps of her fingers.

Something about the momentum of Doctor Roberts's pen, the way it travelled across the page, loosened Marianne's tongue and she was compelled to speak again. She was anxious to unburden herself, to drag every dusty thought from memory. She lowered her hands.

'I wasn't very nice to anyone. Not really,' she said. 'Marie was always lovely and happy. You know how happy people draw you in, make you think you can adopt some of it yourself through close proximity? Being happy is an admirable quality – I think so. She was admired by everyone and there wasn't one person who didn't want her attention for themselves. I wanted it too. I wanted her to love me in the same way I loved her, which was impossible because I was so…' Marianne felt a soreness in her throat then, the old trepidation. *No self-pity! Stop it!* She avoided the doctor's eye. 'Marie kept her distance from me for years. She didn't deliberately – it wasn't coldness that made her do it – she was just, I don't know, independent. Didn't need to rely on anyone. Didn't read into anything too deeply. Didn't even understand what distance was.

'When she got sick, she changed. It's like the cancer had gone from her body, but now it was in her head. We thought she was better, but she was worse in some sense.' Her voice trembled. 'I grew impatient with her. I couldn't believe she was the same person. When she was in hospital and she died...'

Now Marianne felt like her words were congealing. They were merging together and losing their integrity, just as her thoughts were doing. She had stopped because she worried she couldn't separate them anymore and the failure caused a crisis of faith, a desire to retreat from analysis and spare herself the shame. Doctor Roberts was still staring at her, though this time there was no doubt as to her sincerity, the solemn absorption of her face and the stillness of her body. This minor act of respect, so rare to come by, gave Marianne the impetus to finish.

'Marie died twice,' she said quietly. 'The first time she died, she came back, but she seemed to take some of her death with her and carry it around. That sounds silly but it's true. I looked at her and – I knew she'd seen something.' A tear was growing in the corner of her eye, blurring the periphery of the room. 'I think she couldn't be fully *here* again because she'd been somewhere else and didn't know how to talk about it. Or she could only snap at us. I couldn't bear to be in the house anymore – it was suffocating. I didn't like being around her.

'I moved to London not long after that, when the opportunity was there. The guilt was awful, but I thought – I *knew* – I'd miss my moment otherwise. If I didn't get out of there then, I'd lose the nerve. I invited Marie to come and stay with me for a few days but I must have tormented her. I was a big fat show-off, dangling everything I had in front of her nose. I was living with a man, I was earning my own money, I had friends who weren't just *her* friends.' Marianne cast a cautious eye towards the doctor's face. 'I'd always wanted her to be jealous of me. To feel like I used to feel. Lonely and left out. But I didn't want to break her spirit! I had no idea what was going on in her head at the time.' The tear broke free and fell on to the bone of her wrist. 'I'd no idea. I still don't.'

Marianne was still raring to go, sitting on the edge of her seat. She knew her face was wet but she had no interest in any more intermissions and ignored Doctor Roberts's extended hand with the tissue box.

'I'm here because I want to stop thinking about what happened,' Marianne said. 'I don't want to go through it every day. There needs to be some sort of buffer at least. A space between us.'

She looked at Doctor Roberts. It occurred to her then that she may have been unwise in giving so much of herself away. The pity she had thought possible was dwindling in the doctor's face and, on closer inspection, seemed to have been a mirage she'd conjured at will. Once the tension in her head gave way, the face that was staring back at her seemed less amenable than she had hoped, more remote than receptive. Where she had imagined compassion, there was an overriding tautness of perception, attention which was focused but neatly curtailed.

'I want to thank you for giving me a very honest version of events,' the doctor said finally. 'It was a very brave thing to do. And I don't wish to dwell on Marie's story because we're on the other side of it now. I'm going to ask some simpler questions.' She paused and stared at Marianne with a gentler expression. 'You must take your time to answer.'

Marianne nodded. Now that her sinuses were clear, she felt sharper. She took a tissue from the box that had been offered and balled it in her hand.

'Were you prescribed medication from your doctor?'

'Anti-depressants. Paroxetine.'

'How many milligrams?'

'Thirty.'

There was a pause and Marianne took courage.

'When will I get my pills back?'

'I'll give them back to you at the end of the day. We had to check all medication on arrival.'

Doctor Roberts's voice was a little artificially high in that moment. She was still writing, and when she met Marianne's eye, she smiled.

'It's just protocol. Have you taken your pill for today?'

Marianne lied. 'No.'

Doctor Roberts frowned. 'In that case, I'll see if we can speed up the process.'

Marianne was about to ask her what exactly this process was when the doctor tapped her pen sharply on the table.

'Next question. Do you take any other drugs or medication?'

'Only the contraceptive pill. But I stopped taking that about two weeks ago.'

'Was this because you ended a relationship?' Doctor Roberts asked bluntly, not looking up.

Marianne stared at the doctor with renewed distaste. It was strange how the woman oscillated between gentle emotional inquiry and clinical scrutiny within the space of a few seconds. Marianne wasn't sure which demeanour was stage-managed and which was genuine. Her compassion had seemed credible. Perhaps all doctors behaved in this way, speaking in the manner of a concerned yet pragmatic senior figure whose private self has become subsumed over time, after so much practice, so many hours given over to the perfecting of this authority. But Marianne also felt that Doctor Roberts was keeping her private thoughts at a firm, isolated distance, watching Marianne from a secret part of her brain. That watchful part, the thought that wouldn't translate itself, was what she feared the most.

'I sort of ended a relationship but it's not really – it's still sort of – open,' she said uncertainly. Thinking of Richard made her wince.

'And was it a serious relationship?' Doctor Roberts asked. Again, this time she settled for gentle inquiry.

'Yes.' Marianne heard her voice crack. 'I don't know, to be honest. I'm sorry, I don't want to talk about that.'

Doctor Roberts gave her a stunned smile.

'But you're happy to speak about your sister?'

'Yes,' Marianne snapped. The heat flooded through her face. 'I'm sorry, but it's not relevant. My life with Richard isn't relevant. It doesn't need to be talked about. I can choose what to talk about!'

This outburst didn't surprise the doctor. She merely nodded and ducked her head as though in respect to Marianne's wishes.

'Absolutely, as I said – you don't have to discuss anything you don't want to,' she said quietly. 'Do you smoke?'

'No.'

'How many units of alcohol do you consume in an average week?'

'None.'

'Do you have any physical disabilities?'

'No.'

'Aside from depression and post-traumatic stress disorder, are there any other mental health difficulties we should know about?'

'I don't have post-traumatic stress disorder,' Marianne said promptly.

'Alright.' Doctor Roberts wasn't interested in an argument. 'Any other disorders?'

'No.'

'Have you ever experienced memory loss or any cognitive difficulties?'

'No.'

'Good. Now, I'm going to ask you some philosophical questions,' Doctor Roberts said. She'd reverted to a lighter tone, her energy replenished by some sort of progress Marianne wasn't aware they'd made. 'Don't panic. If you don't wish to answer, again, that's fine. We like to know about the world views of our guests.'

Marianne glared at her. This tiptoeing around the edges of the conversation was becoming unbearable.

'Do you believe in God?'

'Am I in church?'

Doctor Roberts laughed and this time it was genuine.

'I know, it's a bold line of inquiry. You're not under duress.'

'I don't believe in God.'

'Have you ever had any spiritual or religious leanings?'

'I don't believe so.'

'Do you believe in an afterlife?'

'No.'

'Do you believe in the inherently redemptive nature of human beings – what I mean by that is, our capacity for good?'

Marianne paused.

'Most people are just selfish and only exist for themselves.'

'Interesting that you say that.'

Doctor Roberts wrote something, smiling ironically, and Marianne grew weary again.

'I'm just spouting things though. I might have a different opinion tomorrow,' she said.

'Understandable. But it's always telling to see what people come up with first, on instinct.'

Was it instinct? Marianne didn't feel well at all. She felt queasy, light-headed and horribly close to tears. For some reason, it felt vital she maintain a semblance of dignity in front of this woman. She had lost most of it earlier but she could claim it back.

'What can you not tolerate in others?'

'I don't know. Self-absorption probably.'

'And what can you not tolerate in yourself?'

'What do you mean?'

'What is the quality you least like about yourself?'

Marianne hesitated. She wanted to say her inability to spot when she was being taken advantage of. She felt it now. She wasn't safe.

'I hate my apathy.'

'And do you believe one day it will be gone?'

Marianne stared at the woman and relished the few seconds before she was obliged to answer. 'No.'

'Do you hope to have children?'

'Probably not.'

'Are you close to your family? Other than your sister, I mean.'

Marianne paused. 'I – don't know. I don't have a big family.'

'Your parents. Are you close to them?'

Marianne hesitated.

'I love my parents but I've never understood them.'

'Do you feel loved?'

'By my parents?'

Doctor Roberts dipped her head solemnly. 'By anybody.'

'Perhaps I am, but it's not enough.'

'What do you mean by that?'

'I mean that it's not reason enough to continue,' Marianne said unhappily. 'Sometimes, it's not enough.'

'You don't wish to continue?'

'This interview or life?'

There was a small smirk on Doctor Roberts's face, and suddenly Marianne felt the urge to slam her hand down on the desk between them. She realised there was nothing she could say or do that was extraordinary, unusual or perverse enough to shock the doctor. That woman was an authority on grief, on endless histrionics, the belief patients held that they were somehow exempt from responsibility and self-restraint because their pain was of a higher value.

She saw Marianne as the hypocrite that she was, someone who hadn't lived long enough to understand the mathematics of pain. How long it took for grief to outlive itself. That time made a mockery of unrelenting pessimism. And there was a measure of dishonesty in defeat, especially if one's life was not seriously compromised by anything. Marianne pitied herself but at the same time, she knew she was safe. She was unconsciously glad to be alive.

She knew deep down that the future was always something to invest in, regardless of its contents. Only Marie had reached that awesome limit of despair which Marianne flattered herself she knew about. It came from a depleted imagination, a failure to grasp the virtue of time. That tunnelled vision made her fearless of death because she couldn't see the full extent of it. It was a horrible snap decision.

'I can see you're tired so I won't keep you much longer,' Doctor Roberts said. Marianne blinked herself back into the room. 'I just want to ask you one more question. After Marie passed, you were confined to a period of grief – one that is still ongoing, naturally. During that period, have you experienced any unusual physical symptoms of depression?'

Doctor Hind must have informed Doctor Roberts of the hair growth on Marianne's back. There was no other reason for this question.

'Yes. I started finding dark hairs on my back. They've been growing there for weeks.'

'I see.'

'Is this common with people who come here?'

Doctor Roberts said nothing and scribbled some notes for a while. Marianne knew she was avoiding the question; she couldn't have that much to write from such a short answer.

'It's not a common occurrence but it's nothing to worry about. It's happened before. You're not an anomaly, don't flatter yourself.'

Marianne was slightly thrown by this last comment. It was spoken lightly, intended as a playfully mocking statement, but the doctor's face had grown dark and vulgar. Her eyes were fixed on Marianne's like the points of someone's thumbs. She had what she wanted.

'Okay, thanks, Marianne. That's all. I'll escort you to the lift.'

'I remember the way,' Marianne said coldly.

'Oh, I know you think you do but it's very dark down here. The lighting is so poor. All the money has been reserved for the luxurious upper floors – no budget left for dull and dingy psychiatry down below.'

This was evidently a private joke she cultivated for her own purpose. But as she accompanied Marianne out of the office and down the dank corridor, her demeanour switched back to the same tense focus she had maintained throughout the interview.

'Thank you for your honesty, Marianne,' she said once they were at the lift doors. When they opened and Marianne stepped in, the doctor pressed the button for the second floor and turned away without giving her patient a second glance.

Once she was back in her room, Marianne was so exhausted she couldn't bear the prospect of going down to see any more new faces. A small tray had been left for her on the table in the corner of her room with a plate of hot food. It surprised her how quickly that had been served, as though there was an invisible attendant who knew exactly when she was due to enter the room. She wandered over and pulled out a chair to eat. She looked down at a plate of warm falafels with brown rice and lentils.

'For fuck's sake,' she said under her breath.

She was angry that she hadn't been given a choice. She would have ordered anything with meat if she'd had the chance to peruse a menu – a sweet chilli chicken baguette or a spicy meatball sub. Or at least something fatty, something rich. But she was hungry; it had been a long time since she'd eaten and she ate with ferocious speed. She drank the smoothie on offer too; it was purple with a thick dark cloud at the bottom. She was surprisingly gratified, though she didn't really enjoy the flavour.

She went to the bathroom and decided to wash her face and hands. She stooped to splash the water on her face and then looked up, expecting to see herself. Instead of finding her face as usual in the surface of a mirror, she saw the blank wall. She turned around and looked to see if it was placed somewhere else. Then she looked in the bedroom, her face dripping wet. There was not a single mirror anywhere. And she hadn't any access to one on her person. She would not even be able to see her reflection using the camera of her confiscated phone.

It didn't matter very much, yet at the same time it mattered a great deal. She was alarmed by it, just enough to feel a little sick. Then her exhaustion entered a final phase and she was paralysed from moving where she stood. A wave of darkness flexed itself at the shore of her consciousness. Perhaps because she had spent so long talking about it earlier – and it had drained her just enough to leave her defenceless – she thought she saw the entry to death inside her brain. Luckily, she was close enough for the bed to save her fall.

Sleep ravaged her thoughts so cleanly that she was convinced she'd never have them back. And inside of that unreality, she saw flashes of what might have been real. The corners of her room contained her. But she began to transpose the two realms, believing that the door of her bedroom was part of her dream. She lay in pain, her chin squashed against the pillow. Through a strange gauze, the colour of a bruise, she saw activity in her room without being able to access it with any coherent thought. The door opened and someone entered. They were wearing a white coat. Someone else was there too but they were too dark to see. She only saw the outline moving through the gloom without being absorbed by it. Her head was propped awkwardly, so that she only saw them when they came in and could only suppose that they were still there. She thought she sensed them watching her, with that disembodied conviction that exists in the province of dreams.

Then the physical world intervened. She felt her body moving without knowingly having directed it to move. Two pairs of hands were shifting her on the bed, rolling her so that she was lying on her stomach and her face was crushed flat on the pillow. It was in no way violent or hurried. In fact, she was moved in graceful slow motion. Then her shirt was pulled up from her back, again slowly. Her eyes were pressed close against the pillow and the warmth of it made her sweat, her breath trapped in that small pocket of air. She felt a small twinge of pain from her spine and she knew, again with delayed and protracted dread, that they had come to take a part of her without her permission. She heard a snipping sound and imagined she saw it, a silver echo in the static behind her eyelids.

MARIE WASN'T WELL ENOUGH TO return to college in the new year. Heather took her to the hospital for a series of check-ups and a bone marrow test. The nurse also removed the stitches from her wound. Marie was disappointed to learn that she still had hairy cell leukaemia even though her spleen was gone. When she was told that she would still have to have chemotherapy, she was initially very childish and told the nurse that she didn't want to go through with it. Heather relayed the conversation back to Marianne when they returned.

'I thought she knew she'd still have to have the drugs,' Marianne said.

Her mother shrugged. She was busy tuning the radio in the kitchen, perhaps anxiously trying to tune everything else out. It kept crackling into canned laughter.

'It doesn't sound too bad actually,' she said. 'The doctor said she can have it as an injection every day for five days or she has it through a drip for seven days. They can even teach her how to inject herself.' She caught Marianne's eye and they both smiled grimly. 'Although that's probably *not* a good idea. It would be better if one of us does it. The nurse will do the first one and then, if it saves a hospital trip, she'll show us what to do at home.'

'Side effects?'

Heather paused and stared into space with her hands on her hips.

'Quite a few,' she said.

Marianne was comforted by the fact that the process would be short at least. But Marie's patience was already waning. She could barely withstand anything for a long period of time and willed things urgently, silently, to a close. She was frustrated she couldn't go back to college and her forced invalidism brought on a bitterness Marianne had never seen in her. She was surly and sarcastic, especially with their father, which Marianne found difficult to watch.

David tried very hard to lift Marie's spirits, but the more effort he gave to the task, the crueller Marie's response to it. She either stared at him through hollow eyes or began to speak over him, loudly, as though he weren't there. Marianne knew it was beginning to wear him down; his face was fixed in a permanent expression of good-natured, magnanimous grief. One day, Marie finally snapped at him to be quiet. Marianne and her mother were stunned and stared at each other. David watched Marie for a very long time with that same bright expression, and then, when she turned away from him, it was still there. There was no resentment beneath it at all; he simply didn't know how to resent her.

Marianne began to find the house suffocating, so she went for long walks down the canal every day. There, she allowed her thoughts to tumble on blackly into the darkening space, barely able to keep up with them. Her breath was short while the images in her head seemed to last forever.

One time, the wind was picking up by the water and the evening was already hurrying towards a close. But she was not ready for it. She didn't want to feel herself through the darkness; she needed to see it from afar. The boughs of the trees hung very low, encroaching on her headspace. Her thoughts quivered beneath them, seconds from expiring. She thought, briefly, that she was perhaps the most alone she had ever felt, and she vowed never to feel that isolated again. She felt bleakly assured that she would take this same route back and forth forever more, endlessly communing with herself. Every compulsion drawn to a dead end. She needed a radically different environment if she was to evolve on the inside. Isn't that how personality worked? So much of it was innately formed, hanging on the way the mind moved and perfected itself. And yet it required material, more fuel with which to power itself; it was an engine that veered dangerously close to combustion.

Marie's illness had drained her, but Marianne suspected something ultimately worse lay behind her own feelings of ennui. It was a powerful notion of emptiness, one that was tied to this place. She had come to the conclusion that every novelty of life could well be exhausted while she remained here, worn down to nothing through endless recurrence. Was it merely that her responses had broken down now the panic of the last few weeks had subsided? It was more than just an aftershock; it was a resoundingly defeatist mindset, one that might have been inherited and could well be permanent.

She thought then of her mother, how her existence confirmed that one could live in close proximity to despair without ever conquering it. Heather was depressed but she had almost accepted this as her default state. She was only occasionally still outraged she felt this way; it was a revolt from the deep, the part of her that resisted sedation, that routinely exposed itself before retiring, exhausted by its efforts.

The sun was bleeding into the towpath at this point. There was barely any light left to see her thoughts. What a strange idea, Marianne thought. But then they grew louder. Once she had less light, they stirred and parted quickly, leading into a rapid succession of ideas that she could hardly contain without panicking. It was like they had been recently oxygenated, given too much life, too much import. She placed her palm on the bark of a tree by the river and forced herself to slow down inside, for her mind to exhale.

She was filled in that moment with a huge amount of remorse and affection for the people she shared her life with. Her parents were braver than she was. She was despicable for thinking of them as futile, provincial people without dreams or drives. Their courage was bound up in their present circumstances, in remaining sane, and together, for the sake of Marie and herself. Something had ruined them around the time of Marie's birth, a desolation like no other, something wildly atavistic and removed from their former selves. They were still living in the aftermath. It had never quite passed into a period of reconciliation but what Marianne had witnessed was something bearably close, bearable enough for relations to continue. Perhaps they should have parted years ago and saved one another the stagnation of living half in fear and half in bitterness, longing for what lay beyond one another but too weary to explore new terrain. The pattern was periodically broken by an accidental retreat into intimacy. Snatches of sudden, exhilarated intimacy. *Is this it? Are we ourselves again?* The illusion was swallowed up by time, a relapse into past pain and all the memories they still shared of Marie's first years.

Marie had always been Marianne's ally against this fragile mode of existence. Now she was slipping into it. She was lost in the puzzling terrain of their parents' lives, watching them circle the same ground as though properly evaluating their worth for the first time. Helpless to detach herself, frightened of what lay beyond it, if there was anything reserved for her. Marianne was about to venture out for all of them. This was it. Her fate was opening itself up and it only required her courage for consummation. *I want to be myself*, she thought stupidly, by the bank of rippling water. She watched the thought swell and grow on the current. She could already feel these wrestling impulses in the dark of her body, the fear of committing to something new and the desire to remain safe. So much of love was just emotional clutter, a hoarder's paradise, the contents blocking her way and pulling her back into chaos. She wanted to see the bare outline of herself, the undisturbed surface, the limit between herself and other people. It would require her to erase an enormous part of what she had always been, who she had always clung to, and she dreaded to see the hole once it was removed. She would have to work fast to fill the gap.

She booked her ticket for the train to Euston where Dylan would meet her in two weeks. She quit her job at the stationery shop and immediately afterwards went into the town centre to look for some new clothes. She had to look presentable for the internship and the old smart clothes she had used for interviews after finishing university had an air of fatality about them, of disappointment. She also remembered how terrified she had felt in those clothes and decided angrily that she had nothing to be terrified about. She marched into every clothes shop on the high street with a vengeful air, rooting through blouses with quick and vicious hands.

It was as she was looking around Marks and Spencer that she saw a familiar face. Eric Mayhew. He was a friend of Marie's from school and someone Marianne had always thought to be unusually sensitive in that warm and insular way that boys rarely are. He was holding a large bouquet of pink roses in his arms, which made her sad for some reason. Perhaps it was the way he held them. His frame was broad, with reassuringly solid arms, but he carried the roses limply, their heads drooping.

'Eric,' Marianne said.

She was close enough to him that she knew he'd hear. She also panicked that she'd spoken. The compulsion was born from a keen interest in seeing how his face would change once it turned towards her. He glanced around and a warmth entered his eyes. She was glad to see it.

'Sorry, you caught me off guard,' he said. 'You're Marie's sister.'

'Marianne.'

'Sorry.' He pushed his hand through his hair. His eyes darted down briefly. 'How is Marie? I heard she wasn't well.'

'She's not. She nearly died.'

She was surprised how loosely those words fell from her mouth.

'I'm very sorry to hear that,' Eric said quietly.

'How are you anyway?' Marianne asked. 'Are those flowers for someone special?'

He bit his lip. The incisors were very sharp, much longer than the rest of his teeth. It was perhaps the only subversive feature in his face. She thought it quite a noble face but in a classical as opposed to an aristocratic way. A Homeric face. His eyes were calm and quietly commanding.

'They're actually for my aunty. My uncle died a few days ago.'

'Oh god. I'm really sorry.'

He smiled. 'Don't worry. I wasn't very close to him, to be honest. He had throat cancer.' His hand moved automatically to his neck and he stretched it, foolishly, to mimic the place. Then his face flushed. 'I have to find something to wear for the funeral too. I don't wear a lot of black.'

Marianne instantly thought this a lost opportunity. She imagined he would look striking in dark clothes.

'Well, roses are a strange choice,' she said. 'They're usually given on romantic occasions – like Valentine's Day. Unless she really likes roses?'

'No. Not really.'

'How about white ones? They're a bit more solemn but still pretty.'

His eyes wandered into space and he nodded slowly. Then they came back to her face. Every time he broke the gaze then returned it, she felt a cold pang in her chest that grew into a suffusing, prickly heat. The heat spread to her legs.

'Sorry, I shouldn't pry,' she said. 'Bit presumptuous of me to tell you what flowers your aunt wants.'

'No, you're being helpful. I think I might get the white roses.' He smiled at her again. 'Thank you.'

He turned as if to leave.

'I really am sorry,' Marianne blurted. 'About your uncle.'

'Oh, don't be. As I said, we weren't close.'

There was a pause. He had lifted the heads of the roses higher so they were angling towards his chin.

'Anyway, please tell Marie – I hope she's alright,' he said.

Marianne felt her face fall. She couldn't help it.

'But it was nice to see you,' he added quickly.

She watched him leave. The shoulders peaked quickly under the heavy coat and spread it tightly across the hollow of his back. He was probably the sort who wore everything without being conscious of how decent he looked, how his body promised so much.

She regretted him mentioning Marie at the end. Was it malicious of her to wish he hadn't? Perhaps it was. But she was beginning to see the virtue of uncensored feeling.

Marianne went with Marie and their mother to the hospital for Marie's first injection of pentostatin. The nurse was quite large and her face was strangely elastic, morphing from one expression to another so quickly that Marianne wasn't inclined to trust it. Her faith in authority was at an all-time low. Perhaps the real task, and one which all hospital staff implicitly understood, was to manage despair rather than disease, to sanitise the thoughts of those in close proximity to what they'd always feared, at least until they had left the building. Here, there was a carefully monitored level of sympathy, its very exaggeration designed to shut down any nuance of thought or uncertainty. The nurse said, in a delicate tone, that the drug would stop the cancer cells making and repairing the DNA that caused them to multiply. Pentostatin would kill the abnormal white blood cells. Her smile returned and her eyebrows curved upwards in the centre. She turned her face towards Marianne, which made her panic as she had been frowning at the nurse the whole time.

They watched her clean the upper part of Marie's arm, then she mounted the syringe. The fluid inside of it was swirling, but Marie watched the point of the needle intently. Her eyes grew black and the pale irises disappeared. When the needle entered her skin and forced the chemical into her blood, she lowered that riveted expression to the floor. Marianne caught her mother's eye. They had both been about to hold her hand through the injection but had sensed she didn't need to be held. In fact, if either of them had touched her, Marianne had the oddest feeling she might have hated them for it.

Over the next few days, they administered the drug at home themselves. Marianne watched while David chose not to. They did it at the kitchen table once he had gone to work.

'Can I not do it myself?' Marie asked the first time.

Heather wiped the upper part of Marie's arm with some alcohol on a wipe.

'No,' she said.

Marie's arm quivered as she held it up and Heather hesitated.

'Just do it. You won't hurt me,' Marie said.

For a moment, Heather looked at Marianne in panic. Her eyes were very wide and she was waiting for something, perhaps an intervention.

'I can do it,' said Marianne.

She took the syringe, which her mother gave up willingly, and she stared at Marie before poising the needle.

'Ready?'

'I've been ready for the past—'

She was suddenly silent as Marianne plunged it in. Marianne had wanted to catch her off guard, but she didn't know why and it made her uneasy. She pushed the silver line through her sister's blood and watched the liquid disappear. Marie's face was frozen as they stared at one another. She was not grateful for the dose, but she was grateful for the force with which it had been administered. Without hesitation.

'Thank you,' she said.

They were careful to monitor Marie for any side effects. By the third day, she had started vomiting. She also stayed in bed for long hours in the day, but Heather and Marianne had an unspoken agreement to check on her every half hour, taking it in turns to bring her cooked meats and glasses of water – lots of water, for she had been instructed to drink plenty. Marie's appetite had whittled down to encompass only one food group. She ate cold cuts with animated vigour, her fingers trembling and her pupils growing fatter until they were so large that they stole the pallor of her irises. She slept heavily and when she woke up, she saw nothing unless it was inches from her face. She could barely get out of bed and stared around the room as though Heather or Marianne were not sitting on the end of the mattress staring back at her with their small offerings. She seemed to think she was alone.

Within that false solitude, she behaved as darkly as she wished. She scratched the space of her skin where the drug had been injected, her nails ripping into the wound and making it raw. They had to hold her hands away from her countless times until Marianne finally brought the pair of scissors from the bathroom to trim Marie's nails. She did this when Marie was asleep, one half of her face buried in the pillow. There was a pathos in the scene that she thought her mother felt too as she hovered in the doorway and watched them quietly, reluctant to leave, leaning into the moment with her whole body. When Marianne made to leave, Heather could not. She had fixed herself to the frame in momentous silence.

They understood one another in those days, more than they had ever done before, and there had always been an unspoken collusive element to the way they conducted their lives. Now the strand of mutual thought was so finely wrought, so complex and vibrant, that they did not even have to glance at one another to communicate it. They existed in a harmony that didn't wish to declare itself. They sat in silence in the kitchen, fortified by one another's presence, staring at opposite ends of the room like twin totems. There was also something valedictory about their silence. Heather had not spoken to Marianne very much about the fact that she was leaving, and that there was every chance she might not return to live in that house again. This absence lingered at the end of their intimacy. The act of caring for Marie helped to keep a vague panic about the future at bay.

In the few days before Marianne was due to leave for London, she packed very few of her possessions. She didn't want to take too much that reminded her of home. In fact, she spent a feverish couple of hours ridding her bedroom of all sorts of items she had suddenly decided were trivial. She wasn't sure why she had clung to them for so long. She had collected notebooks over the years where she'd written things down – her 'musings' – but now she flicked through the lines she'd written with vague distaste for the person she had always thought she was, or at least the person she'd strived to be. She would be different this time, lighter. She ran a bath and soaked all her notebooks in the hot water so that she knew the words were smudged and entirely illegible before binning the lot.

She also gave all her books, including her Norton anthologies with all her annotations, to Marie, who looked at the shelves with dismay on hearing this.

'Why don't you want them anymore?' she said.

'I don't want to reread any of them. I can't take them with me.'

'But you're coming back soon. It's only for a month – right?'

Marianne frowned and decided not to say anything.

The day before she left, her father gave her an iPod. It was a bright green one, square-shaped, which he'd kept for years.

'Wow, this is old, Dad.'

'Oh, I know, but it still works,' he said with a smile. He looked pleased with himself. 'I've put some stuff on there for the journey. Lots of prog rock. You'll like Soft Machine. I listened to them a great deal when I was younger. Some of their stuff gave me an out-of-body experience – helps if you're stoned, mind you. Only – don't do that.'

Marianne smiled and hugged him. She immediately wished she hadn't when he clutched her back. He held her for a long time, until she grew frightened of having to let go of him.

She grew resentful that day because she did not truly believe they wanted her to succeed. It also occurred to her how her family were expertly versed in the art of forsakenness. When her time for self-renewal was close, they drew upon her store of sympathy. They appealed to that instinct she had to root herself to what she'd always known, until she was sucked dry like a fruit, fit for nothing but the bough it balanced on. It was not just Marie who claimed her, though she had been through the worst ordeal. In fact, Marie began to perk up in those last few days before Marianne left her. Her apathy lifted, and for hours at a time her speech was lucid and she could concentrate on everyone again. It was their mother who declined in those few days. She couldn't look Marianne in the eye and remained in her bedroom for long hours. Her face was greyer than Marianne had ever seen it.

When Marianne walked in on her the afternoon of the day before she was due to leave, she was surprised to find her sleeping. She had almost anticipated something violent or perverse, a state of undress or discomposure. But what Marianne saw was a sinuous shape, stretched impossibly long across the bed, silent and still. Her calm form, and the afternoon sun burning through the window, gave Marianne a terrible shock because she didn't know her mother existed like this. Quietly, without implicating anybody else. Softly, without imbuing the world with her sadness. That she could keep her sadness to herself and bury herself for hours at a time was a difficult thing to witness. *I can't do it*, she thought. It was useless, to leave them. They were fragile people, not quite whole and not quite real. She was, in her mother's bedroom, entirely paralysed by the spectacle – one which she had not meant to see – of broken power and seclusion. She stole her mother's power in watching her like this. She stood, frozen, for a few minutes, while she contemplated what to do about it.

It was her father who said he would take her to the station. Heather had been drinking in the night until the early hours and was clearly too groggy to drive. It was a fact Marianne and her father did not want to dwell upon. Marianne felt a flicker of dull resentment when she hugged her on the landing, and though she had hoped they would part with some great feeling for one another, she found there was very little when the time came. She held her mother with some irritation for what hadn't been offered before her departure – advice, approval, encouragement. The courage to leave wasn't there anymore and she knew she had been biding her time, waiting for validation from someone else. At the last minute, her conviction for another life was not granted. She would simply have to leave without it.

Marie was stiff and silent, watching Marianne zip up her coat downstairs. She had grown stronger now the chemotherapy had come to an end, but she was still slightly bruised on her neck and arms.

'You'll come back after a month? A month at most?' Marie said.

'Yes.'

Marianne didn't have the energy to contradict anyone, certainly not her sister. And Marie was different now. For the last month, she had existed between two states, where her mind was either so scant it barely existed or else her thoughts were all on edge, lethally concentrated. That morning, she seemed to have swung towards the latter state. Marianne was wary of her.

'Please get well,' Marianne told her. She took the fraying sleeve of Marie's jumper and shook the wrist inside of it. 'You have to look after Mum too. She's unhappy.'

'I'm not stupid. I know.'

'And don't snap at Dad.'

'I won't. I'll snap at you if you don't come back though.'

Marianne hugged her. She wasn't sure she'd ever hugged her family so much in quick succession. It was strangely disembodying. She hadn't taken into account how physically different they all were, and how much energy was contained in all of them. There were varying degrees of it and Marie's was less muted, more volatile. She could feel a heat between her shoulder blades.

They heard Heather's feet on the landing upstairs and they both looked up.

'Don't be long,' she said to Marianne.

'I'm going,' Marianne said crossly.

'No, I mean don't be away too long.'

Her face was very slender when viewed from below and Marianne saw how much it cost her to say those words. Her mouth was dark, still stained from the wine.

'Bloody hell,' Marianne said. She wanted to laugh. 'You lot are so miserable! Come *on*. Be happy for me. For god's sake.'

She tilted her head towards their mother, who returned an ironic smile.

'Don't be sad. And keep the house warm,' Marianne said.

'Oh, get out of here,' Heather said. She was clutching the banister with a claw-like grip. 'You're becoming obnoxious.'

Marie laughed and Marianne laughed too. She grabbed her bag and turned quickly so as not to disturb the balance. She knew her courage was fleeting and she had to act before it was lost again. When she closed the front door, she saw Marie's blurry outline through the glass window. It didn't move for a long time until her father pulled out of the drive.

When David hugged her at the station, he allowed himself to hold her for a few seconds then drew quickly back. She thought that something was playing on his mind and suspected it wasn't merely her departure. She had to pull the sleeve of his coat to bring him back to earth.

'Sorry. I'm exhausted,' he said.

A voice on the platform announced the arrival of the train to Preston, where Marianne would change. She caught his hand.

'I know,' she said. 'I'm worried.'

'You're worried?' He looked at her critically.

'I'm worried.' She felt tears burning in the corners of her eyes. 'I don't want to leave you if you're all so unhappy.'

He didn't immediately discount what she said. Instead, he squeezed her hand and stared at the oncoming train as it slowed on the tracks. A crowd formed around the doors before they opened.

Then he hugged her again and he allowed his body to lean on her with all of his sadness, as though to make her aware of it and to promise her it would be his alone, that it wouldn't reach the surface again. He bowed his head over her shoulder and said nothing, but she felt everything he had not been courageous enough to say pulsing between them. She wanted to pull back. She was tired of this emotional surrogacy. She couldn't bear another day of it and knew that she would not come back here if she had the chance to stay away.

The tears were on her face and he flicked them away with his fingers.

'No, don't do that. You have to be a tough girl. You're a Londoner now,' he said.

She left him standing on the platform. He wouldn't walk away until the train pulled out of the station again, so there was an awkward interval in which she was sitting in the window staring at him. He put his hands in his pockets, which he'd never really done in front of her before.

The journey was hard. She hadn't anticipated despair. The euphoria she'd felt was still there, but it was losing its effortless quality. That was when she began to think she had imagined her pleasure. But she willed herself not to lose it. The tighter she gripped it, the faster it erased itself. She was finally alone and it was becoming impossible to breathe. She was eventually shocked to discover a man had sat down next to her. In a way, his presence imposed a welcome distraction from her thoughts. The future became a blank and she allowed it to recede from that starved tunnel of thought. Once she forgot what she was arriving at, she relaxed into a purgative silence.

The key was not to care very much at all so that happiness might be stumbled upon, not seized and, inevitably, lost.

Marianne was relieved that she no longer found Dylan attractive. His face had softened and he'd grown a beard, which she didn't like; it wasn't one colour and his sideburns were wiry. He looked older but he still had the same energy trapped inside him, only now it was more concentrated. As he drove Marianne from Euston, he watched her closely when he should have been watching the road, searching her face for cues.

'Rosalie is really excited to meet you,' he said, his eyes jumping between the road and her face. 'She said she wanted to show you round Oxford Street, take you shopping. Liberty's nice. You'd like Carnaby Street.' He looked frightened for a moment and glanced back at her, his eyes paling. 'I mean, I don't know. Will you? Rosalie does anyway. Not that you're the same! But she knows where all the best shops are.'

He lived on the third floor of a terraced house just beyond a cemetery, which Marianne thought looked quite beautiful. When they drove past it, Dylan told her it was Nunhead Cemetery and one of the best in London.

'Do you visit the cemeteries often?' she asked him, surprised.

His self-consciousness was down for a moment and he smiled to himself.

'Yeah, it's a hobby of mine. Don't ask why – I know it's morbid. I think Rosalie finds it odd, but she comes with me sometimes.'

'I'd like to see the cemeteries,' Marianne said.

He glanced at her with a surprised look on his face.

'I'll take you to Highgate. That's my favourite.'

Rosalie must have seen them pulling up to the house, for she was out on the doorstep almost instantly. Marianne saw a very short girl with dark red hair in a French plait and a pale, round, freckled face. She had small eyes that were a lightning blue, not unlike the colour of Marie's eyes, but her features were blunter, leaving no space for ambiguity. There was something child-like and hopeful in the way that she stood on her tiptoes on the doorstep, without being able to keep still, her mouth creeping into an ecstatic shape that drove her eyes into little holes.

'Hi, Marianne!' she squeaked when they were out of the car.

She ran forwards and hugged her tightly. The top of her head met Marianne's chin.

She leapt back and assessed Marianne with frighteningly speedy conviction. Marianne had no time to say anything before Rosalie rushed in and filled the silence for her.

'Dylan's told me so much about you! Apparently, you once locked him in the garden shed with a spider and he nearly wet himself!' She laughed. 'He says you were always so clever, always reading. What sort of books do you like? There's a stunning little bookshop in Mayfair we should go to called Heywood Hill. You'll love it. Also, Hatchards in Piccadilly. Oh my gosh, yes, we must go there tomorrow!'

Marianne followed the girl into the house with a sense of dread. Dylan waited a few seconds before following them. Marianne looked back, wishing he wouldn't. She was already embarrassed and didn't like being held up to scrutiny like this – it felt like she was being ambushed.

Rosalie trotted up the narrow staircase to their floor, making breezy generalisations, parroting more compliments back to Marianne, none of which Marianne trusted. Her whole body appeared to vibrate with the need to exclaim itself. She flattened her arms against her sides, almost squashing them down, until something made them spring back out again. Her fidgeting was alarming; she seemed to wish to readjust something about herself every five seconds, on nervous impulse.

The living room was annexed to the kitchen, and there was a very small bathroom, dominated by Rosalie's cosmetics and perfumes. That left just one bedroom, which Marianne knew she wouldn't be shown. Rosalie had pulled out the sofa bed in the living room for her. Staring at the small corner of the kitchen, Marianne panicked and knew she would have no privacy unless she was in the bathroom. Dylan had not been strictly honest about the amount of space they could spare.

'Do you want a drink? Something to eat? *Waffles!*' Rosalie cried. She whipped round and looked up at Dylan. 'We have waffles, don't we?'

'Oh no, I'm alright. Honestly,' Marianne said.

Her exhaustion was filling her eyes and she began to see everything as an obstacle to sleep; there was so much to be distracted by. Rosalie was everywhere. There were candles and incense sticks, embroidered cushions with little mirrors on and little maneki-neko figurines waving cheerfully around the room. The only safe space was the bed, and they were all suddenly watching it between one another.

'You want to have a nap?' Dylan said kindly.

'Please,' Marianne said. 'Sorry – would that be okay? I'm so tired.'

It was the first time Rosalie appeared confused. But she wasn't capable of relaying any emotion that might impinge on another's desire.

'No worries! I totally understand,' she said.

It became clear that Marianne had altered the dynamic in the flat once she claimed the living-room space. And yet, over the next few days, she was aware that Dylan and Rosalie tried earnestly not to disturb her, to assure her they would comply with any of her wishes. It was comforting to begin with, but Marianne began to feel that every expression on her face was magnified as they watched her constantly for signs of dismissal. She liked to sleep at around eleven most evenings, but Dylan and Rosalie began to watch her stealthily for clues that she was tired from around nine, as the three of them watched television in the living room. For some reason, they sat like bookends at either side of her on the sofa and proceeded to take it in turns watching her from the corner of their eye. They considered themselves an imposition and Marianne found this ludicrous rather than touching, as it had been on her first day.

She was not used to this level of hospitality and it frightened her, made her pine for seclusion again. She began to admit earlier than she normally would that, yes, she was quite tired. They left a small nightlight on for her so she could find her way round the kitchen if she needed to, and the sight of it made her strangely melancholy, reminding her of an older part of her life. She lay on the sofa bed listening to her hosts on the other side of the wall as they sought relief in returning to themselves, that narrow unit which a third party only serves to strengthen or dissolve. They were very quiet once they had escaped her. It unnerved her as she lay on her back, watching the little golden cats waving on the windowsill above her head, listening out for signs of love. For having been so excitable while she was around Marianne, Rosalie soon became silent when she was alone with Dylan.

Then, about four nights into her stay, Marianne heard it. A prolonged sigh of relief. She had not been sleeping well so she was alert to every sound, and that sigh moved her blood. It was the first sound the girl had made in earshot of Marianne that was removed from self-consciousness, from the frantic persona she inhabited while she strove to please everyone and make sure they were happy and that the day was still bursting with promise. This pleasure was genuine. It was also remarkably sad in a way, Marianne thought. Within that sigh, her orgasm had flooded her brain and taken away all the things she thought must be there to ensure her existence was viable. She was slightly reduced, slightly humbled. It was like listening to someone who was surprised by the resounding simplicity of what life amounted to, not disappointed at all – rather, compelled to subscribe to a new minimalism. She couldn't hear Dylan, but Marianne imagined he was forever sustained by the sound that girl had made in those few seconds. Even if he never made love to her again, that knowledge, that he had the power to release her from that pent-up pressure cabin of thought – the secret panic of her own redundancy – would warm his blood for a very long time.

Marianne decided that she liked Rosalie. This decision was strengthened by her first week at *Empowered*. The office was near Soho Square and the two of them took the tube to Tottenham Court Road, only a few minutes away. The office overlooked a dingy street that was sometimes quite beautiful on a sunny day when fashionable-looking people stalked the pavement and employees from neighbouring offices had a drink at the pub on the corner of the road to celebrate an early end to the working day. Sometimes, a group of Hare Krishnas walked down their street in a leisurely fashion, wearing clothes the colour of the sun, flaunting an intimate knowledge of themselves nobody else knew how to reach. It was peculiar to see this disparity. There were also a lot of people who lay in the streets, discoloured, their bare feet black and their faces ravaged with sores. The homeless people frightened Marianne here because they sometimes saw provocation where there was nothing, just the ordinary lapse of time.

Once, when Rosalie led Marianne down a side alley from the Tesco Metro, a middle-aged woman with a gaunt and bleeding face began to follow them, her arms rising from her sides at odd angles. She opened her mouth and nothing came out.

'Sorry,' Rosalie said needlessly.

Her simple response caused the woman to lapse into a state of nervous grief. She screeched at them, spittle flying from her gums. Marianne looked at Rosalie in panic.

'Oh no,' Rosalie said in her high voice. 'It's really awful.'

It was only when a group of young women strode out of Tesco in their smart trouser suits, laughing with one another without giving the homeless woman a second glance, that Marianne realised this was an ordinary occurrence in Soho. That the woman with trousers falling precariously low on her crotch and a torn-open face, who had the appearance of having died many years previously, shocked nobody. She chattered her teeth and that was when she yanked the waistband of her trousers down so far that a great big mound of pubic hair sprang over the top.

Marianne took Rosalie by the elbow and steered her away. Rosalie said nothing until they reached the office. Then she

visibly shook the experience off, rubbing her arms up and down
and grinning emptily around herself.

It was this emotional fragility that Marianne felt bound to
protect, a thing that was nowhere more apparent than in an
office full of women. And she soon learned that the other
women at *Empowered* did not take kindly to simpering, obse-
quious girls. On her first day, she met the editor-in-chief, Anna
Mason, who was particularly unpleasant towards anybody who
exhibited themselves with a confidence that was clumsily assembled. She preferred the women to be slick and effortless. When
she shook Marianne's hand and Rosalie happened to step out
of view for a moment, Anna actually rolled her eyes. Marianne
was immediately wary of this collusion that privileged her at
the expense of another's status. She would learn that these
privileges fell into different hands frequently, though she
suspected that Rosalie, with her hyperactive energy, would
always be excluded.

'If all goes well, you'll soon be able to write features of your
own,' Anna said to Marianne. She showed her to her desk, which
was behind Rosalie's. 'Our first features meeting is this afternoon, so you can take notes and get an idea of what topics
you'd like to research. Our upcoming issue is on female friendships.'

The work was not difficult but Marianne found the atmosphere a strain. Some people thrived in adversarial environments;
others were gradually defeated over time. Rosalie remained her
cheerful self, taking instruction from her editor always with the
same comment – '*Super!* Thanks.' This steadfast optimism
licensed the rest of the women to exploit her in various ways,
whether asking her for work-related favours or asking her to
run errands that were so protracted and unfair that Marianne

sat there in a daze, watching for the moment when Rosalie would finally revolt. But she never did. She was also subject to sneers about the way she dressed. Her prairie dresses and gingham pinafores might have suited a woman whose elegance was understated or whose androgyny presented a pleasing contrast. But Rosalie was girlish to her bones. Her clothes simply dragged out this impression of an almost tiresome and suffocating innocence from which she'd never escape and from which she never wanted to.

Marianne quickly adopted the voice of the magazine once she learned what it was. She began to compose statements which she herself recoiled from, words which would assure the reader that their sex was the most put-upon, the most devalued, and therefore in constant need of validation. This validation was conferred between members of the same sex – it did not require legitimacy beyond itself. Female comradeship was its own religion, a deceptively self-sufficient one. It was defined by men in simply keeping them locked out. And the female friendship that *Empowered* referred to relied upon a series of cock-ups, women pulling one another up from their respective failures and laughing off mistakes and misapprehensions. These women convinced themselves that they were happy for one another when things were suddenly improving in their lives but in fact they never cherished one another so much as when they were both down on their luck. The deception was immaculately preserved.

Marianne was afraid of the women in the office. Sometimes she believed she adopted the tone of the magazine because she had no energy left for transgression, nothing left for the person she thought she might be. And it was easier to bide her time, this prospective personality lying latent in the darkest quarter of her brain. Snatches of it appeared in the day when she said something that caused someone to stare at her for longer than was necessary. Then she panicked. That personality was perhaps never going to be ready for consumption and so she angrily consumed it herself, vowing to remain anonymous. Nobody was worthy of knowing her.

She missed Marie more in the night. She had called her once that week but Marie was sullen and distracted on the phone. It pained Marianne that nothing of any consequence was said. Then her mother rang her at the weekend.

'She does miss you,' she said. 'She won't tell you that.'

'Why not? What's the point in lying about it? I want her to miss me.'

'Exactly.'

'Oh, for god's sake. So I'm being punished?'

'Probably. *I'm* happy for you though. Are you enjoying the work?'

'It's alright. The women aren't very nice.'

'Don't let them know you think that.'

'Why would I do that?'

'I mean, don't pull that sad, serious face you do. Smile. Look lively.'

Marianne thought of Rosalie and rubbed her eyes. It was seven in the morning on the Saturday and she hadn't heard a sound from the other bedroom. The morning light was creeping through the blinds across her bed and she heard the little ticking noises of the cats swinging their arms tirelessly above her head.

'She slept in your room this week,' Heather said.

'Really?'

'Yes. I think she's staying in there until you come back.'

'And what if I don't?'

Her mother paused. 'I don't know. She'll get over it.'

'When's her next check-up?'

'Next week. She does seem a lot better, physically.'

Something in her voice alerted Marianne. It was the way her sentences were tailing off, almost with a sigh.

'What about her mood?' she asked.

'Her mood is – worse. Since you left. She's just gone flat.'

'Oh.' Marianne sat up. 'Have you thought about—'

'Yes. I'm going to ask the doctor next week. If she's put on a mild dose to start with, it can't do any harm. It's temporary. She's shocked. That's all.'

'Do you think it'll pass? Is it a post-traumatic thing? That passes with therapy, doesn't it? She can see a counsellor.'

'Yes. Of course.'

After that call, Marianne resolved to ring Marie. But when she put her phone on the side, she found the whole thing strangely easy to discard from her mind. The sun was growing through the blinds and she could feel the heat of it on her legs through the blanket. She realised too that she was waiting for company, for Rosalie or Dylan to enter the room – it didn't matter who – so that she would be preoccupied. She didn't want to dwell on something that was so very far away, so entirely removed that she couldn't implicate herself with the same urgency. Being in a house that wasn't her own, hundreds of miles from home, had loosened her nerve, and she was beginning to relax for the first time.

She was distracted by what was unfamiliar and close at hand – the smell of other people, the patterns of the plates in the dish rack, the crack in the corner of the bathroom mirror – and she was beginning to recognise how long it had been since she had been genuinely distracted by something new. Back at home, her days had been so similar that nothing stood out to define them in her memory apart from Marie. Though she often believed she could *think* herself free, the connections she saw between things were ultimately grounded in a paralysing sameness of experience. Her thoughts fell back on the same sustenance. She'd been starved of the right diversion – a place, a process, a person – to which her consciousness could cling like a vine to a trellis and finally lead on to something else.

MARIANNE SLEPT FOR SO LONG that she didn't trust what time it was or even what day of the week when she emerged. Perhaps time moved at a different pace in Nede. The cacti around her bed seemed uglier, their heads wrinkled like the sack of a scrotum. She wondered whether it was against the rules to move them.

Someone had placed her paroxetine on the bedside table and she panicked. She didn't know how many days she had missed taking them. The damage would be short-term but the gap in her consciousness was wide, and she reached for the sheet of pills. She popped one out and swallowed it, building up as much saliva as she could to drag it down her throat. Without water, its passage was rough and scratchy. She sat back in the bed and wondered how long it would take her mental state to repair itself.

The sun was gone today and the sky was opaque through the glass wall. There was a thin mist in the garden and it wove around the hedges so that they appeared never to touch the ground. Marianne noticed a statue of a naked man close to an ash tree. His body was slack and strange, very unlike the robust statues of Greek gods and warriors she was used to seeing. He was also distinctly unromantic, possessing none of the human tenderness of a Rodin sculpture. His arms were too long for his torso and they hung limply, dragging his shoulders down, while his feet were large and graceless. The shame inside his body was so palpable that Marianne was moved by the statue in a way she never could be by grandeur.

She knew the folklore surrounding ash trees. When her father was a tree surgeon, she had taken an interest in Yggdrasil, the World Tree in Viking mythology. She used to have a poster of it in her bedroom, which now lay curled up somewhere in the attic at her parents' house. The branches of the tree grew towards the heavens and its roots reached the underworld, so it was connected with both absolutes beyond death.

The Greek poet Hesiod wrote that the first man of the 'Bronze Age' was born from the ash tree, but his species would eventually return to the underworld. Marianne reconstructed the birth in her mind and lent the tree a woman's body. She imagined the surface rippling to relieve itself of the ache inside. The bark still bore the stretch marks where the man within broke the skin. For days after the birth, he would smell the earthy discharge on his body, his limbs full of splinters. Years later, he would see flashes of his former darkness. The memory brought his thoughts to a standstill, and he would wake in a cold sweat on the eve of battle, his muscles paralysed. He did not like to believe he had been held in that body; he was instinctively afraid of it. For when his weapon was down and his lust at bay, something called him back to that original holding place. He fantasised about crawling back inside of it.

Marianne wondered what it was about being in this place that made her thoughts wander so far from the present tense.

It escaped her because she was failing to believe in it; or rather she was losing interest in immediacy. She had reached some sort of impasse where the future had vaguely deserted her, so she foraged for treasures in her past, a place where she had mattered. Snatches of her life bore their fruit: her eleventh birthday party, which her mother had organised and which nobody had wanted to come to; the moment she hit the ground when a girl dragged her to her knees at primary school; the day she told Marie that she was going to go to heaven when she died. At first she was consoled in remembering her part, in bearing pain with patience or promising things that might have been true. Then her mind took a darker turn. She saw herself with less certainty, convinced she had not really been present for any of these things, although the incidents were sharply ingrained in her mind. She relived them without knowing how she had inhabited them.

Had her life been a deliberate act thus far? Or had she been complacent? The earth turned with the same speed whether or not she moved with it or against it. And yet she knew she had resisted torpor for as long as possible, those times where she wanted to go back to bed and try again the next day, hold off life until she was ready for it. *Time waits for no man.* What a sobering thought. There was, lodged inside of her, an instinctual fear of paralysis, of closing up and failing to take charge, allowing the day to fall to waste. She was moved by those small things that had happened, miraculously, because she'd exercised her will against the alternative, impregnating the second with herself before it was fated to have been blank forever.

The first step was to move. She lifted herself from the bed and glanced at the grey clothes draped over the desk chair.

Someone had been coming in and out of her room while she slept and they had left small clues as to how she was to conduct herself. There was a breakfast menu on the desk and a list of activities she was allowed to do for the day. Meditation, massage, gardening.

In the bathroom, someone had left some special shower gels in a basket. Marianne took a shower and opened one of the sachets. She was surprised to find that, instead of a gel, the packet contained a white powder. On the back, it instructed her to wet it slightly in the palm of her hand and then rub it along her skin, especially her back. She wet her hands first and then poured the powder into them. It smelt so awful she wondered what it consisted of but there were no ingredients listed on the sachet. It was a grey paste when she rubbed it along her back, slightly grainy like an exfoliating cream. When she was drying herself afterwards, she noticed the hairs along her spine were suddenly much thicker, forming a narrow bridge on the bone. She was glad there wasn't a mirror this time. She had an urge to see herself from behind but thought it best she didn't indulge it.

She was light-headed and nauseous on leaving her room, still afraid of how much time had elapsed. Having dressed in the grey T-shirt and trousers, she was feeling slightly exposed, wondering whether she should have worn a cardigan. But when she reached the ground floor, she remembered how warm it was there, and instantly knew it was wise to wear as little as she possibly could without being indecent. She passed through the lounge where they had listened to Doctor Cedon speak yesterday – no, it was not a day ago but several days perhaps – and she was already beginning to sweat in the heat. The sound of the water falling from the statue's arms increased her thirst.

She would have dropped to her knees to drink from the fountain if she hadn't been on view.

In the cafeteria, she instinctively looked around for Eric but couldn't find him. There were more people this time, though they were fairly evenly dispersed around the room and nobody really congregated with anyone else. The mood was subdued, though everyone seemed slightly distracted as opposed to being deep in thought. They ate with mechanical weariness, opening their mouths slowly and barely registering what they'd placed inside. Nobody spoke to each other.

She sat down with her menu and looked at the options: quinoa porridge, chia seed pudding, green pepper tofu scramble, smoked tempeh bacon and avocado toast. She wanted to order everything, not because the meals were inherently appealing but because she had a very sharp pang in her stomach. There were more smoothies and juices on the list but she was beginning to associate colourful antioxidant drinks with the stuff of nightmares. She had felt so feeble and groggy within minutes of drinking one the last time.

She looked up and saw a waitress dressed in white heading to her part of the room.

'What would you like, madam?'

Marianne glanced at the list again.

'Avocado toast, please.'

'And to drink?'

'Coffee, please. Two sugars.'

The woman visibly flinched.

'We do not serve coffee. No caffeinated drinks.'

'Oh. I'll just have water then.'

The waitress pointed at the menu in front of Marianne. 'We have a variety of antioxidant beverages.'

'Water isn't available?'

The waitress frowned at her. Marianne conceded defeat as she was anxious for the pain to disappear.

'Okay. Pomegranate and orange juice.'

Once the waitress had disappeared, Marianne noticed that someone had pulled out a chair opposite. It was the woman who'd sat across from her on the coach, who she'd given her juice to and who'd promptly fallen asleep like the rest of the party that day. The woman smiled at Marianne and slumped theatrically back in her chair.

'God, I am shattered.' She attempted to stifle a yawn, but then surrendered herself to it, her mouth gaping wide so Marianne could see the gleaming molars at the back. 'How are you doing? I'm Sue, by the way.'

'Marianne.'

Sue looked around covertly. 'I fell asleep for such a long time, I might have missed a day. What day *is* it?'

'I have absolutely no idea.'

'You too! It's like the worst hangover of our lives.'

The waitress had returned with Marianne's avocado toast and juice. She placed them in front of her and Marianne didn't wait to start eating. She closed her eyes with the first bite.

'And for you, madam?' The waitress turned to Sue.

Sue glanced at her menu hurriedly.

'No eggs, no sausages, no bacon. My husband would go on a hunger strike.'

'There's tempeh bacon?' Marianne said.

Sue cringed and handed the menu over to the waitress. 'Ugh – worse than nothing. I'll have the same as my friend, please.'

The waitress glowered at them both and walked away towards the double doors.

'Have you noticed that none of the staff have Welsh accents?' Sue whispered conspiratorially. She placed her elbows on the table and lowered her head into the gap between them. 'Not one! *Are we really in Wales?*'

Marianne shrugged, her mouth full of food. She was only half paying attention to what the woman was saying as she was so focused on satisfying her hunger.

'Where are you from?' Sue said.

'London.'

'My daughter lived there for a while. Which part?'

'Dulwich.'

'Lovely place.' Sue's eyes wandered towards the glass wall behind Marianne. 'What are your plans after breakfast? Are you going to any meditation sessions? Have you ever tried it before?'

Marianne could barely contain her impatience, her chance to savour each bite of food interrupted by these demands on her attention. Then she decided she didn't care very much about etiquette in a place that had effectively starved her for days at a time. The answer came out dry and hoarse through a mouthful of bread.

'I'm not sure it's for me. Not tried it before.'

'My daughter used to go to these transcendental meditation classes in Greenwich. Apparently it has all kinds of benefits for things like insomnia, addiction, PTSD, migraines. The list is endless.'

Once the waitress brought Sue's toast and juice out, Sue ate with the same unthinking greed. Marianne finished her breakfast very quickly and ended up watching Sue, in awe of how savage she was, licking the avocado from her trembling fingers and forcing the bread into her mouth without bringing herself to close it for any length of time. Every time she swallowed, she did so with a bereaved expression, slightly abstracted and afraid. She seemed panicked into eating what had been given, as though someone was about to take it away at any moment.

Marianne got up and felt a rush of blood to her head. She rested her hands on the table briefly for balance.

'You're going already?' Sue said.

'Yeah. I want to find someone I think I recognised on our first day.'

'Good luck.'

Sue hunched over her plate as Marianne moved away and continued to shovel toast into her mouth, taking increasingly small bites. She was down to her last piece and the dread of her hunger being finally appeased forced her to modify her efforts. She was ravenous in more ways than one. Her manner in conversation was similarly convulsive, rooting for answers that would satisfy a desire for intimacy, no matter how it was achieved. She did not look at all relaxed in her own company.

Before Marianne left the cafeteria, she approached the waitress who was standing behind the counter at the entrance of the room.

'Do you mind telling me what day it is?' Marianne asked her.

It was only when the waitress glanced at Marianne's T-shirt, at an area beneath the collar, that Marianne looked down and realised her room number was printed in tiny black letters.

'It's your third day here, madam,' the waitress said with a smile.

Marianne spent most of the day in the library. She was feeling drowsy and dejected, again wondering whether there was something bad in the juice she'd ordered. The sickly taste lingered in her mouth. She still hadn't found Eric, so resorted to distracting herself with a book about banyan trees which somebody had left open on a small, circular glass table. She sat in the armchair by this small table for some hours with the book in her lap, a monstera plant casting its broad, bright leaves over her head like a lamp.

The illustration that had drawn her to the book was an Indian cloth-based painting of the tree known as Akshaya Vrata. In Hindu mythology, the banyan tree was worshipped for its connection to divinity and its fruit, which had fed the first men. Aside from its wish-fulfilling power, the tree was also believed to have roots that never truly stopped growing and which symbolised eternal renewal, impossible longevity. Guided by this revelation, parents would bury the placenta of their newborn child in the ground beneath the tree, in the hope that their child would live a full and prosperous life. *If only it was that easy*, Marianne thought.

She recalled Marie's first feeble months of life after she arrived in the world the colour and texture of a bruise. How their mother had gradually withdrawn into herself, resisting the hold of this new life and its extraordinary demands on her. It was only when Marie was gone that Heather began to look young again, almost childish; but it was a fragile, feeble disposition, not a second coming or sudden spate of renewed interest in herself. She had taken to hanging off David's arm in public and following him around the house. If she was alone, she was culpable of some nameless evil that had driven her from her child and which she couldn't indulge again. 'I kept away from her,' she had said to Marianne. 'But *she* was all alone. All this time. Why didn't I realise that?'

Move, keep moving, Marianne thought. If she remained still, these thoughts would ruin her.

She put the book back on the circular table and wandered through the aisles. She noticed inscriptions on every bookshelf in tiny gold letters. She read each statement silently, whispering the words to herself. They were all from Carl Jung:

The first half of life is devoted to forming a healthy ego, the second half is going inward and letting go of it.

An inflated consciousness is always egocentric and conscious of nothing but its own existence.

No tree, it is said, can grow to heaven unless its roots reach down to hell.

There was an enormous section of the library devoted to Jung himself. There was also a large section reserved for Jacques Lacan. Aside from psychoanalysis, the library had sections on botany, medicine, human biology, neuroscience, world religions, mythology, ancient world literature and philosophy. Marianne looked around at one point to see if there was a clock in the room but there was none. She wondered whether this was to teach the guests about the practice of mindfulness, grasping which part of the day it was by some untutored, primeval instinct of the body. Her concentration was low and her stomach was aching again. Her weariness had an agitated quality, a belligerent note.

She left the library and made her way to the swimming pool. There were no changing rooms, and when she entered she realised that she would certainly have to lose any inhibitions she had about her body. Guests seemingly had to strip off there and then by the side of the pool where there was a series of wooden shelves for their clothes and another for towels. There were only six people in the room, including her; one was a member of staff, a woman wearing a white T-shirt and canvas shorts who sat in an umpire chair at the only end of the room where guests could enter. She had a silver whistle around her neck. She watched everyone with an impassive expression, glancing around every ten seconds before returning to a small paperback book she had in her lap.

When Marianne entered, she pointed to a sign by the door.

'Please familiarise yourself with the rules,' she said. She looked at the number on Marianne's T-shirt and made a note on a separate sheet of paper fastened to a clipboard that she rested her book against. 'Enjoy your swim.'

There were five rules.

- *No costumes in the pool.*
- *Long hair must be tied up.*
- *No more than ten guests in the pool at one time.*
- *No loud noises.*
- *Guests must not touch one another in the pool.*

This last rule didn't sit well with Marianne. Why would anybody be touching one another anyway? It seemed like an unwarranted addition to the list.

There were three men and one other woman in and around the pool. They smiled at Marianne shyly when she caught their eye. The woman was perhaps in her forties, with long soft hair of a pearly grey colour. It was white around her temples and slightly wavy when it settled around her cheekbones. She moved alongside a rock bed full of purple-headed cacti towards the end of the pool, taking muted steps so as not to slip. Her skin was so white it was iridescent, and the shadows of her back looked like they had formed on the underside. Along her spine were the same black bolt-like hairs that ran down Marianne's. They were not as long but there were hundreds of them and they moved slightly as she walked, shifting themselves independently of her spine. Marianne was stunned to see them. It was strange how indecent she felt in witnessing these same hairs on someone else's body. The sight itself was not unpleasant so much as the freedom with which she looked. She felt an automatic disgust towards herself for some act of violation she knew, rationally, she hadn't committed. Every time her eyes were drawn back to the woman's spine, she felt this same bind, the desire to look and the horror of being able to.

She took her clothes off with shaking hands. She wished she had trimmed her pubic hair and wondered vaguely when she had last bothered to do it. The hairs on her legs were also long enough to ruffle in opposing directions, like an untamed eyebrow. She attempted to cool her armpits with the backs of her hands and tied her hair quickly with an elastic band which was supplied in a small wicker basket on the bench. Then she massaged the small of her back. She was running out of ways to procrastinate.

After a glance from the lifeguard, Marianne made a move towards the pool. She saw momentary flashes of skin, bodies expanding in the water without breaking free of it. The surface of the pool wasn't broken so much as stretched. Cold blue limbs pulsed like nerves inside of an eye, guarded by a taut membrane. There was a rhythmic plunging of heads, a downward glugging motion. Every time someone gasped for air, it seemed shallower than the last time, as though they were forced to expel more than what was there. One woman seemed to forget to lift her head high enough and swallowed the water instead; she pinched her nose to still the pain.

The cacti along the pool were made up of fat globular heads that climbed one another like cells mating for movement. The areoles were small enough that they wouldn't harm her if she brushed against them; the spines lay flat on the surface instead of darting outwards. They also had a dull blue-grey skin, like the hide of something dormant, barely breathing.

She sat at the side of the pool and let her legs hang in the water. It was so cold that she was suddenly excited to immerse herself. It had been so long since she had been swimming, having never found anywhere convenient to do it in London. The last time was when she had accompanied Marie on one of her weekly sessions. Marie favoured the butterfly stroke, where she could smash her self into the surface repeatedly, frightening the children who were being taught in the next lane. When Marie burrowed through the water, she seemed to emerge from her body and, at the same time, withdraw inside of it. She made keen slices of herself until her eyes were empty and bloodshot. Swimming was a kind of amnesiac, a means of perfect distillation, where the muscles bully the mind to submit, forcing it into a temporary extinction.

Marianne dropped. The water shot up to her shoulders instantly and her muscles tightened with the sting. It was deliciously cold without a costume. She opened up her thighs and a series of tiny bubbles emerged from her. She dipped her neck carefully so that the water clamped to the back of her skull. It touched her earlobes and she breathed out slowly.

She lifted her head back up and pushed herself off the side. She chose a breaststroke, slow and steady, her chin dipping through the surface. She saw the other heads bobbing around her, eyes fixed firmly into space. Their bodies flashed beneath the water, but she saw ridges of hairs breaking the surface, all of them cursed with the same dark lining on their backs. She could also smell something that she didn't recognise and which was a quality of the water itself, a powerful chemical. It wasn't chlorine. It made her back sting slightly and she slowed down to scratch it.

She noticed, when she dipped her head underwater, that there was a large, shimmering blue image on the tiles at the bottom of the pool. It was a mosaic of a tree and the roots were gold, glittering between the cracks. Though her eyes were growing bloodshot in the water, she saw the tree clearly through the sting. It was then sharply ingrained on her retina, an echo of itself stored in her vision even when she came back to the surface. Like when one is disorientated and little black spots appear in the corners of the world. The void leaks out beneath the eyelids.

Marianne held the bar at the side of the pool and allowed herself a moment to recover. There was something about the water that made her pores stretch out. And she was troubled by the others, the way they drifted with the same empty languor, sometimes startled back into consciousness like herself. There was the occasional frantic splashing, and Marianne noticed swimmers scrabbling for the side of the pool, as though suddenly convinced they couldn't actually swim. But they had made it to the centre at least. It seemed to roll into their heads halfway across, at the furthest point from the sides.

A dark-skinned man on her left caught the bar and gasped slightly. His hairs rippled away from him, inky black. She saw how they had become one matted shape, a single black wave. Now she was appalled and mesmerised, again, with that same indecent curiosity. The man seemed aware of her, but he wanted to pretend she wasn't there. He tipped his head back and a strained expression entered his face.

Marianne hooked her feet into the silver bar and sprung herself out across the water on her back. The surface caressed her face, closing in on her features when she placed her heels above the silver bar and allowed her head to sink. She sensed a shadow growing beside her and turned to see bubbles forming around the long hairs of the body on her right. She hooked her feet inside the bar again and used the strength in them to lever her upper body back to the surface.

The man beside her had also slid his feet under the bar and stretched himself out. She was close enough that she could sense him shaking inside himself, in a dense space far beneath the skin, but one that still made ripples through the water. He was staring at the ceiling while the hairs along his back wafted sinuously towards Marianne, as though they were sending her a signal. They drifted like weeds on the bed of the sea, extending themselves slowly to a space beneath her. She stared at the ceiling too. A canopy of leaves filled her eyes and there were bright white flower heads hanging free like stars. She watched it for as long as her concentration held out. The hairs on her back were pooling themselves towards the space on her right where the dark man hovered. And they were seconds from touching.

In that small gap between the ends of one another, Marianne sensed the shadow of another life, the very margins of an existence that now lay suspended. His memories were twitching to relive themselves, one greater than the rest. Its echo travelled through the water, a torrent of violence making its way towards Marianne like the roar of an oncoming train.

A latent brutality was nestled in his back. It hadn't emerged from his body; rather it had been inflicted from without and forced to enter it years ago. Marianne could see a pair of hands gripping his head and holding it down. Someone had once pushed his head inside something Marianne couldn't yet see, but would if she waited for their outlines to merge. A tiny phallic symbol on a grubby wall. An image of a dark bathroom stall, the smell of urine.

And she was bound to give up something of her own life in exchange. A moment that she wanted to bury, yet at the same time longed to excavate. A memory of malice. The heat of Richard's bed while her sister lay next door. She leaned back, tired of retention and frantic to release herself. The man shifted his body towards her.

A shrill sound brought her back into her body. The lifeguard was blowing the whistle and it echoed through the room.

'Move apart, please!'

The man beside Marianne blinked, a tear hanging from the corner of his eye. He pushed the heels of his hands angrily into his eyes.

'Ah, shit,' he said.

'What just happened?' Marianne said. She was breathless.

The lifeguard blew the whistle again and Marianne saw her stepping down from her chair. She had an angry compulsion to push it over.

'Move apart! You can't swim close together,' the woman repeated. She gestured with her book and then it fell into the water. 'Ah, bollocks.'

Marianne swam over. The book had already disintegrated but she scooped it up and held it out to the woman. The pages had curled and there was a powdery blue texture along the edges, which caused Marianne to gasp.

The woman snatched it back.

'You have to leave enough space for everyone to swim,' she snapped.

'We weren't actually touching.'

They stared at one another for a few seconds.

'You were very close,' the woman said. There was a faint note of hostility in her voice, something Marianne felt was aimed exclusively at her.

'Why is it even a rule?' Marianne asked.

The woman smiled coldly. It took her a few seconds to contemplate a response.

'Because guests need enough space to swim.'

'There is more than enough space.'

It was with a great effort that Marianne resisted sliding back into bellicosity. She hadn't come here to wage war. She'd come to this place to avoid any strenuous thought, all former grievances against the world. What did it matter that some of the staff were jobsworths?

'You know what, I don't feel like swimming anymore,' she muttered.

'Fine.'

Marianne hauled herself out of the pool, suddenly furious that she was naked and the lifeguard was fully clothed. She turned away and shielded her breasts from her. Everybody in the pool was watching her, clinging to the bars at the side or treading water at the deep end. The room was silent save for the slow passage of water circulating the pool, the hollow echo of the drains. Marianne clutched a bunch of the hairs on her back and felt a wince inside her head, like her brain was clenching itself.

DYLAN TOOK MARIANNE TO SEE the cemeteries in London, as he promised he would. They got the train to Highgate Cemetery and wandered around the grounds in silence, neither of them feeling any desire to speak. They walked around the Circle of Lebanon Vaults on the west side. The tombs surrounded a large cedar tree and imitated Egyptian catacombs, though the place bore traces of the Victorian period when it was first opened to the public. Each dark entrance was the same; it led to nothing. There was a dingy quality about each square portion of nothingness, a denseness that made Marianne feel quite unsafe.

There was something superstitious about the efforts taken to restrain the dead – perhaps the surviving belief that the bodies had never quite passed over, that the life wasn't fully aborted. The high walls of the tombs blocked the trees so that Marianne felt she would never emerge, each vault door insinuating a heavy load inside. She had always found something repellent in Victorian Gothic architecture, about the whole period itself. Its preoccupation with death and the divine was too laboured, too gaudy. The body became a trinket, another keepsake. The mourners staked their claim on the dead more eagerly than they did the living.

Dylan showed her a tree, the roots of which collided with dozens of gravestones, flattened together like bookends without the books, one after another climbing towards the base of the tree. It horrified her but she laughed. It looked as though the dead still fought for space even when it was of no earthly use to them. They converged towards the tree as though to return to the centre of something again and continue an organic relationship with the world. They seemed to rotate around the trunk, to climb, to knock against one another. But the stones had been planted there by living hands and the earth had slowly moved them without anyone's consent.

Marianne spent some time by herself in Nunhead cemetery, which was located just across from Dylan and Rosalie's flat. The Anglican chapel was its dominating feature, a single empty path leading towards it through the trees, but Marianne was more interested in the angels who guarded the tombs. One of them knelt to inspect a grave, the robes of her gown rippling at the sleeves while she clutched her hands, her eyes drawn to the ground out of genuine curiosity, it seemed, rather than spiritual condescension.

One angel was leaning back slightly in the shadow of a linden tree. Her eyes were downcast, giving an impression of despondency, but the way her head tilted towards the light through the leaves suggested she was seconds away from looking up.

Marianne spent a long time trying to decipher that pose. Finally, one Sunday afternoon, when the light was burning the edges of the trees, it struck her that the angel was forsaken. *Yes, that's it*, she thought. She was a postlapsarian figure, hoping to be saved and refusing to believe she was lost. Her slight air of anticipation, her chin cocked upwards even while her eyes were on a downward slant, was like that of a child who had been told they were excluded from a game – a game that seemed to last forever at the bottom of the garden – but who was still convinced, with unfailing self-belief, that they would be absolved.

Some evenings, Marianne closed her eyes in that place and she saw something red beneath her eyelids. The light seemed to part her eyes from their lids, and she was sure she saw her veins moving across them. It was not really a light; it was more of a darkness, but one which was visible, a sluggish red shadow sitting between herself and the world.

She became frightened and convinced herself she would never open her eyes again. Her lids seemed to pulse as she tried to open them. She became dizzy, nauseous. A strange humming in her ears prevented her from shouting out, for she feared she'd never transcend it. The red darkness had a fluid, propulsive quality and swam across her eyes, like a wave breaking over a shallow pool. The sound in her ears was vast and lonely, one note.

When she prised her eyelids back, she was standing beneath the linden tree.

Marianne was offered a full-time position as a features writer at *Empowered*. Anna called her into her office one afternoon on a Friday and she sat on top of her desk, her thighs bulging through her trouser suit, while Marianne sat in the chair opposite, staring up at her. Anna told her, curtly, that she had proven herself to be a conscientious worker with a flair for finding an original take on things. 'Your piece on the etiquette of WhatsApp was – very good,' she said, without smiling. Marianne had a strong suspicion Anna did not enjoy giving compliments. She would probably prefer her staff to be starved of adulation so that they might grow ruthless in pursuit of it. Her magazine profited from ruthlessness.

Marianne was appeased but she was also vaguely worried about her present living circumstances. She would now have to look for somewhere else and she had no idea how to search for a place. But her life was taking shape so quickly, as though all the good fortune she had been denied earlier was now revealing itself at once.

Dylan and Rosalie went out to celebrate Marianne's job offer at the Adam and Eve in Soho. Dylan approached a tall man he knew at the bar with dark, wavy hair hanging down his neck. Before he turned, he seemed stiff and retentive, his long back arching away from the crowd. When he turned and saw Dylan, his face was warm and rich, the eyes a very light blue. He had a large mouth, though his lips were thin and drew far back over his teeth, which Marianne liked. He had a lovely, civilised manner but his mouth was slightly vicious, the teeth exposed without the lips. His shoulders were broad, but he was extremely elegant, his torso thinning at the waist like a woman's.

'This is Richard,' Dylan said, turning back to Marianne. Rosalie evidently knew him already and hung back. 'He's my mate from Techolyte. Works in the sales department.'

Richard smiled and bobbed his head.

'Marianne's staying with us at the moment. She's just been offered a job at the magazine Rosalie works for.' Dylan slapped Marianne on the shoulder and left his hand there. 'We've been friends since we were, what – five or something?'

His hand was shaking slightly on her shoulder.

'Congratulations,' Richard said to her. His eyes were so light they made her feel more keenly scrutinised. 'So what do you make of London?'

'It's like living in ten places at once,' Marianne said.

Dylan laughed and finally removed his hand, but he could barely stand still, looking anxiously from Richard to Marianne. He was beginning to resemble the boy he used to be, his face quivering from one expression to another. It struck Marianne that he was quite similar to Rosalie.

They found a booth in the corner of the room. Richard and Marianne faced the other two so that Marianne had prime viewing of their receptiveness to him. Rosalie was attracted to Richard, and she was not good at concealing anything she felt. The best she could do was not to flaunt it like she flaunted every other emotion she was pleased with herself for having. Instead, she watched him avidly, hungrily, quietly. And Dylan watched him with a mixture of admiration and mild dismay. For his friend was magnetic in a way he would never be. Richard had the gift of projecting himself idly, without much effort but with maximum effect. When his face was still and unselfconscious, he was not remarkable. It was when he spoke, laughed, listened, that he unfurled himself cleanly, concisely. He had perfect control over himself and never seemed to say the wrong thing. Dylan, on the other hand, tried very hard to make an impact, leaning forward on his elbow until it slipped from under him and he banged his wrist clumsily on the table. Rosalie placed her hand over it automatically.

'So, you're looking for a place?' Richard asked Marianne, turning to her with his whole body. The other two were dismissed for a period. 'There's a flat I'm interested in renting – it's in

Dulwich. Has two rooms and a separate living room, bathroom. You should take a look.'

She was surprised how little time it took him to propose this: they had just met, after all. In angling himself to talk to her in that booth – his arm stretched across the green cushioned seat until his hand was just above her head, his elbow sharply balanced on the table allowing his other hand to dangle over the edge so that his fingers were softly hanging towards her thigh – he had somehow managed to position himself in such a way as to make her recklessly responsive.

'I'll take a look,' she said.

Marianne waited for Richard to get in touch with her about the flat. Then a week went by and she lost courage in the whole thing, deciding it was too rash and impulsive. She barely knew him and only had Dylan's word for it that he was perfectly normal, without any secret fetishes or dirty habits.

'Wouldn't he want to live with a friend? Someone he actually knows?' she asked Dylan.

'He's in his late twenties. Most of his friends are probably coupled up or starting families.'

One evening, Richard texted Marianne a time to see the flat on a Thursday after work. It was on Crystal Palace Road in East Dulwich. Rosalie informed her that it was a lovely neighbour-hood.

Marianne arranged to meet him outside the flat, where the letting agent would let them in and show them around. She had checked Google Maps before she made her way there and realised that there was a small cafe in Peckham Rye Park, which she would cross from Nunhead. She headed across the green, hoping to buy a coffee and steady her nerves before meeting Richard again.

His face had grown sharper in her mind. Her memory had a knack for retrospectively filtering out the redeeming values of any incident and clinging to those parts that had seemed darkly significant. That he'd looked blank on occasion and there was an edge to his blankness. That he was calm but he sweated and his hair was slightly wet around his temple. That his eyes had a funny habit of changing between one remark and another, the pupils growing second by second until she felt he was seeing her through the prism of something else. Her impression upon him – the idea of herself she'd wanted to display – had contracted and folded under the weight of his consciousness until she wasn't sure what he saw in her. Perhaps she had managed to project a version of herself that would not stand her in good stead. *Stop ruining everything! Nothing is as sinister as you think!* She walked through the park and pushed her shoulders back to relieve the tension mounting in her back.

The park was not in full bloom – it was early March after all – but the trees carried a latent promise of an almost violent fecundity, their empty boughs suspenseful and alert in the cold air. There were so many different types – ash, oak, horse chestnut, crack willow. There was a species that she remembered her father telling her was called Persian ironwood; it flamed blood-orange and yellow. She saw colours beginning to emerge as she made her way to the cafe and found solace in the smallest things. A great black labrador lunged towards her and she heard its breath from deep within its throat, sharp and jagged. A throbbing tongue emerged from the darkness of its mouth.

She had an urge to touch everything she saw. She scratched the peeling bark of an old yew tree with her nail. The trunk was an elongated tendon, always flexed. It did not seem to grow at all and would always seem entirely still – but there was a steady power biding its time inside of it. If time elapsed more quickly and one saw a decade compressed into the space of a minute, the transformation would be startling, almost brutal. God would have to knit several lives together to witness it.

Marianne's father had once taken her to see the Fortingall Yew in Perthshire, the oldest tree in the United Kingdom. Nearly five thousand years old, it had endured long enough to morph into a different sex. It had originally been a male tree until it started sprouting berries, which was something only females did. Its trunk had split in two and her father told her that funeral processions would sometimes pass through the middle of the tree, and that Pontius Pilate was born in its shadow. These myths consoled her and made her feel like the earth had a custodial purpose, that these natural phenomena were not entirely removed from the human race.

She had managed to lose her dread of Richard by the time she met him. When she saw him waiting outside the flat, she considered how different he was from this angle, when he was being watched without his knowledge. He was slightly hunched and his head was down while he looked at his phone, the hair hanging over his ears so that the tips of them poked through it in an elfish way. He must have sensed her walking towards him, because he turned and smiled. She thought he looked tired and his expression, which was friendly enough, was slightly delayed.

'Are you alright?' she asked.

'Yeah, sorry. My mum's in hospital at the moment.' He looked at the screen of his phone again. 'I'm seeing her after this.'

'I'm sorry. Is it...' Marianne hesitated.

'It's serious, yeah. Bowel cancer. Stage three. She was diagnosed in November.'

'I'm really sorry,' she said.

'Thanks.' He genuinely seemed grateful. 'She's not doing well. Her spirits are low.'

Marianne watched him and waited for something to emerge in his face or posture, a collapse of reserve. The muscles in his face seemed to shrug and he smiled with half of his mouth. The right side of his face was a little slow to keep up. It was only in that isolated slackness that she recognised something bordering on grief, but she could have imagined it.

'I'm going to ask the agency to bring the rent down by a couple of hundred,' he said. He looked up towards the bedroom window of the flat. 'See if we can get away with twelve hundred a month without bills. How does that sound?'

'I already know I want to live here,' Marianne blurted.

He looked back at her and smiled, but it was a different smile. 'You do?'

'Yes. I just took a walk through the park. It's beautiful. I want to walk past those trees every day.'

'Me too. It's one of the reasons I wanted to move here. It's out of the chaos a bit.'

The letting agent arrived at this point, a dark-skinned man with eyebrows that met over the bridge of his nose. He was flustered and walked up to the door with a key before turning back to them, as though it had only just occurred to him that they were needed.

'Sorry I'm late,' he announced. 'Step this way.'

The flat was cheerful and had a second-hand vibrancy from the previous tenants, who'd painted the walls downstairs a turquoise blue. 'They were charged for that. It's not allowed,' the agent said. He tripped over a corner of the carpet on his way to the stairs. They followed him carefully as the steps were very narrow. A window on the first landing allowed a shaft of golden light in and Marianne bathed her face in it on her way up. They looked at both bedrooms and a small bathroom, which stood in between the two, next to an airing cupboard. There was a skylight in one of the rooms.

'Which room do you fancy?' Richard asked Marianne.

'Either,' she said.

When it came to discussing the price, Richard's negotiation skills were admirable. His voice was delicate but had an unbreakable quality. He gave the impression you would be securely placed in the world if you were in his favour. Marianne watched the agent battle with the desire to please Richard, to thrive under a different set of conditions, one which contradicted his position. But Richard's attention was a powerful inducement to transformation; it was irresistibly involving. The agent finally relented, his skin fired up and blotchy.

It was settled and Marianne was elated. When they left the flat, which was now theirs, they walked through the park together, and she was drawn to him in a way that made her panic slightly. Drawn by the manner in which he delivered himself to the world at large, fully formed, as though he'd never been a child. His feet turned slightly outwards as he walked and she liked this too. She could have liked anything about him. If he had told her, in that same cold, elegantly vital way, that he was a murderer, she would still have liked him, and her guilt for liking him would only forge a deeper connection. She knew dimly that she was behaving like all the idiot girls she'd ever known through high school, college, university, and it wasn't that she didn't care about it – she would always care enough to hate herself for this – but she wanted to indulge it. She believed in some way that she deserved to be excited and if she required someone else to deliver that feeling, then so be it.

Living with Richard was not really like living with anybody in those first few months. Marianne soon learned that she would hardly see him; he worked long hours and went to the gym after work until he was sure there was no energy left to spare. At the weekend, he saw his mother and spent hours at the hospital. He went shopping for her too. Then he would go running and always come back sweating and shaking, his veins pulsing through his temple.

He treated time like it was his adversary; the seconds swallowed him up if he didn't load himself into them quickly and brutally. It struck her that he probably dreaded stagnation and fought it off with an instinctive violence. If his thoughts slackened, he simply closed them off by heading out for another run or a swim or a cycle, purging his mind of that recurring impulse to wander. He motored through every day as though he was afraid of losing it, of the day outrunning him. His indefatigable life was disturbing to Marianne and she was beginning to tire of being a witness to it. She was also lonely, for she arrived home from work to a flat that was ghostly in its immaculate state. Richard was scrupulously tidy and she was almost afraid to cook anything for fear of leaving behind a trace of herself that she hadn't realised was there.

When she was alone those week nights, Marianne felt a hard lump forming in her throat. She had wished for solitude so many times, even while she lived with Rosalie and Dylan, and now that she had it, she had no use for it. She changed into her pyjamas as soon as she was home and remained in her bedroom, not daring to venture to the kitchen for fear she'd meet Richard if he returned home early. She stared at everything for a long period of time, dreading to lift her eyes away from a single point of reference for she was afraid of slipping through the gap between things. The lump in her throat was heavy. She wasn't weary of anything, quite the opposite. She sat in a state of unbearable tension, waiting for something to happen and willing it to.

It was at some point during this time that she began to feel a dull ache in the wall of her body. The pain travelled down from the top of her spine and she winced when it finally arrived in the small of her back. She took painkillers, but they never seemed to do anything. It was like an electrical current shooting through her blood in a single taut line, causing the hairs on her skin to rise. She would go for a long walk to exercise it off but there was now a stiffness in her body that gripped her and wouldn't relent its hold. The ache was also in her head. At the end of the day, she saw the trembling outlines of objects, as though a dark heat was suffusing everything. She thought of her brain like a large, hot lump of coal, glowing red as it simmered. Sleep, as always, was out of the question – her brain was too hot for it. She wondered whether to see a doctor but was too idle, in some sense too disheartened, to do it.

She spoke to her mother on the phone, who passed it on to her father and finally Marie. They all wanted to know when she would come home to visit. Marie's need of her was urgent and Marianne sensed it in the way she feigned indifference at the beginning of the conversation, then grew hostile when Marianne fielded questions about her return. It wasn't that she didn't miss them. She craved them. And her craving was unhealthy, a return to a former weakness. She wanted to be embraced by all of them, to disappear inside that fatal intimacy until there was nothing left of herself. She worshipped them deeply in the silence of her new home. While she was physically removed, she was divorced from the impulse to cling to them.

Those lonely evenings were purgatory. She had to wait for the tension to subside, and to do this, she had to avoid thinking seriously about anything. She watched action films without emotional content, read *Closer* and *Heat* magazines – much to her shame – to soak up inane gossip about actresses and pop stars. She listened to podcasts about serial killers. She created a Twitter account and deleted it three days later. She developed an almost fascist interest in personal hygiene, shaving every hair on her body apart from the ones on her head until she was agonised that she'd have to wait for a few days to do it again.

She listened to some of the songs her father had loaded on to her iPod, bringing them up on YouTube so the sound filled her bedroom and blotted out the silence. She had fallen in love with a track by Caravan called 'Nine Feet Underground'. It had the quick, breathless energy of jazz and the operatic scope of something classical. The guitar had an echoey quality, like an owl mewing. The sound found its way through her skin and resonated with her darkness until it was gone.

She didn't hear Richard open her bedroom door one night as she sat at her desk. She had just begun to play the track again and was staring out of the window behind her desk at the moon hovering over the lamppost on the other side of the street, creamy and slightly grey. She was used to seeing her reflection from the glare of the screen; the shadowed muscles of her cheeks were barbaric in the light. She was shocked when she saw another shape emerge in the reflection, just to the side of her head. She turned round.

He was different. She couldn't place the change, but she knew one had occurred. He leaned in her doorway, not quite daring to come in.

'That sounds nice,' he said, indicating the sound coming from her laptop.

She said nothing and watched him, wondering what he wanted.

Without saying a word, he wandered towards her window to stand beside her. His movements were more fluid, less punctual. Although there was still a cold, abstracted quality in his face, something she was suddenly tired of seeing. She wished she knew how to make him laugh. The organ tripped into a lovely part of the song, hurtling forward and rising without losing its intricacy. It was sad without being joyless, conveying a melancholy that was relieved by the lightness of its form, its restless, soaring notes. The pitched wail of electric guitar answered the lusty breath of a saxophone. She looked up at Richard. He looked down at her as though she'd demanded, silently, to be seen. He looked quite angry for a moment. Then he leaned over and kissed her, prising her mouth apart.

They both moved quickly, as though they didn't have much time before the impulse was lost. She was afraid of losing her clothes as she hadn't been naked in front of anybody for a long time. She realised, however, that he was fixated on her face. In spite of her nudity, his eyes remained on hers and wouldn't leave them. She was glad of it. And then it frightened her. He willed her into doing things she wouldn't normally do simply by watching her. He watched her into the bed. He watched her spread herself and lift her thighs apart until she felt the air in her crotch. He moved towards her with that same serious expression, his head gliding towards hers as he travelled along her body without touching it.

When he dipped inside her, he did so quickly, without prefacing himself. A single concentrated stab. She had almost forgotten how vulgar the practice was, unbidden and extreme. As he moved back, he breathed out heavily. Then he came slicing in and squeezed his eyes shut. She began to watch him more carefully than he watched her, until he was not seeing her at all; when he opened his eyes again, they were dull and empty. He was watching nothing. He dived into a muscular darkness and chafed himself against her. The bones of her knees hovered in suspense. He whittled himself down to a single slice, moving back and forth like a saw through the branch of a tree.

She had thought he might be a heartless lover, cold and imperious. In fact, he made her feel like the heartless one. And she began to enjoy it, to push her thighs around him so he was compressed, forced to expand inside. He groaned. The mechanical grace of his body and face was gone. He had become raw. The sounds he made behind the wall of his mouth – he could never bring himself to open it – echoed a barely realised despair that crept through his blood and then hers too, so that she was implicated in the swooning, suffering aspect of it all and was held responsible for helping him find the end of it.

Marianne now knew she had the power to bring him to this state. She wondered whether he would hate her for it.

Richard stopped going to the gym after work and brought home bags of food from Waitrose. He cooked for Marianne and was surprisingly inventive in the kitchen, serving dishes she hadn't tried before. He used ingredients she'd only heard of since moving to London, such as kimchi, quinoa and jackfruit. When she admitted she'd never eaten avocado before he was genuinely stumped. He ate it with almost everything.

When she asked him why he never ate much meat, he told her it didn't agree with him. 'For ethical reasons?' she asked. He declined to answer, and she never worked it out. She couldn't help thinking his diet – so rich in superfoods and antioxidants, so low in fat, salt and sugar – was another part of his ongoing campaign to punish himself in some way, to deprive himself of things he believed he was too evolved and cerebral to indulge in. Sometimes she wondered whether he was malnourished. His skin had a faint grey tinge some evenings when he came home from work, and his body was hollow in the middle so that his shoulders looked too far apart. She was relieved he had stopped going to the gym so much.

He was a martyr to something, of that she was sure. There was a black spot in the recess of his mind, something Marianne knew without being told that she was not to inquire about. It seemed to migrate to the forefront of his consciousness sometimes, which was when he grew silent and walled her off. He never spoke about his mother, his childhood or his previous girlfriends. These were topics that were strictly out of bounds. With everything else, he was painstakingly articulate, supplying Marianne with the kind of detail that she would seize upon in the moment and guard with miserly interest for the future.

He talked about his father, who died eight years ago of a heart attack. If a wry little aphorism emerged in conversation,

Marianne soon learned to attribute it to Richard's father rather than him. His father's advice had often been about making irreversible decisions quickly, or severing ties with 'futile friends', people who carried negative energy or were unfortunate in life. The universe was an inhospitable place but one could only take their own measure of pain; one couldn't be held accountable for saving anybody else from theirs. This latter advice ensured Richard would never be held back by somebody else; but it required a ruthless, quick-fire evaluation of another's character. If he came into contact with self-pitying types, he was careful not to affiliate himself with them. It was a trait that Marianne didn't believe was native to his character.

She knew she had made her own ruthless judgements of people, but she had been mistaken about almost all of them in some way or another. Life was too long and too brief to maintain any opinion of anyone in an absolute sense. The seconds erode all thought from the inside until the passion that informed it – that someone is cruel or kind, ridiculous or remarkable – is no longer there. And everyone changed so quickly, Marianne knew, leaving behind their former skins with the seconds that informed the next one. No external judgement or interior development of character was ever perfectly synchronised.

Richard was never the same person from day to day, so Marianne was never quite sure which edition of him would emerge from the shower or step through the door after work. She considered his shower the beginning of his consciousness, the moment it reconfigured itself. They slept in her room now, and when he pulled himself out of their bed, he did so with a terrible sadness. She sensed it in the way he sat on the edge of the mattress briefly and dipped his head towards his chest, his hands clutching each other in the space between his legs. He always sniffed very loudly when he was ready to move, snapping his head back up and slapping his thighs so the skin shook beneath. She once asked him to stay with her another five minutes. He turned back and she saw that same sharp edge to his vacancy, something territorial, as though that silence was his alone. She was not even supposed to acknowledge it. She was certainly not supposed to fill it for him.

Sometimes he came home witty and licentious, banging cupboard doors open and shaking his hips when he cooked or leaned over the kitchen island to read a book. Other days, he came home silent and reproachful, not of her but of some generalised evil. She knew he worked very hard and that he was eager to please without ever seeming so, but some days he was not sufficiently rewarded. And briefly, without ever fully giving into it, he lost his complacency and the secret pains taken to keep it. He gave into simpler desires. He watched *South Park* late at night downstairs, without laughing. He scrolled through Reddit for hours, his sullen features cast into shadow by the glare of the screen. Marianne would try to make conversation with him, and while he was never uncivil, she found his answers desultory, as though he had plucked them at random from his subconscious.

Marianne found herself booking a train home when she felt her loneliness creeping back. She did it in the early hours of the morning while Richard lay sleeping beside her, her laptop balanced on the duvet. She had an urge to leave him for a week, perhaps longer, just to see whether her absence would prompt anything different to emerge in him. She was genuinely curious to see how he would be without her.

She didn't tell her family that she was coming to visit in a fortnight. Something stalled her from doing so. Perhaps it was a desire to see them when they weren't prepared to be seen. She considered the plan vaguely cruel – it was rather like an ambush – but she wanted to see them as authentically as possible, to go back to her home for the first time without feeling in any way bound to it, even to the atmosphere within its walls.

When she told Richard she was visiting her family, he said something that surprised her.

'You've been very secretive about them.'

It hadn't occurred to her that Richard would notice her reticence. She had remained very careful about which details she wanted to impart to him. She hadn't mentioned Marie's illness or her mother's depression. And she never wanted to discuss her father; some prohibitive impulse came out of nowhere and forbade her from giving him away. She guarded him fanatically, frightened of letting him slip into conversation. She didn't know why she did this. She was not ashamed of him. She wondered whether it was because she knew there was something easily broken and quietly borne in her father's nature, something melancholy without the drama of despair, and she wanted to keep his essence safe from scrutiny. She could only conclude that she didn't trust Richard enough to share her father with him.

She took the train to Lancaster on a Monday morning, grabbing a coffee from the cafe at Preston between changes. What she was doing felt traitorous. It had seemed an affectionate thing to do at one point but now she wondered whether they needed to be ready for her, whether she was asking too much of them by forcing herself into their lives again just when they might have begun to accept that she was gone. She burned her mouth on her coffee, searching the departure screen on her platform. When she saw her train was delayed by three minutes, her heart dropped. She was suddenly anxious to be home as soon as possible, and though she'd been away for months, each minute she had to wait now seemed so much harder to bear.

She got the bus from the station, feeling too idle and impatient to walk with her suitcase all the way to Chancellor's Wharf. When she arrived, it was midday, and she wondered who would be home at this time. She rummaged in her bag for her key and, as she walked down the lane, her suitcase bouncing off the uneven path, she realised she didn't have it. Marie was watching her from her own bedroom window when she walked up to the house. Marianne noticed something wasn't right about her straight away, a physical change she wasn't quick enough to identify, for Marie's face wasn't very close to the glass and she moved it back entirely once she caught sight of her. Marianne walked to the door and waited, trusting Marie had gone downstairs to let her in.

When Marie opened the door, Marianne saw the change at once. All her hair was gone.

'Fuck,' Marianne said.

Marie stood frowning at her, her hand still on the handle of the door. Her head was entirely different without the hair. Her scalp was slightly grey where the roots hadn't yet emerged, and her ears were very sharp. Her features were magnified to an alarming degree. She had the look of one whose thoughts raced forward until they were irretrievable.

'Fucking hell,' Marianne said.

'You just going to stand there and swear?' said Marie.

'Is that from the chemo?'

Marie looked murderous.

'No. I did it.'

'Sorry. But – why?'

She shrugged and said nothing.

'Aren't you pleased I'm here?' Marianne said.

'You didn't say you were coming.'

Marianne was suddenly irritated. She couldn't bear to see Marie standing woodenly, barring her way like she didn't belong there. She also couldn't bear it that she could see the bones of Marie's face leering through the skin. For it was not just her skull that was so dramatically exposed; her cheeks and jaw were more pronounced and there was a meagreness of spirit in those hollow spaces. Her eyebrows were heavy and seemed to overtake the rest of her face, the hairs darker than usual.

'You look awful,' Marianne said. She knew she'd regret it, but she was feeling bitter. 'Why haven't you been looking after yourself?'

Marie turned and wandered down the hall towards the kitchen. Marianne followed, shutting the door behind her. She left her suitcase at the foot of the stairs. The house was chilly. She'd forgotten how much colder it was in the north and wished she'd brought warmer clothes.

'Aren't you freezing?' she called. There was no answer.

When she entered the kitchen, Marie was sitting at the table. Every time Marianne saw her head from a different angle, her horror was renewed. There was something quite cruel about it, something vulgar about the closeness of bone to the skin. It was appalling to think how close one's thoughts were to extinction through being literally exposed. The neural tissue was buried only a few centimetres below. Marianne was afraid of baldness because she imagined she was seeing the blue

shadows of thought beneath the skin. Marie no longer resem-
bled the child who lived calmly and leisurely on the inside.
Her newly shaved head forced itself on the eye as rudely as
possible.

'Seriously, why did you do that?' Marianne asked, pulling out
a seat in front of Marie.

'I don't have to wash my hair now.'

'Because it was such an effort?'

'In a way. Also, it's pointless because it doesn't stay washed.
You have to do it all over again the next day.'

Marianne nodded. 'How are you feeling now? Are you still
having blood tests?'

'Yes.'

'And you're all clear for now?'

'Yes.'

'That's great!'

She reached out and took Marie's hand quickly before she
had the chance to take it off the table.

'I'm on anti-depressants,' Marie said. She cupped her hand
softly over Marianne's knuckles.

'I thought you would be. Mum said.'

'I don't feel good.'

'How long have you been taking them?'

'Three weeks.'

'Perhaps it takes a bit longer?'

'I think they're already doing something but it's not good. I
don't feel anything.'

'You will. Just give it time. Are you still off college?'

'I'm off until next term. I start the year again in September.
I missed too many lessons so I've got to do it all again.'

Marianne was afraid that would be the case. She couldn't imagine having so much spare time in which to dwell on herself.

She saw then that Marie wasn't just sick; she was bored. She had become bored of herself without being able to divert her attention away from her own condition. She was still in the house that held traces of her illness, circling the same spots where she'd slipped into a surreal half-consciousness. She had wavered between sleep and that terrible vagueness of thought where nothing materialises.

She told Marianne that it felt as though she were underground and the earth was hot with her thoughts. That they were escaping but not quite leaving her, hovering instead just out of reach. Sometimes she thought she saw the ends of them, like roots dangling in the undergrowth.

She had lost that sluggishness in her face and had become much sharper for it. Her eyes seemed to burn into everything, wherever she looked.

'I don't feel anything, Mari,' she said. 'I don't know what to do about it.'

'What do you mean?'

'I thought you weren't coming home again.'

'I was always going to come home again.'

Marie frowned and said nothing.

They heard the door open then and someone paused in the hallway. Then their mother's voice.

'Mari?'

She must have seen the suitcase. She stormed down the hallway and into view, shaking slightly. As soon as she saw Marianne, she darted for her quickly and gave her a tight hug.

'Are you staying the night?' she asked.

'I took the week off but I don't have to stay that long.'

'You can stay for as long as you want.'

Heather made Marianne a cup of tea and asked her all the questions she had probably wanted to ask on the phone but had felt obliged to let go. She asked her how safe the city was, what the security was like in her flat, whether she was keeping healthy. 'You look like you've lost weight,' she said sternly. Marianne felt a small stab of satisfaction, though she was ashamed of it. She was asked about her job and whether she could afford where she was living, whether the flat was in good condition, whether Richard was pleasant to live with. 'I wish you'd told me more about him before moving in,' Heather said. 'Are you sure he's trustworthy?'

After this interrogation, Marianne said she wanted to go out for a bit and asked Marie to join her. Once they left the house, they turned down the path to the canal and resumed their old walk. It was a cold day but the sky was bright and clear. The willow trees dipped their leaves languidly towards the water, never quite touching the surface. The branches seemed to be lowering themselves in slow motion to the ground, their boughs like bones.

'Mum seems better,' Marianne said.

Marie nodded. She was walking much faster than she used to, so that Marianne found she was making an effort to keep the same pace.

'She's okay,' Marie said. 'But she's so anxious. She finds it difficult to leave me alone for too long. I feel like I'm being stalked in my own home.'

They ducked beneath a low-hanging canopy where the sun was blocked.

'I'm worried about you,' Marianne said. She looked at Marie, but Marie was still looking straight ahead. 'I don't like what you did to your hair.'

'It's just hair!'

'It's not though. Without it, you don't look like you.'

Marie said nothing, but her eyes hardened in the gloom.

'You'll get back to feeling like your old self. Just let it happen,' Marianne said.

'I don't even know what it means any more – to be *myself.*'

'Alright. I mean, you'll feel better.'

'I don't believe it. And I wish Mum didn't put me on those pills. She made the decision without me – she acted like what I wanted didn't matter. But coming off them now is apparently even worse because it will "drive me over the edge". It can't be much worse than this. I wouldn't *mind* feeling on edge. I feel nothing most days. Nothing at all. And I think of things I never thought of before – I don't know why I'm thinking them. They're not my thoughts.'

'Like what?'

She paused.

'I – don't know how to explain. I just… I don't know. I think about the gaps between things. You know? I can't close the gap.'

Marianne could see that Marie was afraid of herself. She had developed a habit of clawing at the skin on her arms when she spoke. But whenever she began to hint at what was happening inside of her, she immediately lost the energy to articulate what it was. The words teetered close to some sort of precipice, which made her draw them back. She stared anxiously up at the leaves above them.

A man was approaching from down the path, and they moved into the shade of the trees while he passed. He eyed Marie with suspicion, her naked head catching his eye. When he was ahead of them, he couldn't help turning back for another damning look.

Marianne took Marie's arm and directed her back the way they came.

'You need a change of scene,' Marianne said. 'Why don't you come and stay with me for a while? You could get the train back with me.'

'Are you sure?' Marie looked at her in awe.

'Yes.'

There was a forlorn expression in her face, but a smile was worming its way along her mouth. She nodded rapidly before responding.

'I'd love to.'

'Then it's settled. You're coming back with me.'

MARIANNE RETURNED TO THE CAFETERIA after her swim.

She ate slowly this time so that she might not miss Eric. She'd ordered a roasted courgette, chickpea and lemon salad but without any juice this time, not wishing to be influenced by its powerful flavour again. Then she ate caramel poached peaches with blueberries. This time, she was vaguely pleased with her choices on the menu and no longer felt that gnawing emptiness in her stomach. But when she finished, she sat back and looked around the room, and that fatal heaviness of spirit came back.

She knew it might take a while for her mind to readjust itself after missing one of her pills, but she was impatient for the numbing sensation to return, the safety of feeling nothing or at least very little. Now she could sense something more dangerous taking hold. Since her swim, she was feeling fragile and couldn't work out why her heart was beating so slowly. *Surely* it couldn't be down to skipping a pill? She had done that before by accident and she had never felt this unsteady afterwards. What informed her mood was not even strictly confined to a series of thoughts. It came from something very much at the bottom of her consciousness, frighteningly remote and resistant to interference.

It was a sense of depletion, draining her of the imperative to continue. It was built on nothing at all but its very power was rooted in the negation of everything. A conviction lurked out of sight – that nothing mattered. Marianne reached out for reasons to resist what she knew was a baseless foundation for despair, but its roots were far-reaching and they continued to spool into darkness. Quite simply, it was a depression so ingrained in her body that she could not think her way out of it.

Keep moving.

She had pins and needles in her arms and legs when she stood up. She decided she would return to her room and sleep off her sadness. There was nothing she wanted to do.

It was then that she saw him.

He'd entered the cafeteria with a sullen face, ignoring the waitress who greeted him and slouching down the aisle to find a seat in the far corner of the room. There was a book tucked under his arm and the waitress immediately spotted this and hurried after him.

'Sir, you can't take reading material from the library.'

'It's a notebook. *My* notebook,' he replied.

She looked at the book. Then she took a mental note of the number on his T-shirt.

'Okay,' she said.

'I'll have the tofu fried rice,' he said coldly. 'And instead of dessert, I'll have another bowl of the tofu fried rice.'

He then planted himself down and shook his head softly. When the waitress left him, he opened his notebook and glanced down at the last page.

'That's a lot of rice,' Marianne said.

She was standing in front of him and he looked up warily. As soon as he recognised her, something terrible happened to his face. His mouth struggled to stay still, trembling open. His eyes were sharp and watery at the same time.

'It's Marianne,' she said lightly.

'I know! I just can't believe it.'

She pulled out a seat in front of him and he sat back as though he was afraid of her. She wanted to take his hand but thought better of it.

'I saw you on my first day. You were right here. I wanted to say something but—'

'No, I get it.'

They stared at one another for an uncomfortable amount of time. Marianne had so much she wanted to say, but the urgency to speak stifled her.

'What are you doing here?' she asked finally.

Eric's eyes widened. 'I should ask you the same thing.'

'Sorry.'

'No. *I* am.' His voice faltered. 'I'm sorry. I heard what happened—'

Marianne froze and the look on her face silenced him.

'How did you know?' she said.

'It was announced at college. There was a memorial service for her once exams were over. I was there.'

Marianne nodded.

'I'm so sorry. I didn't realise she was... I hadn't seen her for a while.' He waited for Marianne to speak but she didn't. 'I should have come to the house but I didn't know what to say.'

'Were you friends with her for long?'

'Not really. I knew her from a few classes but never really got to talk to her until the final year.'

They were both deeply uncomfortable with the line of conversation and Marianne wasn't interested in pursuing it. The
waitress brought Eric's meal out and set it in front of him with
a curt smile.

'To drink, sir?' she asked.

'Nothing, thanks.'

She hovered for a few seconds and Eric looked up at her with
open hostility.

'Thank you,' he repeated loudly.

She drew herself away with some difficulty. They watched
her walk down the room without speaking for a while.

'You're not thirsty?' Marianne asked him.

'Of course I am. They drug the drinks though.'

'I thought that too. Are you sure?'

'It's obvious. Have you looked around?'

Marianne knew exactly what he was alluding to. She had
studied the guests and they all exhibited the same signs of mental
apathy and emotional vacancy. There were varying degrees;
some had progressed more deeply into their seclusion. For that
was what everyone seemed prone to here: a seclusion that
became more concentrated over time. Only Sue, and a few other
members of Marianne's intake, were still resistant to this muted
atmosphere and sought the novel kind of distraction only
strangers can provide. Marianne had watched a young man she
recognised from her coach enter the room that morning and
his face was open and eager, hopeful of engaging someone in
conversation. But after a time, he was disconcerted and appalled
by everybody. He tried to catch eyes with someone, anyone.
He managed to latch on to someone's attention several times,
but they stared back with total incomprehension. The expression
was stunted, barred from revealing anything, not through an

act of deliberate self-effacement but genuine weariness. Nobody gave themselves away because nobody seemed to know how. They had forgotten how to speak to one another.

'How long have you been here?' Marianne asked Eric.

'About three months. I keep forgetting which day I'm on. But that's all part of it, I suppose.'

'Part of what? The healing process?'

'Who knows? I'm not convinced there's any healing going on. The staff are haughty and the atmosphere is just – unnerving. That speech Doctor Cedon gave on arrival – ' He winced.

'I know, it was a bit pretentious.'

'It's all just very *creepy*. I don't like it. And I feel like I'm being sized up constantly.'

'What do you mean?' Marianne asked quickly.

Eric lifted his eyes to the waitress, who was hovering at the side of the room. She was staring straight ahead at the opposite wall but her head was poised in a way that suggested her attention was peripherally drawn to them.

Eric lowered his voice. 'I haven't met a staff member who behaves naturally. They're either really rude and condescending – or they have this shifty, sad look about them. Like they pity you but don't want to be too open about it.'

Marianne noticed his right eyelid was beginning to twitch slightly. She wasn't sure if it was related to stress or just something that had happened randomly, without any subtext. She wished they were alone.

Eric began to eat but he took each mouthful slowly and deliberately.

'So you're not drinking anything?' Marianne asked him again.

'Just water from the tap in my room. Honestly, it helps get rid of the drowsiness.'

Marianne nodded.

'This is awful,' she said quietly.

Eric stared at her silently. She was struck by how much older he looked. She could barely believe he was only nineteen. Yet the features of his face were very fine and, in some ways, effeminate. His eyes, with their grey tints, were alert and sensitive. She was nervous of being scrutinised by them.

'Is there a mirror in your room?' she asked.

'No. I don't think there's a single mirror in the building.'

'It's odd.'

'I think it's probably symbolic. There are so many books on Lacan in that library. It's probably an attempt to reverse "the mirror stage". You know, when the infant recognises himself for the first time.'

'Oh god, that's ridiculous.'

'Lacan is pretty ridiculous.'

'Eric, why are you here?'

Marianne's head was beginning to ache. The pain made her impatient to know more before she was completely overwhelmed by it.

Eric put his knife and fork down. 'I did really badly in my exams. My dad was horrified. He wouldn't speak to me. My mum didn't care because she was still upset from Uncle Ben dying. My best friend was a year above me and he'd gone on to study medicine at Oxford, so I knew he'd have little time to see me. I was in a shitty place – and then I found this weird growth of hairs on my back.' He reached behind him.

'Yes. Me too.'

'My doctor told me I should take time out from education and work on my mental health. He gave me a leaflet for Nede and said I could skip the waiting list.'

Marianne nodded. 'Same story.'

'Yeah, well, I can't wait to get out of here. It's given me some perspective, that's for sure. To get over myself, at least.'

'Surely we can leave if we want? How long have you been here again?'

'Three months.'

Marianne felt a hard knot of pain in her stomach. Eric was staring at her intently.

'Why that long?' she whispered.

'Who knows?'

'But – haven't you spoken to someone?'

'Of course. I just get told that Doctor Roberts hasn't signed off on it or they think I'm too valuable and I've made "too much progress" to quit now. There's even a financial reward if I continue to stay and *progress*. I mean, I could do with the money, but fuck knows what progress they think I've made. I wake up some mornings and it feels like my head has been through a grinder.'

Marianne nodded fiercely. She realised she had been nodding so hard for the last few minutes that she might have seemed agitated. Then she thought, *I am agitated*. She didn't feel the need to hide it from Eric, who was so clearly distraught yet taking care not to advertise it too much. He was transmitting great waves of fear across the table and she was readily absorbing them. It was a relief to speak to someone who felt this same overpowering conviction – that something wasn't right.

'I know what you mean and I've only been here a few days,' she said. 'I don't know why I feel so drained though – I thought it was something in the water, so to speak. But you said you've stopped drinking—'

'Yep, still feel like a wreck! A nervous wreck.'

Eric's voice had grown very loud. They looked around and
realised simultaneously that they were the only guests left in the
cafeteria. Marianne spotted four new members of staff by the
entrance. Along with the waitress, three concierges were staring
directly at them from the other end of the room. One conferred
with the waitress and she murmured something into his ear.

'Jesus Christ. They really want to drum every good feeling
out of you, don't they?' Eric said.

'Are we supposed to leave?'

'I'm eating at my own pace. But I don't think that's the issue.
I reckon they don't want guests being overly chummy with one
another. It ruins the process.'

'But I don't understand. What *is* the process? What harm
does it do to talk to one another?'

'No idea. I just know it's not encouraged. If they spot people
being overly friendly they'll try and split them up. You just
watch. I've seen it before.'

As if on cue, a female concierge walked towards them. Her
pace was measured and her shoes echoed on the floor. Her
hands were clasped firmly behind her back and the smile on
her face was shallow.

'Madam, would you like anything else?' she asked Marianne.

Marianne shook her head.

'Are you perhaps interested in our meditation class that begins
in ten minutes?'

Marianne glanced at Eric and he raised his eyebrows comically.
'Um, okay.'

'Excellent. Step this way and I'll escort you.'

Marianne exchanged a final look with Eric. He shook his head
in disbelief. Then she heard something almost inaudible leave
his mouth.

'You won't like it.'

It might have been intended as a joke, but Marianne detected a very clear warning there. She left with the woman and looked back at him again, but he was making notes in his book.

Marianne was escorted to the oak-panelled room she'd seen on her first day. Doctor Cedon was standing in the doorway, ushering everyone in with a tight smile. She saw Marianne and nodded. Once inside, Marianne was part of a group of ten guests. They all stood cautiously against one wall and had grown silent. The succulents glimmered on the shelves.

Marianne quickly realised what everybody had become so nervous about on entering. Placed at even intervals in rows up and down the length of the room were large, black, rectangular boxes. Each one was about seven feet long.

Cedon stood behind the boxes, across the room from the guests. She raised her arms in welcome.

'For those of you who are new to this practice, let me explain,' she said. 'Firstly, there is no reason to panic. Each of you has a box and each box is filled with earth. The earth is full of nutrients. You are going to lie inside your box in the earth for as long as you feel you can endure. This session is designed to remove you from the world. We want you to lapse into that darkness and live inside of it. You will still have enough space to breathe once the lid is closed. And I must stress to you all –' she paused and lowered her eyes to the box directly aligned with herself '– you will not be held against your will. If you wish to come out of the box, you must knock *once*.'

Cedon stared at everyone with equal weight. When her eyes landed on Marianne, the pupils had almost outgrown the irises. There was an energy there that Marianne did not like. She looked at the door.

'I'm going to ask you all to undress,' Cedon announced.

About half of the room stared at one another in undisguised horror.

'What the *fuck*,' a woman whispered to Marianne on her right.

'This exercise will only work if you give yourself to it, without inhibitions. Please, if you don't feel up to what is a very fulfilling challenge, then by all means leave.'

She said this in a sharper tone and nobody moved. After a few seconds, a woman in her forties stepped forward and began to move quietly towards the door. Marianne wondered whether to leave herself. But her curiosity was a powerful thing and she was beginning to grow excited. Her heart had begun to beat faster than it had for a long time.

Cedon waited for the door to close and turned on everyone.

'Is anyone else too afraid to commit to this?'

Nobody moved or spoke.

'Get undressed.'

Marianne removed her T-shirt with surprising readiness. Because everyone was reluctant to be seen, they avoided staring at one another. By the time all clothes were removed and piled on the floor, the sight of so many naked bodies in varying degrees of age and sexual maturity was novel enough to remove the tension from the situation.

It struck Marianne that once everyone was bare, they appeared to her in fragments. The woman on her left was awarded a permanent place in Marianne's memory by virtue of her freckled breast, the mark lying just outside the nipple. A man further along on Marianne's right had a dark penis, slightly purple, like it hadn't moved for a long time; the veins in the head were full and heavy. She saw too that he had beautiful wrists. There was a contrast between the sharp knuckles of his hands and the flesh of his hips, which she felt was of great importance and which she wanted to remember.

She felt the heat rising inside the room and, along with it, a primal bodily smell. Something that released itself in certain moments. A scent she recalled from her own skin when she fought her way along the underground carriage, her hands falling on to someone's thighs to steady herself. *No, don't go there.*

Cedon instructed everyone to open up their box. It was filled with dark earth that shimmered on the surface. Marianne pressed the bottom of her foot into it lightly and realised it was wet, more like mud, and gave way very easily.

Cedon circled the room.

'Please lie back in the earth and I will come round and close the lid. Again, if you wish to come out – knock *once*.'

The woman on Marianne's right caught her eye. She was about the same age, tall and broad-shouldered. Her pubic hair was shaved off and Marianne couldn't help staring at her exposed vulva. The idea that this part of her would be buried in the earth without any final intervention, no space in between, offered up a strangely carnal dimension. She hesitated from getting in her box.

Cedon approached.

'There is nothing to be afraid of.'

Marianne stepped into the wet earth and it gave way slowly, her feet sinking down to the bottom. The box was deep enough that she would be almost fully submerged in the earth with just enough air to breathe. She lowered her bottom and then proceeded to lie back, dropping her neck slowly. The mud climbed up her face. Her back slid deeper with each passing second.

She continued to fall until she was suddenly convinced there was no real bottom to the box and that she had been tricked into a premature burial. Then she felt the mud settle beneath her. The earth had a way of finding every crevice and filling it like caulk, absorbing her sweat.

When Cedon closed the lid, she did so with a quick snap. Then darkness.

Marianne quickly understood that remaining calm held the walls at bay, while panic drew them in. The space became tighter as the body naturally expanded in protest. She forbade her muscles from twitching. She breathed evenly. The lid of the box was close to her nose and the heat of her breath was terrible. The soil continued to move into the lines of her skin. Her vagina was precariously open to receiving it. She panted when she thought about her confinement. The trick then was to think of nothing at all. She closed her eyes and tried to divorce herself from her body.

It was impossible. Her body was the ultimate boundary between herself and nothing. It was tight and involving, no matter how hard she tried to convince herself of some disembodied truth. She was, however, determined not to fail a task that was effectively designed to defeat her. She was to be mortified. And she would pretend to comply. There were two options – to rail against her confinement or adapt to it by surrendering thought altogether – but she espoused a third. She lay still in the damp earth and kept her breathing steady, thinking of herself. She would harbour all the thought this coffin sought to steal from her.

But time was a heavy thing inside that space. She began to ache and one shift of her right buttock caused a momentary crisis of confidence. The earth slipped deeper into her bottom and caused her a few minutes of grief. Every time she tried to move a little more to reverse what had happened, she made it worse. She was horrified by what she couldn't keep out. Her clitoris was trapped like a pressed flower. It occurred to her that the earth was violating her in slow motion, eroding it without the explicit evil of violence. The tension inside of her paralysis was so great that she believed her muscles were slowly divorcing themselves from her brain and she could no longer accurately foretell what her limbs might do.

Then something occurred in that space between thought and physical life. Perhaps because she had reached some limit of despair, she dulled her efforts to transcend it. She surrendered, for there was no other way. She inhabited her darkness with the emotional vacancy required to fill it. Her blood grew quiet. Her arms and legs were entirely numb. The soil was pregnant with her slumberous form.

Gradually, she felt a sensation in her spine that made her imagine someone was stretching it. Her skin was prickling along her back. It felt as though someone had pinched her skin on the bone and now began to pull it at different points of pressure. At around the same time, she saw that familiar dark red film in her vision. The blood burned beneath her eyelids. She stared into what looked like a dark uterus of blood, an image of where she once existed before she entered her life. Her spine sent a series of sharp vibrations through the soil where her mind began to root itself.

She was falling through herself. Through her past. A reversal of evolution, the ecstasy of rushing back towards the crib. But as she pulsed through these strange dark rings of consciousness – through words and whispers, garden gates, night lights and needles – she saw the outline of someone coming into view, close to the bottom. She felt the dense magnetism of someone who refused to vacate her mind, who continued to cling to the walls of her thoughts and slide across them into the next room, and the next one beyond that, no matter how many doors were slammed against her. Someone that drugs wouldn't dissolve and sleep couldn't sedate. Who trembled in the ends of Marianne's nerves while keeping them taut. The memory of her lay at the bottom of her soul, at the limit of her sanity. Marie was in that coffin with her. If she hadn't been there, the line dividing memory from oblivion would have been crossed. Marianne refused to go further, refused to be lost. She lay at the bottom of her world, horizontal at last, and sobbed beside her sister.

There was a sudden sound beyond Marianne's box. It was a series of sharp knocks against wood, somewhere down the room from where she lay. The knocks were strident and frantic. They came so fast and with such certainty that there could be no doubt that whoever was knocking was in a great deal of distress.

Marianne opened her eyes and the red film parted. When she recognised her predicament, she was shocked. It was like coming back to a part of history so remote from the timeline she had leaned into that it was effectively redundant. She no longer felt trapped by the box and the earth inside of it; she was suffocated by her own skin, by the rush of blood to her back, the memory of herself that came round like an animal from a long hibernation.

A voice came low and distant from somewhere in the room.

'Please, let me out. *Please.*'

Nothing. Then another loud thump against wood.

'Please. Get me out!'

Another three knocks came from somewhere on Marianne's right. She was forced to orientate herself and she was angry about it.

'Open this! Get me out!'

Panic caused anarchy in every box. Now that the guests realised they were not being freed when they so wished, their incarceration was a genuine nightmare. They were each convinced that their private apocalypse was unique. And Marianne slowly came round to this way of thinking. She too knocked on the lid of her box. But she did so once and without really believing it would matter.

In a matter of seconds, the lid was removed and she saw Doctor Cedon hanging over her in the gloom. The rush of air made her gasp. Then she attempted to move her arms. The soil had dried and her body was caked with mud that fell away in dull heavy blocks.

It was strange to sit up and hear those agitated noises coming from inside every box. She stared at Cedon.

'Why don't you help them?'

'You were the only one who obeyed my instruction,' the doctor said calmly.

Marianne understood and hated her. She pulled herself out of the box and shakily stepped on to the floor.

'Just knock *once*,' she called out.

Cedon continued to stare at her and did nothing. The room went silent.

Marianne moved to open the box on her right. There was a gold clasp that she hadn't seen before, which locked it on the outside. Her fingers were trembling. Cedon took her waist from behind and pulled her away from it.

'Get off me!'

'Don't interfere,' Cedon snapped.

Then the knocks came back again, a single echo from each box. It was solemn and plaintive, like a child finally relenting in its campaign for a mother's attention. The silence afterwards was difficult to bear.

Doctor Cedon walked down the hall to the first box at the end of the room, close to the door. When the lid came off, the man inside was sobbing. He rubbed his face when he sat up and he was blinking rapidly. Marianne had never seen anyone so wholly impotent.

She did not want to see anyone else emerge. She brushed herself down, picked up her clothes and dressed quickly, her arms and legs still shaking. The earth was brittle in her knickers. Then she marched down the room and out of the door. She ran down the corridor to the lift and, once inside, jammed her finger on the button to the second floor. She also pressed the button for the basement floor, angry that it was denied her and savagely suspicious of it.

When the door opened, she froze, confused again. Slipping along the corridor was like sliding into the world newly born. There were seconds in which she recoiled from her body; her consciousness lapsed back out of it again as though it was no longer viable. She managed to locate her room after remembering the number on her shirt, which cost her a great effort. When she looked at her door, her disorientation was so extreme that she forgot where she was in her life. She was convinced she was home, at her parents' house. Marie was along the hall. She didn't have the key for her room because she believed there was no key. So she continued to try to open her door, pushing the handle up and down with increasing violence.

She saw a female figure approaching out of the corner of her eye. Long blonde hair sitting on her shoulders. Marianne didn't look directly at her as her vision was disappearing and she thought she might be sick if she tried to force herself to see.

'Marie,' she said, 'I can't get in my room.'

The girl came closer and placed her hand on Marianne's back. It was a mistake.

'Marie, don't,' Marianne cried. 'It hurts.'

Then she fell sideways into her darkness, unconscious before she hit the floor.

MARIANNE LED MARIE TO THE Underground at Euston station. Marie looked down the tunnel as she heard the echo of the oncoming train, her naked head hovering in the darkness. And then she stepped over the line.

'It's there for a reason!' Marianne said, pulling her by the elbow.

People were beginning to stare at her, at her strange baldness. She didn't pull back until the carriage emerged from the dark with its violent red face. Then she leaned backwards into Marianne. They'd both marvelled at the tiny mice scurrying along the tracks minutes earlier and wondered what kind of refuge they found beneath the body of the train.

There was a grubby, dingy quality to the air and it pressed against everyone. It made people guard their personal space with peculiar avarice, watchful of stray bag handles and elbows. Someone was always on the edge of hysteria. Marianne detected an undercurrent of suspicion and hostility. It was depressing how this forced proximity to strangers was enough to incite a basic primal response that should have been tamed a long time ago, an instinct to rage when one's space was stolen. Nobody knew one other and would continue not to know one another once the journey was over, which made it so much easier to erupt there and then without ever having to apologise for it.

Marianne found that she wanted Marie to be darkly impressed by everything. She was glad when horrible things occurred in front of them – a drunk savagely calling down the carriage to someone who wasn't there; an old woman mouthing at her own reflection in the window opposite; a homeless man smelling of dried piss hauling himself between rows of people to ask for change – because all of this only served to demonstrate how dauntless one must be to survive in London. Marie would come to realise the extent of Marianne's courage, her instinct for survival. For Marianne was ultimately proud of herself for staying away from home.

When they got the overground train to Nunhead, Marianne asked whether Marie wanted to see the cemetery now or later, as they were still carrying their bags. Marie was looking drawn. She'd gone silent.

'I'm a bit tired,' she admitted.

'We'll head to the flat.'

It was twenty past three on a Friday and Richard wouldn't be there for at least three hours. They had plenty of time for privacy. Marianne hadn't told him that she was bringing her sister back and she was slightly nervous. She wished that Marie still had her hair.

Marie's first impression of Dulwich was favourable. The sun was shining with more warmth than usual, and she took off her denim jacket and tied it round her waist as they walked down the street. She attracted a few more stares, but perhaps people thought she had a grungy, punkish energy; her outfit suited her baldness – a black T-shirt with navy dungarees and post-box red Doc Martens. She never wore any make-up now. Perhaps it was the effect of the sunshine, but Marianne was beginning to believe in Marie's beauty again; her skin was very pale but it gleamed with a rare translucency. Her eyelashes were still light and strong. Her face had not lost its fine-boned delicacy; in fact, the lack of hair magnified the exquisite shape of her head. She was thin and still had that undernourished look, but the day was bright and lent her illness a kinder aesthetic.

She loved the blue wall downstairs in the flat.

'Did you do that yourself?' she said.

'No. The people who lived here before us did it.'

When Marianne said 'us', some of that earlier seriousness returned to Marie's face. She brushed it off quickly and climbed the stairs, ahead of Marianne. She looked in on the bathroom and then wandered without prompting into Marianne's bedroom, which was now shared by Richard.

Marianne panicked when she saw Richard's Bose headphones on the bedside cabinet. She hadn't originally planned on bringing Marie back, and she hadn't told her that she slept in the same bed as him, so there had been no opportunity to hide things. She was suddenly grateful that he was the kind of person who rarely left traces of himself, always disposed to pack his life away when he was gone. But Marie's instinct was sharp and she noticed the headphones. Her eyes also lingered on a pair of silver cufflinks. She said nothing.

'What do you want to do?' Marianne asked her. 'Take a nap?'

Marie smiled and nodded.

'I feel like taking a nap too,' Marianne said.

'Let's do it!'

Marie unclipped her dungarees and flung them into the corner of the room. Marianne discarded her jeans with the same childish glee. Then they flopped into her bed and instinctively drew close to the centre, facing one another. They smiled without saying anything for a while.

Marianne fell quickly asleep. The revelation that she was tired occurred a few seconds before giving into it with the kind of yielding, yolky warmth one has when sleep is the single most desirable thing imaginable, the only thing imaginable. It only occurred to her later that Marie might not have slept at all that afternoon. She had opened her eyes through her dream at one point, and in that second of alertness she remembered that she had locked eyes on Marie and that Marie was sharply awake. They had looked at one another through the void. Marianne was closer to it, sinking gently out of consciousness again as her dream resumed itself. Perhaps Marie was beginning to smell something she didn't recognise in the sheets. It must have haunted her when she realised she was sharing the same space as one who'd known her sister more intimately than she, who'd left a carnal imprint of himself that now curled suggestively around her shoulders with the weight of many hours. When Marianne finally awoke to the sound of the front door closing, she saw that Marie had shrugged the duvet away and was lying flat on her back, staring emptily at the ceiling.

'Richard's back,' Marianne said. She looked at her watch. It was half past seven. 'Shit, we must have slept ages!'

'I didn't,' Marie said coldly.

Marianne sat up and rubbed her face, then stared at Marie.

'Why didn't you tell me about him,' Marie said without looking at her.

'I was going to. I don't know.'

It was true. It was suddenly absurd that she hadn't told Marie. She didn't know why she'd kept the relationship a secret. She leapt out of the bed and forced her legs into her jeans, then hurried downstairs before saying anything else to her.

Richard was hanging his coat on the hook by the door when he heard her approach. He turned and she was honoured by how pleased he seemed to see her again. His face assumed a bright expression, his mouth curling upwards without being able to contain itself.

'You never said you were coming back early!'

'I know. Look—'

He marched towards her and took her in his arms gratefully. For a terrible moment, she wished she hadn't brought Marie back.

'Listen. I hope you don't mind but I brought my sister back with me,' she said over his shoulder. 'Just for a few days or so.'

He pulled back and touched her face. 'That's okay. I'm glad to see you again.'

She beamed. 'So you missed me then?'

His pupils flared for a second but he nodded.

They heard Marie padding slowly down the stairs. Marianne's heart stopped and she turned to see her slouching forward, one of her dungaree straps hanging from her chest.

'Marie, this is Richard. Richard – Marie, my sister.'

He still held Marianne while he smiled at Marie. Marianne sensed him tightening his grip on her arms and she felt a tingling sensation in her armpits, the kind of itchy, nervous feeling before one begins to sweat.

Marie looked at him without smiling.

'Hi,' he said. He stared at the top of her head and they both saw it – a tiny bemused frown on his face.

Marianne extracted herself as softly as she could and moved into the space between them, looking earnestly at Marie. Marie was not going to make this easy.

'Cup of tea?' she said.

As she made a show of dragging cups out of the cupboard and clanging the teaspoon inside each one, she sensed a rigid silence behind her back. Richard leaned across the island in the kitchen and watched her filling the kettle. Was he sulking? She didn't recognise this pattern of behaviour, having assumed he was too sophisticated for infantile demonstrations. Perhaps he didn't like Marie. Or he found her strange. Marianne inwardly cursed herself for failing to instruct him in advance, for never giving so much as a hint as to how ill her sister had been. Perhaps it was because she had believed her relationship with Richard would not last anyway. But this was simply not true. There was a permanence about them that had developed quickly. Richard eyed her hungrily and she knew she was not going to be able to shrug him off, even for Marie's sake.

Marie sat in the single armchair with her tea and watched Marianne curl her legs into Richard's thigh on the sofa. She said very little and darted her eyes to Richard's face every now and again to steal a glance at him when she thought he wouldn't notice. The problem was that he was always aware. And he became loquacious, his old humour and easy social grace returning after that temporary loss of dignity and confusion. Marianne couldn't help but glow with pride for who she'd found and she knew she was willing Marie to be impressed by him, just as she had wanted her to be disturbed on the Tube. She leaned into Richard, demonstrating how easily she slotted there and how readily he allowed it. A dizzy pleasure crept into her blood and she was profoundly receptive to everything.

Richard talked about Dylan, and Marie must have felt another pang of remorse, for Dylan had also come between her and her sister, having intervened in the not-too-distant past to deliver Marianne from obscurity. Marie was part of that obscurity, that redundant stage of adolescence and early adulthood that Marianne had nothing to do with anymore. Marianne knew Marie better than anybody else so this sense of exclusion, of expulsion almost, was not difficult to read on her face. Even her ears looked sad against that shadowy blue head. The problem was that Marianne could not resist giving in to a predominant urge to punish Marie in some way. To taunt her with her new self, her new life. She was growing addicted to this new sensation, of being wanted by more than one person, of being sourced and singled out. She watched Marie's body shrink back in the chair, her toes curling and overlapping one another in her purple socks.

Richard cooked them a stir fry, which Marie ate very little of, and they sat in silence around the table that overlapped the kitchen and the living room. Richard attempted to ask Marie questions, feeling generous after having secured Marianne's affection, but she refused to expand on anything. He asked her things that intimated his lack of knowledge about her, about her illness. When he asked her when her exams were, she looked at Marianne with a dark, accusatory expression. Then she said she wanted to go to bed.

Marianne went upstairs after her and stopped her on the landing.

'Hey, are you alright?'

She shrugged.

'Why wouldn't I be? He knows nothing about me so I've nothing to be concerned about.'

'Look, I didn't tell him because we still don't know one another that well.'

'Doesn't seem that way.'

'I'm sorry. It's a strange subject.'

Marie stared at her neutrally.

'I guess it is,' she said.

Marie knew not to return to the same bedroom then, sensing that nobody slept in the vacant room across the landing. Marianne returned downstairs with a ruthless edge to her thoughts. She was dealing with a sulky teenager. It was perhaps the first time she openly thought of Marie as being one, as she had always been something quite different growing up. Now Marianne was inclined to think her cancer had been a catalyst of some kind that had prompted a late puberty. She sank into Richard's arms in the safety of this knowledge. Nothing was ever as sinister as she originally believed.

That night her malice grew and turned into something quite extraordinary. Knowing Marie to be across the landing, she pulled Richard into herself with brutal urgency. She performed the pleasure she'd never truly been able to feel, not caring whether it was real for Richard's sake, knowing it was real to Marie. He cried happily and seemed to see her this time. She rolled into the darkness of the bed, pulling him with her, chafing herself against him quickly and frantically.

She saw the lurid outline of his shoulders and was suddenly frightened how passionate he was in return. It was when she saw how hollow her passion was, how calculated and cruel, that she lost courage in it. He wasn't ready for closure and when he recognised that dawning lassitude, the fallacy of movement in her body, he held her sadly, his hands shaking on her skin. She let him finish what she'd started, though she was lapsing out of herself, receding from the moment as though it had not been possible after all. She felt a white-hot spasm of grief shoot inside her. Then she rolled over and fell asleep.

Marie overslept that Saturday morning. By the time Marianne finally went to knock on her door it was nearly midday. She heard a voice but not the content. She opened the door and looked in to see Marie sitting up in bed and staring at the wall.

'You okay?' Marianne said.

Marie turned and nodded. Even her head looked tired. The roots of her hair were returning, a fine grey cloud across her scalp.

'I might go home today, if that's alright,' Marie said.

'Of course. But – you can stay the whole weekend if you want.'

'No. It's okay. I'm intruding.'

'You're not.'

Marianne came forward to hug Marie but she leaned away.

'I need a shower,' she said quickly.

Marianne left some spare towels in the bathroom and headed to the kitchen, where Richard was brewing up. He had left a cup out for Marie.

'We're probably going to head out,' Marianne said to him. 'I'm going to show her the area, the cemetery.'

'Alright. How long's she staying for?'

'I don't know. She said she wants to go back today.'

He must have seen something sad in her expression as he placed his hand on the small of her back.

'There's a lot I haven't told you about her,' she said. 'I should have mentioned that she was ill for a while. Very ill. And she's still not really better.'

'I got a vibe from her,' he said. 'I mean, I can tell something's not right.'

She moved away from his hand. 'It needs a lot of explaining. She actually used to be a lot different – not that long ago.'

'Was it cancer?'

Marianne glared at him, though she had no reason to be angry. 'Yes, but not a serious form. And that's not the reason she's bald. She did that because she wanted to.'

'Okay.'

'She had sepsis after her spleen was taken out and she nearly died.'

Her voice caught on that word, and she couldn't say anything else. Her impression of him was much weaker that morning. She wanted to hoard Marie from his inquiring eye, his clinical curiosity. She wandered upstairs and sat on her bed, listening to the water running in the bathroom.

When Marie was dressed, in the same outfit as yesterday, they left for Nunhead cemetery. The sky was overcast and they suspected it would rain. Marie had borrowed Marianne's anorak as she said she was cold, though it was still slightly humid from yesterday. She looked at the gravestones morosely, pushing the tip of her shoe into the grass just beyond where the body might have lain.

There was a large ash tree with a split at the bottom that gaped like the parting of a woman's thighs, dark and cavernous. Marie crouched and peered inside.

'Not big enough for you this time,' Marianne said, smiling.

Something strange happened as Marie smoothed her palm across the bark. Marianne felt a pain in her back, like the pain she'd experienced shortly after moving to Dulwich, but this time it wasn't gradual. It was more concentrated, a single straight line all at once. The pain was also there in her head and she felt a sultry heat infuse the space behind her eyes. A dark red film, like watered-down blood. She took Marie's arm for support.

As soon as she touched her, there was a tiny intake of breath.

'I miss you,' Marie said.

Marianne held her hand.

'I miss you too.'

They stood in silence. Marianne blinked the pain away and was surprised how quickly it receded now that she was holding her sister's hand.

'I'm happy for you,' Marie said. She looked at Marianne and her face held something of that old softness. 'I'm glad you live here and you found someone.'

'Thank you.'

Marie curled into her then and hung from her middle. Marianne closed her arms around her back, where she felt a quiver. Her bones were very small but sharp.

'Hey, you're shaking. Are you really that cold? Shall we go back?'

'Okay.'

Marianne accompanied Marie partway of the journey to Euston. Once they got to Victoria, Marie said she could take the Tube on her own as there were no changes and little possibility of making a mistake. They walked down to the platform together and Marianne swept her into a hug.

'Look after yourself,' she said when the carriage rumbled forward.

Marie nodded and smiled. A tear slipped down her face and curved into her mouth.

'Go on, quick!' Marianne said, nodding at the opening doors just ahead of them. They were standing at the back of the platform so people could get past.

'It's alright. I'll get the next one.'

'I'll wait with you.'

'Honestly. You're making it hard.'

There was an urgency in Marie's voice that Marianne hadn't really picked up on until now.

'Okay,' Marianne said uncertainly. 'Well – look after yourself.'

Marie nodded and another tear flew from her face.

'Bye, Mari,' she said.

They shared a secret smile, a knowingness of one another and a deep-rooted closeness that extended far beyond any isolated moment. And yet Marie was a lonely, anomalous figure on that platform. Nobody was quite like her. Marianne did not linger because she knew Marie did not want her to.

When she got back to the flat, she saw Marie's antibiotics on the bedside cabinet in Richard's old room. It was the only object that really caught the eye: the room was virtually empty otherwise, the duvet smooth without any creases, as though nobody had slept there at all.

She figured Marie would be at Euston by now, so she tried to call her mobile. The dial tone didn't go through. An hour later she tried again. She waited another couple of hours before ringing home, thinking Marie had forgotten to charge her phone.

Her father answered.

'Hey, are you alright?'

'Is Marie back yet?'

'No. I didn't think she was coming back today!'

'Yeah. She got the four o'clock train. She should be back by now.'

'Maybe it was held up?'

Marianne said goodbye quickly to check the National Rail website. She found nothing. The train to Preston, which was the first one Marie had caught, had been on time. No trains from Preston to Lancaster were running behind either.

She had recently set up a Twitter account again to keep up with London transport updates and something prompted her to check the TFL account. She looked at the recent tweets for the Victoria line, scrolling down the feed until she saw one that said there were severe delays. Another one said it was due to 'an incident on the tracks', which seemed to have originated at Victoria and which had brought the carriages to a standstill for a long time. She typed 'victoria line' in the main feed, which brought up several tweets alluding to the delay.

A woman had tweeted about being on the Victoria line when someone jumped off the platform and she'd felt the impact judder through the carriage. A young girl had thrown herself in front of the oncoming train. Then there were hundreds of replies to one particular tweet where a woman mentioned that she had been standing on the platform when it happened. Everybody swarmed in on this one, asking her what the victim looked like and whether she had seen any signs of distress moments earlier. 'Not really,' she replied. 'I didn't notice her until she ran past me. She was young (a teenager maybe??) and very thin and she had no hair. Everyone screamed when she ran off the platform. I can't get it out of my head.'

Marianne heard a strange sound leave her throat. She slipped off the bed and knelt on the floor, gathering her nerves for what was coming. There were a few seconds of silence as she marvelled at what was possible. Then she felt the numbness subside from her head and the darkness unloaded itself. She sobbed until she couldn't breathe.

MARIANNE HEARD SOMEONE KNOCK ON the lid of her coffin.

'Stop it,' she called.

Another knock. She opened her eyes and saw the ribbed face of a cactus. She was staring at it from across her bed.

It was then that she realised someone was impatient to see her. She tried to haul herself off the bed, but she was still trapped in a myopic state and couldn't see very far. The periphery of her room had erased itself and only the centre throbbed with her thoughts.

'Hang on,' she said quietly.

She got up slowly so as not to fall. When she reached the door, she opened it to see Eric staring back at her.

'Oh god, you went through with it.'

She had absolutely no idea what he was talking about. It was only when she caught sight of her soiled hand on the door handle that she recalled her burial.

'Oh, yes. I did. It feels like a long time ago.'

Eric sensed her impending vacancy and manoeuvred past her into the room. He closed the door and took her hand.

'Don't panic, just come over to the bed,' he said.

She was vaguely irritated by him, though she didn't know why. She allowed him to guide her to the bed and she thought that he wanted her to lie down, so she sat on the edge and lowered her back. He put his hand there to stop her.

'No. Stay awake. Keep conscious.'

'What?'

'We need to talk.'

She felt, beneath the palm of his hand, a terrible weight on her spine. It was not an internal weight; it existed on the surface of the skin. Eric instantly felt it and moved his hand away as though it burned him.

'Can I look?' he asked her. They both knew what he was referring to.

'Yes.'

He lifted up her shirt from her back and she shivered. She knew the hairs had grown almost three times as long since she'd last felt them. She knew that it had happened while she was buried. She reached out and felt the ends drift softly against her hand. The roots that emerged from the spine were now so thick that she was amazed she had once tried to trim them off in the shower. It seemed like years ago. How foolish to think she could uproot them.

'Can we seriously not just leave?' Marianne said.

Eric looked at her and his eyes were glossy, the whites slightly clouded.

'I didn't mention this before, but it seems like *some* people can leave and some can't. That coach sometimes picks up tiny groups of guests from the entranceway – I've seen them lined up with their suitcases. Maybe they've been here as long as I have or longer, but they didn't look like they had.'

'What do you mean?'

'You know how sluggish you feel now you've been here for even just a few days? Like you're tired of carrying around your body?' Marianne nodded. 'The people in the lobby waiting to go – they didn't look that way. They seemed a bit tired but kind of cheerful and they were chatting among themselves, not anti-social like the rest. Anyway, I saw them getting on that coach. Couldn't get through to the lobby because they keep the door locked – have you noticed that? You need a member of staff to let you back in there. I could see through the glass though, obviously. Someone I met on my way here was part of the group last week. Never saw any real change in him while he was here. He was reunited with his phone – I saw him calling someone outside just before he got on. Seemed very animated, emotional – not in a bad way. I think he was obviously relieved to speak to whoever was on the other end. He's very likely gone home now.'

His eyes had grown dark and hollow, almost as though they had moved a few inches further back in his head.

'I don't know why some people are held here,' he said. 'I don't get this notion of *progress*. Once, I caught eyes with someone I'd seen in the cafeteria for months, like me, and he just...stared back. I was glad someone finally had the guts to make eye contact and to hold it. We both had this moment of recognition between us, like a shared panic but the kind you can't explain because you can't account for it. Then a few days later – he was there again, same time as me, and he was visibly shaking. He looked so tired and his hands were trembling so he could barely hold his knife and fork. His eyes kept darting up towards the exits, then the staff, then he stared at his plate again. Same thing, over and over. Wouldn't catch my eye again.' His voice began to shake. 'And I didn't want to upset you earlier, but I have seen someone try to leave. Someone who didn't have permission, it seems.'

Marianne's heart was beating so quickly she thought she could hear it thumping in her skull.

'How?' she said.

'I saw this woman beat her head against the garden fence. It was so strange, I thought I was hallucinating. One minute she was sitting with her back to one of those oak trees in the garden, totally calm, the next – she just sprang up and darted towards the fence. Slammed her head against it.' He threw his head forward to demonstrate, nearly cricking his neck. 'Like with all the force she could possibly have. The pain must have been unreal, but she didn't seem to feel anything.'

His voice sounded like there was too much air in his lungs, his imagination pumping his body with adrenaline. Marianne's bowels felt heavy, the familiar sensation of panic trickling through. She was afraid of a sudden purgatory impulse and looked towards the door of the bathroom. In spite of everything, she was wary of losing her dignity. She placed the palm of her hand on her stomach, beneath her T-shirt, to soothe the pain.

'What happened to her?' she asked.

'I wanted to help,' Eric said faintly. 'I didn't know how. You know when someone is obviously so far gone that nothing will help them? And she had these really intense eyes, one of them a bit off centre. Anyway, she was held down and sedated by about six members of staff. They told everyone else there to stop staring and go inside.'

'You said she was trying to leave.'

Eric nodded. 'Oh yeah, and I think she believed that was what she was doing. You could see it in her face. She genuinely believed she could break through that fence. The way she kept crushing her head...' Marianne groaned. 'She was trying to knock it down. Or knock herself out. She went literally insane.'

'What did she look like? One eye was off centre?'

Eric frowned. 'She had a bony face and lots of wavy black hair down her back.'

Marianne gasped. 'I spoke to her on my first day. She was sitting in the corridor across from my room.'

'Really?'

'She said her friend was in the next room and she was upset because she'd been "taken".'

The word brought discomfort to both of them, and they were silent. Its brevity frightened Marianne, the claustrophobic import of its perfect tense, one that signified an unresolved yet irreversible conclusion. No subject lay before it, no destination after.

'She said some very strange things,' Marianne continued quietly. 'Like "don't give them your thoughts or you won't get them back."'

Eric stood up and moved towards the glass wall, where the garden could now be seen in the half-light of the sun. Its angular lines of privet hedges provided a series of sharp intersections all the way down towards the gate that divided the garden from the forest.

'You might think she's insane,' he said, 'but she might be telling the truth. At least about the "taken" part.' He pointed ahead at the gate leading on to the forest. 'On two occasions, I saw someone being escorted through the garden in the early hours of the morning. I couldn't sleep so I'd been staring out the window. The first time, it was a woman – a bit younger than you – and two large men were sort of guiding her. I think she was really out of it. She was taken into the woods. That wasn't long after I came here. Then it happened again a few days before you came. A man – I'd say he was in his fifties. He was walking oddly, kept bending over and they had to wait for him to straighten up again. They were both absolutely exhausted.'

'Where were they going?'

'I don't know. But I don't think anything good happened to them.' He scratched the hairs around his temples in a quick, angry fashion. 'I honestly thought I might have been dreaming. My dreams have been really weird since staying here.'

Marianne looked at the cacti surrounding her bed.

'What do we do?' she said.

'We need to see what's happening downstairs.'

'You mean the basement?'

'Yes. That whole floor has so many rooms that we don't have access to,' Eric said, staring again through the window. 'I think something odd is happening down there. Like really odd. When I go to see Doctor Roberts, I'm always blown away by how many doctors are down there wandering around, sometimes in big groups. What are they doing? There's no way they're *all* therapists.'

'How do we get in? We'd need a fob for the lift.'

'There's a staircase behind a door at the end of a corridor downstairs. It's near the lounge. I once saw a man in a surgical coat come out. It's so they don't have to use the lift, I guess. Maybe to avoid other guests? He locked it afterwards.'

'He looked like a doctor?'

'Yeah.'

Marianne rubbed her hands against one another. She was anxious to see the dirt fall away.

'I need to have a shower,' she said.

'You do. You'll feel better.'

The conversation had exhausted them, and for a moment they sat facing one another wearily. Marianne's mind was losing its footing again. Every time she tried to remember something tangible or to think further ahead, to apprehend a future in which she existed, she felt a peculiar dizziness, a cold sensation at the back of her head. There was no such thing as tense, as volition, when she vanished into this pain. Her mind entered a new dimension, one in which it couldn't survive. The hairs on her back felt singed, like her skin was aflame. She could still see Eric, his shadowed eyes, but she saw him as one who lived on the other side of something vast and unbreachable.

The image of that man Eric had seen in the cafeteria suddenly returned to Marianne and it spurred her into movement. She could still be shocked out of her reverie, which was consoling, especially if the trigger was internalised. She stood up abruptly and went to take her shower.

Strangely, she felt more exposed now with Eric in the other room than she did in the meditation hall before all those strangers. Her nakedness was more tangible when she thought of how close he was to it on the other side of the wall. She hadn't locked the door. Once under the head of water, she switched the temperature to a scalding heat then scraped the soil from her skin with her nails. She had slept with it inside her knickers and her groin was dry and dusty. She opened her legs apart on the shower floor and rubbed her vagina frantically with the heel of her hand. The only cleaning product available to her was the strange powder she'd used that morning. When she applied it to the hairs on her back, they softened again and fell thickly into the palm of her hand. They were so long that when she tugged them, a jolt of pain was sent to her head.

When she dried herself, she flipped her hair back from her head and expected to see a mirror, forgetting that there was none. It was the longest amount of time she hadn't seen her face and she wondered, stupidly, if it had changed a great deal. She could not believe she would see the same person staring back.

She dressed and opened the door to find Eric hunched over on the bed. He was softly running his finger along one of the cacti.

'I want to go outside,' Marianne announced.

He turned round and stared at her.

'Okay. Do you feel better?'

'Not really.'

She looked at Eric and he must have sensed that she was appealing for an intervention. He moved towards her and linked his arm with hers.

'I've got you. We'll move at your pace,' he said.

Eric guided Marianne to the garden through a pair of double doors at the back of the building. There was a small patio where some guests were sitting and staring emptily into space. Beyond this, the garden was quaint and modestly proportioned, with trees still in their infancy, guarded by mesh cylinders that looped around the trunks. Marianne noticed that the garden lost its tranquil, pacifying atmosphere the closer it got to the forest. The yew hedgerows began to dominate the landscape about midway; they were enormous and one could never quite grasp the layout of the land unless viewing it from the upper floor of the house. It was quite easy to lose oneself past this point. The hedges formed a maze, though its pathways were narrow and unyielding, sometimes barely opening up to allow for more than one person to walk through. Though the walls seemed sharp and streamlined from the outside, when one journeyed deeper into the recesses of the maze, the foliage began to bulk out so you had to flatten yourself through the passage and brush against the bloated shrubs. One space was so contracted that Marianne felt a sharp branch snag the corner of her eye as she pushed her way through, her eyes mercifully squeezed shut. Occasionally, these walls yielded to secluded pockets of grass, where there was space to breath. One would find a bench and a small fountain or statue, along with a different species of tree in each corner, the tops of which Marianne had glimpsed from her window, breaking up the monochrome lines of the maze. These trees were vibrant and lavish, the colours a salve for the senses. They were varying shades of scarlet and pink – Japanese maples, katsura, mountain ash, weeping purple beeches and purple-leaved plum trees. Marianne and Eric came upon a corner of the hedgerows where a cherry tree presided over a small stone bench. *Autumnalis Rosea*, Marianne mouthed to herself. It was one of those that thrived in winter, the flowers still a tender pink, unbearably soft. The colour was so gentle, so vital, that Marianne could barely look anywhere else. The foliage calmed her and consoled something very far back in her mind. She closed her eyes and the colour was still there.

'It's lovely,' Marianne said after a while. Eric murmured something but she couldn't hear. 'I want to stay here. I'm not going back inside.'

'They round everyone up and send them back in,' he said.

'Surely you can find a spot to hide out here?'

'No. I've stayed out until the sun's gone down. Trust me. After dark, nobody's left unaccounted for.' Eric massaged his upper arm closest to Marianne and his knuckles brushed against her. 'There are security men that patrol the garden after eight. One of them grabbed my arm when I wouldn't follow and it was – *vicious.*'

Marianne looked down and realised she hadn't noticed a blue shadow there, just below the arm of his T-shirt.

'What do we do?' she said lamely.

He looked at the ground and said nothing.

Marianne stared at the foliage again, but even those brilliant colours couldn't change the darkness building in her head. She was lapsing back into her memories and then continuing to fall through them, gathering speed in the wake of what was left behind. The sensation was of plummeting to a climax instead of climbing towards it.

Her recurring thoughts were not so much of Marie as of her mother and father, the two people who had once existed independently of them. She missed every second of their lives together, including those seconds she was not witness to. She steered her thoughts towards the past, piecing together small incidents that yielded new possibilities she hadn't been clever enough to make use of at the time. She had missed her chance – all those little moments when someone had opened up to her ever so slightly, ever so carefully, and she didn't enter. When she had failed to see a sign, the way certain words imply resistance but are really invitations, appeals, admissions of loneliness. She was thinking of her parents – her mother's hard tenderness and her father's gentle dignity – precisely because she knew there was a point in the not-so-distant future when she would never think of them again. That knowledge had already insinuated itself into her body, making it difficult to breathe.

Then she began to cry.

'It's alright,' Eric said. 'We're alright.'

'I don't know why, but I feel like I'm not getting out. I really feel it.'

She pointed to her head when she said this. He took her hand and placed it in his lap, which consoled her.

'I want to go home,' she said stupidly.

'We *will*.'

'I mean...' She shuddered and her voice was trapped in her throat.

'You mean *home* home?'

She stared at him in surprise: he knew what she meant. 'Yes.'

He gripped her hand for a few minutes while she hunched over and cradled her forehead in her other hand. When she hung her head towards the space between her thighs, her sinuses cleared quickly and the rush of air through her nose made it sting. There was a physical ache for what she was convinced she no longer had any recourse to. The presentiment of loss was powerful and it began somewhere out of sight, out of reach. She could not see where this conviction stemmed from but she only knew it existed somewhere at the bottom of her consciousness, the bottom that erased itself every time she seemed to reach it. Her thoughts were too small and too sensitive to survive what dragged them down.

Eric sensed what was happening inside her and she felt his body jolt quickly, angrily, from its paralysis.

'We have to stay alert. Keep thinking. Move about.'

He pulled her away from the bench and led her towards the edge of the garden, where they saw the high-security fence. She was sobered by the sight of it. The fluid quality of her thoughts – that odd quality they had of running away from her – was momentarily stymied. The shock of being held in some unspoken way *against their will* recalled an old recalcitrance she'd not felt for a long time, a dark heat inside her skin.

'Where are we?' she said to Eric.

'I honestly don't know,' he replied.

He was watching something further along the wall, away from the house. A large oak tree stood against the fence in a way that intimated its space was being stolen, though not enough to completely censor growth. The trunk appeared to be leaning, pressing, with a slow and gradual urgency, upon the fence. The foliage climbed over the top and the roots tumbled beneath it, the entrails clawing for space on the other side. There was a small gap between the earth and the fence at the bottom, small enough for someone to push their hand through.

Before Marianne said anything, Eric seemed to have noticed something in the gap. He pulled her towards it.

'He's back,' he said quietly.

'Who?'

Then she saw him. A small boy lurking behind the tree on the other side of the fence. His hand was on the mesh panel where the trunk was pressing its weight, his fingers exploring the bark through these small holes. He was in the process of crouching to the ground when he saw them and froze. He was only about eight years old. His head was pale, his hair very light so that he looked like a figure in a photograph bleached of colour and expression.

'He's here almost every day,' Eric murmured to Marianne. 'He's the son of someone who works here. Likes to gawk at everyone from this spot.'

As they approached, the boy continued to lower himself to the ground and finally squatted on the largest root of the tree. It was a mildly alarming position as his crotch grazed the root where it tipped at a sharp angle and he flattened himself around it, bending his knees like a locust.

'What's your name?' Marianne asked him.

'Peter.'

'Peter, where are we?'

He lowered his gaze slightly and smiled in an abstracted way. There was no humour in the curl of his mouth. He was carefully distancing himself, while at the same time managing to satisfy his curiosity.

'Are we in the Wye Valley?' Marianne asked.

'I've asked him. He doesn't answer that question,' Eric said.

Peter's eyes drifted upwards very slowly and settled on Marianne's loose hand. The one which Eric hadn't taken. Almost instantaneously, Marianne untangled herself from Eric and walked towards the boy. He shrunk away from her, though his smile was still frozen to his face. It seemed to grip the muscles of his mouth, and he had no control over it.

'Peter, please tell us where we are?'

Marianne crouched to the boy's level and she eyed the hole beneath the fence. Inside that hollow, beneath the root that traversed the gap, there was a small collection of stones, a feather, the speckled shard of an eggshell and a red petal the size of her thumbnail.

'Do you keep things here?' she asked him gently.

He nodded and pushed his forehead against the fence so that his skin bulged through it slightly. When he pulled it back she saw the tiny indented crosses before they faded.

'Peter,' she said slowly, 'I only want to know where we are. We've been told we're in the Wye Valley. Is this true?'

She held out her hand, the palm upturned, through the hole. He hesitated and then he touched her fingers as though to test

that she was palpable, not some simulacrum designed to trick
him. His own hands were clammy and gritty from the soil.

'No,' he said.

'Where are we, Peter?'

She moderated her voice so that even she didn't recognise it.
It was so light, one would never guess the panic beneath it.

'Ennerdale,' Peter said.

It slipped out of his mouth as though he wasn't even conscious
of what he was doing. He continued to watch Marianne through
the fence until his complacency chilled her enough to release
his hand.

'Ennerdale Forest,' she said to Eric.

'Where—'

'We're in the Lake District. We're nowhere near fucking
Wales.'

Peter curled his body away from them like an angry tadpole.
His head seemed suddenly enormous, the golden hair too fine
to hide the shape of his skull.

'Thank you,' she said. 'Will you be here tomorrow?'

He said nothing. He was growing quickly dull and resentful
of them. Before they could say another word to him, he picked
himself gingerly from the ground, his knees pockmarked from
the little stones in the earth, and scuttled towards the path that
led to the forest. They watched him walk, then run, then settle
for a kind of lunging through the air. Marianne was certain he
had deleted them from further thought.

'He's been told not to talk to us,' Eric said.

Marianne turned to face him.

'I'm not going to stay here another day.'

'You think I haven't tried to walk out?' Eric said sharply. 'I
have. I didn't care if I got lost in the forest for a few days. I

didn't care about my luggage. I asked the receptionist if she could open the gate for me. She said my time wasn't up. They needed further progress from me and Doctor fucking Roberts hadn't deemed me well enough to leave. I've told you this.'

Marianne fingered the items Peter had left in the hole. The petal was a very dark shade of red, and when she laid it on her palm she felt how firm it was, the veins like stitching.

'We don't consent,' Marianne said in a daze. 'We should be able to leave at any time.'

She looked up and stared back at Eric, and realised he was slipping inside his own panic. His eyes were gaping at the hole in the ground without actually seeing what was there.

'Let's go back,' Marianne said. 'Tomorrow, we will…think of something.'

They didn't know what time it was, only that the sun had begun to go down. The sky was darkening slowly. As they walked towards the house, Marianne thought the air heavy and she was burdened with having to breathe. She caught the eye of a female statue at the end of a hedgerow, standing emptily with her arms behind her back. Marianne remembered her from a photograph in the brochure. The eyes were a dark red stone.

Before returning to her room, Marianne asked Eric whether she could borrow some paper and a pen, remembering he had brought his notebook to Nede with him. She had brought a writing set with her, but the paper was decorated with little flowers and she felt it was too glaringly sweet, not suitable for the words that were thrashing around in her mind. Eric gave her a single sheet of blank white paper. Before parting in the corridor, they stared at one another, and Marianne felt the impulse to take his hand. She wondered whether she had ever felt so compelled to do this with anybody else before.

When she was alone again, she sat at the desk in her room and began to write.

Dad,

I'm writing this from that therapy resort I told you about. It seems like I've been conned into coming here for some kind of medical research or experiment and I don't know what it is. I only know that I'm in Ennerdale forest.

You took us here when we were little. Marie fell from a tree and we all thought she'd broken her spine! Mum couldn't stop laughing afterwards. Then we watched it again on my camera because I'd been filming her in that tree before she fell. We watched it over and over and I don't think I'd ever laughed so much before. I can't believe how something so scary could turn into the funniest thing in just a few seconds.

I miss who I was when we came here. I don't feel like I'm that person anymore. I can feel my grasp of things slipping, my memories. This place is designed to make us forget who we are. I thought that would be a good thing but it's a form of brutality – I can already feel it working and it frightens me. I just want to come home.

I am no longer here of my own will. If you get this, please come and find me.

I love you.

Marianne

At this point, Marianne placed the pen down because her hand was shaking. Her breath was short and shallow. There seemed so much of it that, every time she exhaled, she felt the pressure mounting to take it back in.

She looked through the glass wall towards the garden. The moon was a bald white knuckle. Everything was still and yet she intuited movement everywhere, a ceaseless conspiracy. The darkness prompted a steady circadian rhythm, cells expanding silently. The trees devoured the sunlight which they'd trapped earlier, consuming it quickly like gold. She felt the hairs rising on her spine and they were long enough to push the fabric of her shirt away. Again, she felt her thoughts hurling themselves irresistibly towards their end where she was no longer the subject.

Since she had been buried, she now knew there was a darkness that succeeded her, which dismantled the pronoun without destroying its contents. She would end, but she would not be over. She remembered the heat of the earth with herself inside.

She wrote 'Marianne Marianne Marianne Marriane Mariane Mariaane Marrianne Mariene Mariee Marie' across the page. The name soon became strange to her and she realised that the harder she clung to the outline of herself, the greater its collapse, like an object she tried to whittle down from clay, spinning rapidly out of control. What she wouldn't do for a photograph. A mirror. The old notebooks she had drowned in the bath! What sacrilege led her to dispose of her history, no matter how clumsily it had been assembled?

She heard a knock on her door and she jumped.

'It's me.'

She folded her letter before rushing to open the door.

Eric's face was pale and his eyes were shining. One of his tear ducts was very red and a pink cloud was branching off from it towards his pupil.

'I'm sorry. I wondered whether you wanted company. I can't sleep.'

Marianne said nothing and ushered him inside before closing the door. Then she gestured to the bed.

'Do you want to just lie here for a while?' she said quietly.

Eric nodded. He walked slowly around the other side of her bed, taking care to avoid the cacti. He lay down on his back and stared at the ceiling without saying anything further.

Marianne hesitated. Then she lay down beside him. For a few minutes, neither of them spoke. The light of the moon was shifting the shadows of everything, each cactus angling its shadowy twin along the floor, as though in a twilit desert.

Without the aid of the juices supplied by the staff, neither of them was tired enough to sleep, and the fugue they shared had gradually abated, like mist. For a few hours, they were miraculously alert, their minds raw with a new kind of tension. Marianne could tell Eric was experiencing this same shift as his pupils were expanding and his breathing was laboured. She suddenly felt explicitly conscious of both herself and Eric, of their outlines, which were barely touching. They turned at some point in the early hours so that they were back to back. Marianne felt the hairs along her spine trembling towards the other body, meandering across the space that divided them. He must have felt this happening to him too, for they both lifted their clothes slightly to see what would happen. He turned his head and she saw the glossy line of his earlobe, the tender folds in his neck, his left eye, which was looking at a spot of the room where she knew, instinctively, that he thought of her. She filled his mind from that space on the bed and he was bracing himself to enter her.

The hairs became entangled, embedded. And a curious thing happened to Marianne's consciousness. She was able to apprehend Eric – his fear, his loneliness, the unspeakable fragility of his dreams – at exactly the same point of intersection where she too was apprehended. Their thoughts wound themselves together more tightly until Marianne felt a murmur in her blood, an almost incestuous intimacy with another life such as she had never known, which she hadn't thought possible.

She leaned into his life as though it were her own. In her mind's eye she saw him watching her and her sister as they walked through Williamson Park. The Turner girls. He had seen them on so many occasions, without their realising he was ever there on the periphery of their lives. He watched Marianne laugh in a way he had not witnessed with other girls. She was a little dark, a little defensive. She was thinner than Marie, her hair a dirty shade of blonde, and her eyes were relentless, the kind of eyes one always felt wary of being watched by. He spoke to Marie so that he might one day be courageous enough to insinuate himself into her household and learn more about that angry, beautiful sister who guarded her.

The hairs fastened themselves to Eric and formed a dense network so that she saw him intermittently throughout the night. Marianne was also illuminated. The sensation was like being at sea while a lighthouse trained its eye on her every few seconds, her body appearing in white flashes, her terror subsumed in the light that caused it. He was seeing her in an entirely fluid sense, bathing in her life and stealing some of her thoughts, just as she stole his. He saw Marie as Marianne saw her and his remorse entered her blood, making her shiver. Marie lay between them as they directed their thought towards her, until she was so close that Marianne moved her hand through

the air, thinking she would find her sister's warm skin somewhere in the bed.

Once their backs were knitted tightly together, Marianne saw
something in Eric's past that turned out to be the end of the
line as far as her consciousness was permitted. She was staring
up at a woman who shared his eyes and who stooped over her
with a knife in her hand, her mouth moving in wild, contorted
shapes. The knife swerved through the air until a spasm in her
wrist caused it to drop. Marianne screamed through Eric as they
simultaneously watched it fall to the floor, pinning itself to Eric's
foot. The pain reverberated in the memory, novel enough for
Marianne to feel a prick inside her skin. She revolted from him,
the hairs of her back wrenching free of his own.

At the same time as she had seen Eric's mother, he had
entered a space at the back of Marianne's consciousness that
she had taken pains to avoid these past six months. He was
sitting in the dusty carriage of an Underground train, staring
at the other faces who stared back blankly. Then, inside this
memory, he saw another one, this time more deeply encased.
It unloaded itself like blood from a wound, leaking into the
present until he was convinced – as Marianne had been that
day, her first day back at work – that he was running through
Marie along the track, that he was disturbing her grave. The
train was diving into the void where she lay. She was everywhere and nowhere in the darkness, flitting through the
windows. Eric cried through Marianne, his blood vibrating
with her own. He got up and looked around for the emergency
stop, stumbling over passengers' legs, until he found it – a
bright red button.

When Marianne and Eric parted on the bed, they were
breathing fast and held one another's hands quickly. Marianne

could not even remember reaching out for him. She couldn't believe he had been in her life for such a short amount of time.

They sat up and stared into space, though they could barely see anything. They were still contaminated with one another, Marianne's thoughts entwined with Eric's, like interlaced fingers. The familiar red shadow filled her eyes and pulsed with every recollection. For she had also seen fragments of a life that moved her, which filled her with hilarity and which she wished she had known about much sooner. That he had seen her own mental life, her history, her outline, filled her with shame and relief. She was aroused by their mutual voyeurism, compelled to share every last detail, to strip her mind to the bone.

Eric had moved to the edge of the bed. He sat with his back to her again, his hairs tangled as though he had emerged from a large pool. They looked shorter now. Marianne wondered whether she had imagined them withdrawing in the skin, even as she watched him.

He must have been too disturbed to stay with her as he got up to leave, tucking the hairs beneath his shirt. Before he reached the door, Marianne grasped his wrist and forced him to stare at her.

'I...'

She'd had the impulse to speak, without the words. But he sensed what lay outside of language. He held her in his arms so that her head was against his chest. His body was damp beneath the shirt.

When they released one another, he slipped out of her room and closed the door quietly. She watched the space where he'd lain for what seemed like hours, too wary of disturbing the outline of his body.

After he left, Marie entered.

Marianne had finally buried herself in sleep to find her sister sitting calmly at the other end of consciousness. They were both very close to one another and they were naked. The dream spread towards the margins, the scene filling itself in, until Marianne glimpsed the water that held them, the gleaming taps, Marie's foot on the side of the bath, her toes splayed, as she leaned back into Marianne. The water was still running and it sloshed precariously high around the sides.

Marie's back was facing Marianne, and when she looked at her sister's body, she knew instinctively that the cancer had returned. A series of bruises had worked their way down from Marie's head – still bald and blue like dusk – and emerged along her spine. One mark yielded a small crop of hairs, which sprouted just like the ones on Marianne's back. Automatically, Marianne reached out her hand and smoothed those hairs down so they lay flat across Marie's skin.

'That's nice,' Marie said.

Marianne continued to press the pads of her fingers along the bone. When her fingers glided across the muscles, she relaxed them, knowing when to relieve the pressure. Marie tensed and shivered. Gradually, Marianne watched the hairs slide back through the pores. There was still one hair that remained, thicker than all the rest, and it came from the base of her neck.

A loud bang on the door made them both jump. Marie sat up, suddenly rigid with tension.

'Marianne, are you there?'

It was Richard. He sounded impatient.

'Tell him to go,' Marie said. She turned and looked at Marianne with a pleading expression.

'Marianne!' he repeated gruffly.

Marianne stood up, and as she did so, the water crashed towards the rim of the bath.

'What do you want?' she said.

'You can't help her,' he said.

Marianne stepped over the rim of the bath and walked to the door. She was in the process of unlocking it when –

'Don't let him in.'

Marie was standing now, and all the blood had drained from her face. The hairs came charging back, unloading themselves from an intensely active yet hidden part of her body, bleeding down her back in fraught lines.

Marianne hesitated, her hand still on the door. The slower her response, the faster Marie seemed to dismantle herself. She began to tug at the hairs on her back, to unravel each and every one. They were long and some were split, the ends forked and frayed, but she found them all. They fell into the water, where they disintegrated. Soon there was only one left, dangling from the base of Marie's neck. It was at this point that Marianne realised that hair was the literal end of her sister. The last thread of thought.

Richard hammered his fist on the door and Marianne jerked her hand away from the handle.

'You can't stop her from doing it!' he said.

Marianne watched Marie as she clenched the root. Marie stared back. Her eyes were not shining with conviction; they were dark and dull. She seemed to have suddenly lost the capacity to see beyond what lay inside of herself.

She yanked the hair like it was a cable connected to an enormous electrical appliance. Then she collapsed abruptly. Her body shrank as it fell, folding into itself. It bombed the surface of the water and there was a large thud when her head hit the rim of the bath.

'How *could* you?' Marianne said.

She knelt by the side of the bath and took hold of Marie's wrist, pressing her fingers into the cold, wet skin.

'Marie, you had *me*!' She tapped Marie's knuckle on the rim of the bath. 'What about *me*?'

Marie's eyes opened.

'I'm sorry,' she said. Her face turned grey when she realised what she'd done.

That morning, Marianne swallowed her pill and skipped taking a shower. She massaged her temples with her fingers and stared out at the garden.

There was a knock at her door and she assumed it was Eric. She was relieved and got up to answer it. But when she opened the door, she was faced with the man who'd escorted her downstairs on her first day.

'Hi, are you free to chat with Doctor Roberts for about half an hour this morning?'

Marianne immediately looked at the small bag around his waist.

'Yes,' she said.

'Good. Are you ready now or would you like me to come back in ten minutes perhaps?'

'I'm ready. No, wait. Just hang on.'

An insane idea had gripped her. She closed the door on him and walked over to one of the cacti. Her bag was lying close by and she pulled a small white scarf from it, wrapping it several times around her right hand like a bandage. She carefully tipped the pot of the cactus to the side, then selected a spiky swollen arm, the part where it branched off from the main body of the plant, and placed her foot on top of it. It was like severing someone's spine, only this was wildly shaped, dipping and diving beneath her shoe. She stamped on it quickly. She did this several times until it snapped off.

When she returned to the door, she was wearing a large jumper from her suitcase, which caused the concierge to frown.

'Are you cold?'

'No, but I thought it was quite cold down in the basement last time.'

He nodded. 'Yes, it is a bit.' He caught sight of her bandaged hand. 'You've injured yourself.'

Marianne gave him a little laugh.

'Oh, I managed to scrape it on something thorny in the garden. It's not that bad.'

He walked ahead of her to the lift at the bottom of the corridor and Marianne began to feel sick. This time, her nausea came from what she was about to do. She watched him take the fob from his little bag before he pressed the button. They waited in silence for the doors to open.

A sudden spasm in her body made her do it. When the man turned his head to speak to her, she pulled the cactus branch out from under her jumper and smashed it against his cheek.

He reeled back in surprise. She saw blood and hit him again, quickly. On the second blow, the spines pricked his eyes and one lay nestled inside the folds of his eyelid. He could barely draw breath to express the pain. She forced herself to hit him again, but this time he caught her hand. He twisted her arm sharply and she thrust her knee towards his crotch, a gesture that frightened her more than wielding the cactus.

He fell back against the doors of the lift, groaning in disgust, and for a moment Marianne repented. She was caught off guard when he grabbed a fistful of her clothes at the neck, dragging her face towards him. The doors parted and he fell backwards, bringing Marianne with him, his back landing with a sharp *crack* on the lift floor.

Marianne pinned him down and hit him with the plant one more time, forcing the spines into his pores until he cried. She froze.

'I'm sorry,' she said automatically.

His eyes were bloodshot, the lids puckered and twitching. She was horrified by the fear she had brought into his face and she dropped the remains of the plant by his side. She pulled the fob out of his hands and he let go of it as though it burned him.

'I'm sorry,' he said suddenly.

She stared at him for a second but he wouldn't meet her eye. The blood had begun to cloud his pupils, and he seemed to see only this tiny explosion of pain in the forefront of his world.

Marianne turned away and held the fob on the sensor. Then she pressed the button for the basement floor. She held her head against the wall and felt a drop of sweat fall from the nape of her neck and run down her back. She rolled up the sleeves of her jumper and tried not to look at the floor where the man quivered out of the corner of her eye.

Her heart was thudding when the doors opened again. She'd expected to see Doctor Roberts standing there, waiting for her. But the corridor was just as dark and empty as before, a flickering light in the centre of the low-hanging ceiling. Two flies

crowded the dying light, furiously trying to get close. There
was the sound of dripping water. She left the man on the floor
of the lift. He looked as if he was about to say something else
to her, but the doors closed on his crumpled outline. She exhaled
slowly, her breath shuddering.

When she looked towards the light again, she was drawn to
it in a way she couldn't explain to herself. The dark spots on
its surface gave it a charred look, a smouldering, stymied glow.
Now and again, the filament inside glowed red and the glass
appeared clouded with blood. Marianne knew she was imagining
it, but this in itself troubled her. A bead of sweat was hanging
in the hairs of her eyebrow. She felt, in that moment, a tension
that would hold her captive forever if she consented to be still.
No. Keep moving. She tore her eyes away. The bulb rippled across
her vision, stinging her retina.

The lift made a sound like it was being hoisted upwards,
leaving no immediate escape route at hand. Marianne stag-
gered forward. She didn't want to walk down the corridor
ahead as she knew Roberts's office lay that way, so she made
a random decision to take a right. She leaned her head against
the first door she came to, on her left. Silence lay on the other
side, so she opened it slowly. It was dark and she found a light
switch, the palm of her hand sliding across the wall. An electric beam from the ceiling buzzed and flickered, revealing a
room with large wooden tables in rows and filing cabinets at
the back.

On each table was a large but shallow tray of earth. She
looked closer and saw that some of the earth was darker, glittering in the overhead light. There was a repulsive smell from
these trays, a chemical odour that made her eyes sting. She
almost thought it was the stench of her own distress; it lingered

around her skin as though waiting to be reabsorbed. The soil in the trays seemed to be shifting slowly when she was not directly looking at them. Possibly another hallucination. When she looked up, there were several diagrams pinned to the wall. One image was of the inside of a tree, with what appeared to be a single black line passing through the trunk. The line was annotated with countless symbols, formulae, inscrutable comments that she didn't understand.

She headed to the filing cabinets and pulled one of the drawers open hurriedly, causing the whole tower to shake. The tabs at the top of the files didn't mean anything to her. She saw the initials 'NT' repeated over and over. *NT Methodology. NT Administration. NT Mission Statement.* Another filing cabinet held a file labelled *NT A Concise History.* Marianne took the file and, with an urge to keep moving, headed quickly to the door. If she was to remain rooted somewhere in time and space, she was certain not only of being apprehended, but of being doomed to a prolonged dissociation, a panic that drained her of autonomy. She could feel the shimmering coldness of herself in rivulets down her back and the strange thing was that it soothed her, this annihilating fear. Some part of it was pacifying. A tiny portion of her brain was leaning into it, the loss, the certainty that she would be freed from the effort of guarding herself. She jerked her arm too quickly when closing the door; it shut with an echo and she was afraid she'd alerted someone.

She knew she couldn't return to the lift. A series of voices grew louder from that direction and she thought she heard Doctor Roberts commanding someone. She turned and continued. There were two more rooms down the passage and she could hear lots of activity behind the doors; her heart throbbed as she moved past them, dreading the moment when her good fortune gave way. What she had found, what she had done, was too easy for peace of mind. She should have been challenged but instead she had been able to explore as freely as though in a dream she hadn't yet recognised as such.

She found a staircase at the end of the corridor and guessed it would lead to the first floor, where Eric had seen the doctor coming out. But that door would be locked. She stood still and finally gave into panic, her body stiffening.

A door opened behind her and she instinctively thrust the file inside her jumper.

'What are you doing?'

Marianne turned and saw a young woman in a white coat frowning at her. Her face was sharp and androgynous, the mouth a thin, white line.

'I'm sorry,' Marianne whispered. She hugged herself, pressing the papers against her chest. 'I got lost. I came to see Doctor Roberts but I don't know the way out.'

A coldness gripped Marianne's stomach and she felt a heavy pain descending towards her bowels. It was quite possible the doctor considered Marianne very ill from the expression on her face.

'Didn't she escort you?' she asked.

Marianne shook her head. 'No. She was busy.'

The woman didn't believe her. But she was evidently stressed by something she had been attending to in that room, and anxious to get on. Her eyes flickered from Marianne to the staircase ahead.

'Come this way. I'll let you out here,' she said. 'You can't wander around on your own down here.'

Marianne followed her up the stairs. The woman's movements were sprightly and energetic, though looking at her face one wouldn't imagine her capable of such animation. On the first-floor landing, she took a bunch of keys from her pocket. They were attached to a small accessory – a red flower on a silver chain. When she opened the door, she did so slowly and looked out to see if anybody was nearby. A man was walking into the library just ahead and she pulled the door back slightly to wait for him to disappear.

'I shouldn't be doing this. Please don't come here again,' she said to Marianne. There was a pained note to her voice.

'I'm sorry,' Marianne said. She meant it.

Once she was out, the doctor closed the door quickly and locked it. Marianne turned and watched the lock dreamily as she heard the sounds of the key scuffling through the hole on the other side. She was lapsing back again with the sound, deleting her former line of thought. Then it came back when she felt the corners of the file against her chest.

She moved away and walked quickly towards the double doors leading out to the garden. She picked up her pace and ran along the lawn. Her hair was hanging damply on her temple. The sun was harsh on the top of her scalp and she felt daunted rather than refreshed by its warmth, accosted by everything.

She headed to the oak tree where they'd seen Peter the day before. She almost cried with relief when she found him there again, kneeling at the foot of the tree and pouring something into the ground.

'Peter!'

She ran towards him and he hovered on his haunches, bouncing slightly. He would take flight like a terrified bird if she continued to panic.

'Peter.' She softened her voice. 'Peter, I'm so glad you're here.'

She crouched to the ground and saw he'd placed five scarlet petals inside the hole. He had been spreading them around an invisible point in the soil.

'Peter, I want you to do something for me,' Marianne said. She was breathing heavily and he eyed her with hostility. 'I want you to post a letter for me.'

She took the letter out of her pocket, tucked inside its envelope.

'It needs a stamp. Do you know where the nearest post office is? Is it quite far from here?'

Peter nodded slowly.

'But you can take it there? You know the way?'

He glowered at the letter. She pushed it into the hole, taking care not to move his petals from their place.

'Please, Peter. It's very important. Please.'

He took the letter from her and turned it over to see the address.

'It's for my dad,' Marianne said. Her eyes began to sting. 'Does your daddy work here, Peter?'

'No. Mum.'

'Your mum? What does she do?'

But Peter was finished with her. He had her letter and she was no longer interesting. He stood up and slid his fingernail beneath the seal.

'No, no. Peter. Please don't open it.'

She had a horrible feeling that anything she said was redundant. But she couldn't count on the boy's disloyalty any more than his cooperation. He would likely operate on a whim, a series of arbitrary impulses that ruled his mental life.

When he walked away from her, the letter at the end of his fingertips, Marianne massaged her chest where her heart was beating.

'Thank you, Peter,' she said in a high voice. He didn't look back.

A voice had been calling her name while she watched the boy disappear along the path to the forest. She turned and saw Eric marching up the lawn, pale and sweating.

'Are you alright?' he said once he'd caught up. 'I've been looking for you.'

'I went to the basement floor.'

'How?'

'I can tell you later. Look, I took something from one of those rooms – a file.' She indicated what she was holding on to. 'We need to go to your room. They'll be looking for me.'

Eric nodded and took her hand. Their palms were both wet but she felt assured, righteous, the moment he held her.

They were more careful about heading back into the house. It was difficult not to give in to the impulse to run but that would immediately alert the staff. Marianne dreaded the lift. When the doors opened, she thought she would see the concierge again, his oiled hair dark with blood. But the floor was clean and the lift empty. When it reached the first floor, nobody was there to meet them.

It was going to end badly. Marianne knew that their luck would run out; it was half fantasised anyway and so offered little consolation. She believed that she was being enabled in some way, granted her moment of triumph until the time came for retribution. There would be some punishment for what she had done and she waited for it excitedly, the adrenaline prickling through her back.

Once she was in Eric's room – which was identical to her own – she spread out the papers from the file on the floor and motioned for him to join her. Then they hunched over the pages and began to read.

The first known case of cerebral roots forming in the spine was in November 1979. A 28-year-old city banker from London, Daniel Garrick, complained of a large growth of hair on the back of his neck. A CT scan revealed that the 'hairs' were in fact roots that were connected to the central nervous system and which came from the cerebellum in the brain. These neural roots appeared to cluster around the brain stem, where they travelled down the vertebral canal of the spine and eventually through the skin, appearing like thick hairs on the surface. The cause for this extraordinary development was initially unclear. Sarah Clarke, a neurobiologist from King's College, studied the location of the roots in the brain and concluded that they were connected at different points of contact to the cerebrum, cerebellum and brain stem, and there was every reason to believe that neurons travelled through these passageways. Where the neural activity ended was difficult to determine.

Garrick's mental health declined rapidly during the month he was examined at King's College, and he committed suicide on 5 January 1980. Garrick's psychiatrist of two years, Alan Dunn, who practised privately in London, actively ensured no doctors spoke to the press about his peculiar history. He was interested primarily in the connection between Garrick's psychosis and the emergence of what Clarke had referred to as 'cerebral roots' in his brain. Garrick had reported being highly stressed and anxious during the two years of his psychiatric evaluation. He was medicated for depression and his dosage was adjusted in increments. In March 1979, Garrick's wife was the victim of an assault on her way home from a restaurant, and it was following this traumatic event that his mental state deteriorated rapidly. The attacker was never found and this caused Garrick extreme emotional distress. His wife was traumatised by her ordeal too and partook in extensive CBT sessions and was treated for PTSD. Garrick spoke of an emotional fatigue brought on by the fundamental idea that he was impotent. He experienced a psychic breakdown that destabilised his cognitive abilities. For hours he seemed to lose consciousness and reported seeing a red light in the forefront of his vision. It was during this period that he noticed the growth of what he believed to be hairs along his spine.

By 1990, there were thirty-three reported cases of these cerebral roots. Clarke assembled a small group of neurobiologists to research the connections between cases and their findings were as follows:

- Each patient had a history of mental health disorders which included but were not limited to: depression, anxiety, obsessive compulsive disorder, personality disorder and dissociative disorder.
- Each patient had experienced a traumatic event (within the last year) which caused a dramatic deterioration in his/her mental health.
- Each patient had a blood relative who had had cancer or who had died from cancer – most commonly breast, ovarian, colorectal and prostate cancer.
- Each patient reported a neurocognitive deficit such as hallucinations, poor motor coordination and confusion.

It was only in October 2005 that Clarke's team of neurobiologists learned of a potential connection between the individual and his/her exterior environment, which made a very large difference to the evolution of the neural network. In one case, Martha Brown, 38, spent a week hiking in South Wales and noticed that, during that time, the roots on her spine grew very quickly – almost four times as long. She spoke of losing consciousness on several occasions as she walked through Wentwood Forest: 'I fell asleep in the shadow of a very large sycamore tree and when I awoke, I forgot who I was. I can't explain it very well. I didn't even think in any recognisable language. The words were gone. I had no concept of the divisions between things – every living thing around me merged seamlessly into the whole.' Brown claimed she had not ingested any drugs and her disorientation was not caused by exhaustion, hunger or dehydration.

Clarke refrained from publishing her findings until she reached a conclusion about the purpose of this expanding neural network. She formed a research group called NT (Neural Transference) and the members agreed to advertise for desirable candidates in general practices throughout the country. GPs were asked to refer any patient who exhibited the physical symptoms of this unique condition – namely the appearance of these neural nerve endings along the spine – to a facility set up and run by the research group. Their patients would be cared for and could opt out of the experiment at any time. Some would also be eligible to assist the team for a monetary reward.

It was soon clear that a large percentage of patients with cerebral roots were undesirable candidates for study. Clarke noticed that some were capable of spontaneously 'curing' themselves, where the roots gradually returned through the pores of their skin. This left a small proportion of patients who invited closer scrutiny, and this seemed relative to the degree of mental distress they were in during this period.

Clarke wished to concentrate on the impact of environmental factors, and whether dramatically increased exposure to natural surroundings influenced the patient's neurobiological development. She was particularly interested in one patient's account of losing consciousness while walking through Sherwood Forest in Nottinghamshire in August 2006. Charlotte Blair (22) told Clarke that her last memory was of sitting against the base of an oak tree with her back against the trunk. What struck Clarke as important was the way these roots had traversed the small gap between Blair and the tree, for when she regained consciousness Blair felt 'like [she] had tunnelled backwards in her mind'. She felt biologically reorganised.

In the interval between losing and regaining awareness of her surround-ings, she remembered being vaguely sentient and spatially dislocated. She insisted that she was blind but that she could 'feel' her way through the back of her body and anticipated an arrival that never came. She explained that 'it wasn't a dream. My blood seemed to carry me forward and I was aware of travelling without moving my body. I speak of "me" because I still felt like I had a self, but it wasn't going to last. I had the distinct feeling I was being erased. It's strange because it horrifies me now, but when it was happening, I wanted to be carried. It felt a bit like I was being evicted and the house was my body. I was about to be homeless. But I knew I would still exist.'

The National Institute of Public Health in Japan actively encour-ages the practice of *shinrin-yoku* or 'forest-bathing'. Studies have shown that the bioactive substances released by plants and trees have anti-inflammatory and neuroprotective qualities. Breathing in the forest also boosts the immune system by causing an increase in the count of the body's Natural Killer (NK) cells (people who spend just one day in the forest have more NK cells in their blood for seven days afterwards).

Blair volunteered to undergo 'forest therapy', ostensibly to help her anxiety (which she had suffered from for several years). What Charlotte was primarily interested in was relieving herself of a series of painful memories surrounding her childhood, namely incidents of abuse and coercive control at the hands of her stepfather (who died when she was sixteen). In September 2006, she travelled with Clarke and five members of NT to Sherwood Forest. Clarke suggested placing Blair in a shallow grave to see whether the soil had any impact on the roots. Over the course of half an hour, the roots grew almost three inches into the earth. Blair spoke of how she experienced the same mental disorientation. She described the experience as deeply nour-ishing in a way that sickened her once it was over. She was keen to stress that she remained conscious while 'buried' and that, if anything, her consciousness 'expanded'. She described herself falling back into a darkness that was temporarily infused with a red light. She was convinced that the red light was a 'signal' for the death of herself.

The experiment continued for three months. Blair was buried eleven times with a tube for breathing. Her longest submersion lasted for an hour and it would be her last one. When she was brought back up from the ground, she displayed signs that she was pathologically disturbed. She was violent and inconsolable. By this point, the roots had grown to almost fifteen centimetres. Her speech was incoherent and one member of NT, Nathan Kelly,[1] described her as seeming 'like a foetus that had fallen out of the womb too early. She'd been "miscarried" and she remembered it.'

Blair was given the choice to opt out, as her mental state had deteriorated rapidly. After weeks of experiencing disturbing dreams, delusions and persistent feelings of despair, she committed suicide in December 2006. Whether this is directly connected to the burial remains unverifiable – there is no concrete evidence that it precipitated her death as she had stated that she was prone to suicidal ideation before the experiment took place.

Before she died, Blair spoke to Anne Morton, a psychiatrist at Circle Nottingham Hospital, for a month, and their sessions were transcribed at a later date (file xi. *NT Conversations*, April 2007). A particular conversation (dated 15 October 2006) interested Clarke greatly:

Blair: The memory of being underground doesn't leave me. I recall falling so far back into my mind that I knew those were my last thoughts.

Morton: Can you describe what those last thoughts were?

---

1 Kelly left NT in November 2006. He agreed to sign a non-disclosure agreement for the group and would not publicly speak about the experiment. He admitted to his colleagues that he was disturbed by what he had seen and insisted Blair's mental health had been compromised, though she gave full consent to the procedure.

Blair: I thought of my mum's hands. I don't know how the image got there but it was so strong – the idea of her hands.

Morton: Did you imagine those hands touching you? Or was it a static thought?

Blair: I think they were still and there was something final about them.

Morton: Did you believe you would end at this point?

Blair: Yes and no. I believed that I was ending but my consciousness wasn't.

Morton: You spoke before about expecting a transformation.

Blair: Yes. I was about to arrive somewhere.

Morton: And when you say 'I'…

Blair: I mean my… I don't know how to—

Morton: Without the ego?

Blair: Exactly.

Morton: And this arrival – it was imminent.

Blair: Yes. It didn't happen because there was nothing…receiving me.

Morton: What was missing, do you think?

Blair: I don't know. I was rushing into space – I felt I was leaving my body but the space outside of it was too vast.

Morton: You wanted to be contained again.

Blair: Yes, but by something else. I didn't want to return to myself again.

There was a knock on Eric's door.

'Oh god,' Marianne said, and a tear slipped from her eye.

Eric clutched her hand, her arm and finally her face, working his way closer to the sadness inside of her. Her face shook in the palm of his hand.

The door opened and they saw a woman dressed in white with long blonde hair. She was surprisingly gentle and she moved towards Marianne without implying force. But they saw the syringe in her hand. She crouched down in front of Marianne and placed her hand on her shoulder.

'There's no need to be frightened. You're very distressed and this will calm you down,' she said softly.

'No. I don't want it,' Marianne said in a high voice.

Marianne pulled herself away along the floor, but the woman's face was so calm as to be mildly, inoffensively bored. She seemed to want to wait for Marianne to lose that last bit of energy before she took over; she knew it was inevitable with the assurance of one who had seen a great deal of emotional violence played out. There was a man at the door whom they hadn't noticed, and he came forward quickly to restrain Eric. Once he was apprehended, Marianne was alone on the floor.

When the needle sank into her arm, she was almost relieved.

She awoke with difficulty. Her mind was sluggish, and the brief interval of unconsciousness had cancelled out all former impulses. Now she was entirely desolate, slow to come round and slow to engage with her surroundings. She made out her own form first and it took her a while to realise that she wasn't wearing any clothes.

That small stab of panic made her quicken back into consciousness. She was lying on her back on something rough and dry. She lifted her head but the effort cost her and she banged it back down with a sigh. The hairs along her back had anchored her, stretching slowly into a space she couldn't see but which held her aloft. She could smell what was beneath her – it was earth – but she knew instinctively that she wasn't outside. There was a harsh light over her head which made it difficult to stare directly upwards. This was the same room she had entered hours earlier, in the basement of Nede. She was lying on a shallow tray of soil on top of a large work surface.

It took her about fifteen minutes to lift the upper part of her body, tugging herself up by inches, so that she could see the room clearly. She shared it with nobody and the electric light overhead was the only one switched on, so the corners of the room were dark. She felt exposed, frightened. Her eyes moved slowly around, straining to locate something, anything, which would relieve her. Her palms were pressed into the soil and she raked her fingers through it, the dirt riding up her nails.

The door opened and the same blonde woman who had sedated her walked through. She was a blurry shadow to Marianne's eyes, her vision still drifting in and out of focus. The woman wandered round behind her and Marianne tried to turn to see what she was doing, but twisting her body made the sting return in her spine.

'No, don't move. Just stay still,' the woman said. Her voice was silky and sensitive. 'You have absolutely nothing to be afraid of. This will soon be over and you'll be able to go home.'

'What will soon be over?' Marianne said. She had struggled to get the words out. Her whole face seemed to be paralysed and yet her mouth was trembling.

'We're going to send you home tonight. Inside of an hour, you'll be on your way.'

Marianne wanted to press her, but this last statement made her weak with relief.

'Are you sure?' she whispered. 'Am I really allowed to leave?'

Then she jumped as the woman placed a hand on her back. It was cold because there was something wet inside her hand, a sort of gel which she rubbed up and down Marianne's spine.

'What is that?' Marianne asked slowly.

'Just an ointment. It's to relax the tension in you. You're very tense and there's no reason to be.'

Marianne closed her eyes and began to enjoy the sensation. Once the woman had spread the ointment along her spine, she patted it into the nape of Marianne's neck. It was cool and refreshing. There was something about it that gradually reduced the pain riding up her body and brought it to a standstill.

'Thank you,' Marianne said stupidly.

'You're welcome,' the woman said, and she placed her clean hand on the top of Marianne's head. 'Now, if you'll step down, I can give you something to wear.'

Marianne obeyed and lifted herself out of the tray. She had regained feeling in her legs, but she was still shaking. She looked down and realised that she barely recognised her body because it was so reduced. The bones of her pelvis were sharp and shadowy. The veins in her feet stood out and looped around her ankles. She was alarmed by the change but vaguely unin-terested in it at the same time. She saw her feet as if from a great distance, suspended from seeing herself properly.

The woman gave her a large dark-blue robe with a deep hood. She was asked to put it on and draw the cord around her waist.

'Where are my clothes?' Marianne asked her.

'You won't need them.'

Then she tied Marianne's hair and swung it over her shoulder so it wasn't touching her back. The robe didn't stick to her skin where the ointment had dried into it.

'Ready?' the woman asked kindly.

'For *what*?' Marianne asked.

There was a knock on the door and the woman went to open it. Two men walked in dressed in long dark coats of a dense, heavy material. Their faces were slightly grey and impassive. They might have been undertakers. Doctor Cedon was also there behind them and she was carrying an iPad.

'Is she ready?' Cedon asked the attendant.

'Yes.'

The two men took Marianne by the arm and they walked her along the same route she had taken to escape that morning, though it felt like weeks ago. Time was reshaping itself in her sleepy brain, stretching her thoughts out then cramping them into nothing. She was incapable of concentrating on anything and moved like one condemned to forget every step of the way. They took her up the same staircase and then across the corridor of the house to the double doors that led to the garden. The house was dim in the silence of the night, the garden surreal, devoid of any stateliness it had in the light of day. The hedge-rows towered over Marianne and leaned in towards her. The path was not straight and her balance was compromised. They had her firmly in their grip though; every time she swayed to one side, one of the men was quick to push her back. She was so dozy that she was beginning to enjoy their presence. They made her feel curiously protected, insulated from the darkness. The forest was closing in on her and she was feeling short of breath.

She waited for them to open the gate and then proceeded through. But as soon as she left the garden behind, Marianne's panic resurrected itself. The space between the trees was dense and she worried herself into it, forced to continue in spite of an incomprehensible dread of moving forward. She struggled and felt her energy returning, her blood rushing back.

'Please, I want to go,' she said. Her voice was so small in her ears that she doubted they heard her.

'This will be quick and then you'll be home.'

It was Doctor Cedon who said this, and Marianne looked at her, trying to glean something from her face. Cedon was ignoring her and looked directly ahead. Marianne wondered why she could see her features so distinctly. It was then that she realised there was a light ahead of them. Cedon stared at it with complete concentration, never blinking, never looking down to guide her feet across the bracken. Marianne was sickened by the voracity in her face.

There was a clearing in the forest and a spotlight on the ground drew their attention to an enormous ash tree. Its body was stark and terrible in that glare; it seemed explicitly alive. Marianne was afraid of it, instinctively horrified. She shivered and a spasm ran through her arms. She shook them, and those hands that had been restraining her all this time finally tightened without remorse, squeezing her until the pain stole her incentive.

The blonde woman stood in front of her and placed her hands on Marianne's shoulders.

'It's alright. You'll be free once this is over,' she said.

'I don't consent!' Marianne said quickly. She knew there was something she needed to say and she finally remembered the words. 'I don't consent. You don't have my consent.'

'It's for a cause much greater than yourself,' Doctor Cedon said.

They took Marianne towards the tree, where two women were standing either side. The symmetry of everything was sublime and Marianne was confused by her impulse to admire what they were doing. There was a darkness in the design that took her breath away. Someone untied the cord around her waist – she was no longer conscious of who was doing what – and the robe was removed. She stood, trembling, in that immense place, finally without anything to protect her from being absorbed by it all. Now she saw her white body as a foreign entity, a thing so easily discarded. And she knew it was about to happen.

She shook so violently that they had to hold her arms and legs to prevent her from stumbling. She also felt her back begin to quiver, to split. She was reeling backwards, her thoughts dropping like flies from a burning light.

'Anaesthetic, please,' Cedon said.

Someone slid another needle into Marianne's skin, this time in her back. Instantly, the sting subsided. Then she grew numb. She saw a flash of silver as one of the women who had been waiting by the tree produced a sharp instrument from a layer of cloth on the ground. The woman disappeared behind her. Marianne squirmed beneath her touch. She could feel the blade tearing into her skin without the searing impact of it, a small tingling as it sliced her open. And then warm blood running through. The blood slid down her back and glided down her tailbone until it reached the curve of her bottom. The blade sliced deeper and deeper until Marianne knew it had reached her bone.

Once she was soaked in her own blood, they pressed her back against the tree. She finally knew what they were doing. Where she was going. In response to the bark, the hairs along her back moved of their own accord and knitted themselves to the surface. Her thoughts were sliding out of her skin, magnetised towards what lay inside this tree, a place where nothing could be recalled. The roots of her life were really there, knotted in the blood of her back, hot and wet. It was never a dream! She cried, for it was a possibility she had vaguely anticipated in a way that never quite declared itself in the surface of her mind. Now there was no surface. Every thought that she had ever had merged, pulsing at this broken seam. She knew that what had broken the surface of her back were the tail ends of her consciousness. They would grow through the tree. Her mental life was being installed inside it.

For a few seconds she imagined what this would be like. A free-floating consciousness moving through time without being, in any sense, bound by it. She recalled, briefly, her sister's ordeal in the hospital – those minutes in which her brain turned dark. A wave of darkness, like a tsunami, which ransacked her thoughts, only to fall back at the last minute. Marianne would know the wave, would ride it forever, her consciousness free from all living impulses. The roots pulled at the skin of her back, urging her mind towards its end.

But she had an overwhelming urge to exist and could hardly breathe for want of breath. She knew now, with a conviction that had perhaps always lain somewhere at bay, that she was loved. That she would be loved beyond this point, even if she couldn't return it. This was the saddest part of life – not being able to tell someone in time how valuable they were. She sought a last image of Marie in the dark heat of her mind, and there was a succession of them, coming in sharp, hot flashes like dying embers. She would have loved again in that urgent fashion; there was a man who might have claimed it, a child. It would all go to waste. She prayed that someone would slice the tree open, or failing that, burn it to the ground. *Dad*, she thought, *please come find me!*

The roots quivered and wormed their way slowly through the bark. Her eyes were still open and the pupils were enormous, as though she had seen eternity in a second. Once the roots entered the tree, her consciousness ejected itself with such force that her spine vibrated and almost snapped in two. But its energy was sustained. It was like an orgasm, a state of perpetual arrival, without end. The tree held her inside and she filled its dark body without memory, only with an eternal immediacy. For consciousness forms itself through time, building a series of structures that rely upon a definitive end. Marianne's stream of thought finally lost its urgency. It was no longer furiously building towards something or despairing for what it lacked. It occupied a flat and featureless horizon. Its sound, humming indistinctly inside of the tree, was one note.

Marianne was tied to the tree so that she would remain upright. The small party watched until the animation in her face disappeared later that night. Weeks passed, and her final expression had evolved into one of flat hostility. The sun burned through the foliage and a shaft of light gilded her feet so that her skin was briefly warm again.

The roots moved slowly into the heartwood and then the tree finally altered itself, producing tiny pink buds along its branches. Cedon continued to monitor the growth, recording all the changes. Though their method was ugly, its purpose was pure, and they had effectively trained themselves not to be appalled by what they saw. Yet when they departed the forest at the end of each day, a few members of the party looked back furtively, imagining that the girl might return to herself when nobody was watching. As though her consciousness could be recalled within seconds of them turning their backs. That expression on her face, though it could not logically have been an *expression*, appeared acrimonious, her mouth gripping itself instead of growing slack like the others. She also seemed to have erected herself of her own accord, her white body like a totem pole, though her spine had broken. Their superstition drove them slightly mad and one woman remained behind to give Marianne the sign of the cross. 'God will take you in the end,' she whispered.

It was about a month later, when Marianne's body had grown cold and her skin was blue, that Doctor Cedon saw what she had been looking for. On one of the boughs of the tree, a stark, red flower. It had a pronounced stigma and a dark ovary. She smiled. It was done.

ACKNOWLEDGEMENTS

I'll be forever grateful to my agent, John Ash, for taking on this book and plucking it out of obscurity. His tireless enthusiasm, intelligence, humour and generosity has helped me feel less of a nervous wreck throughout this process, always daring me to trust my instincts and to take pleasure in what I have created. I can't adequately express how much I appreciate his help in shaping the manuscript before submitting it to editors. I'm also grateful to the team at PEW Literary Agency for reading the book in its initial stages.

I wish to thank my UK editor at Oneworld, Juliet Mabey, as well as my US editor at The Overlook Press, Chelsea Cutchens, for publishing my book. They have been wonderful, providing me with excellent feedback and helping me to develop the story in a way that would make it more powerful. Polly Hatfield has also been a brilliant guide – her close reading of the text was truly impressive and really benefited my writing.

I wish to thank Helen Szirtes for a very thorough copy-edit, leaving nothing to chance. Thank you to Hayley Warnham, who designed the cover for the UK edition, as well as Devin Grosz, the designer for the US cover – both wonderfully compelling and eerie designs. I'm really grateful to everyone in the production, publicity, sales and marketing teams at Oneworld and The Overlook Press. Having worked in sales and marketing myself, I know how much passion, thought and care goes into these publishing campaigns. I'd also like to extend my gratitude to Candie Earle-Hutton, who took my headshots for the book.

Though this book is about a deeply troubled family, I am very lucky to have such a strong relationship with my own parents and my younger sister, Rachel. Like Marianne, I will always feel the desire to return home where I feel safe and loved. And I am very fortunate to have my nephew, Benjamin, in my life, as he is the purest source of joy. When he is (much) older, I hope he enjoys this book.

Michael, the fourteen years I've spent with you have been the best. You alone know how exhilarating yet terrifying this process has been, and you've shared all my highs and lows. Thank you for everything.

Lastly, I am indebted to Ralitsa Chorbadzhiyska, who recommended I submit my book to John Ash at the PEW agency – a brilliant suggestion and one that changed everything! Rali has been an incredibly supportive friend to me and is one of the kindest people I know.